The
Young Oxford Book
— of —
Folk Tales

Other Oxford books for children by
Kevin Crossley-Holland

Beowulf

The Green Children

Short! A Book of Very Short Stories

The
Young Oxford Book
of
Folk Tales

EDITED BY KEVIN CROSSLEY-HOLLAND

OXFORD UNIVERSITY PRESS
Oxford • New York • Toronto

Oxford University Press, Great Clarendon Street, Oxford OX2 6DP

Oxford • New York

Athens • Auckland •Bangkok • Bogota • Buenos Aires • Calcutta
Cape Town • Chennai • Dar es Salaam • Delhi • Florence • Hong Kong
Istanbul • Karachi • Kuala Lumpur • Madrid • Melbourne
Mexico City • Mumbai • Nairobi • Paris • Sao Paulo • Singapore
Taipei • Tokyo • Toronto • Warsaw
and associated companies in
Berlin • Ibadan

Oxford is a trade mark of Oxford University Press

First published 1998

British Library Cataloguing in Publication Data
Data available

Cover illustration by Rosemary Woods

ISBN 0 19 278141 3

Typeset by
Mike Brain

Printed in Great Britain by Biddles Limited, Guildford and King's Lynn

For Sally and Dick and their children and grandchildren

Contents

Foreword

Yes, most human beings are born with arms and legs. No, they do not have tails. Yes, they are able to look forward and look back, and sometimes they laugh. No, they have no wings.

Of course humans are alike, in the sense that they share many more characteristics with one another than with any other beings. That is one point made by this anthology. A Welsh hill-farmer and a young couple in Armenia both feel the same emotion of love; a Basuto girl and a boy in Hawaii both display the same courage; a Japanese woman and town councillors in Germany pay for the same greed; a girl on a Pacific island and a Polish boy both understand how humans and animals depend on one another; and a Canadian poultry farmer and three Burmese brothers rejoice in the same power of the imagination.

But this anthology also makes the opposite point. It reveals how utterly different human beings are. You are you and there is no one in the world like you. Not within your own family. Not in your or any other country.

These tales demonstrate not only individual difference but also difference between tribes, nations, religions, environments: the different ways we talk and eat and dress; the ways we make and renew relationships; our ideas of good behaviour and bad behaviour; the ways we treat children, and treat the old; the different beliefs we have about what will happen to us after we die.

Difference is more interesting by far than similarity. That is why cloning is at the same time highly fascinating and extremely boring. The most astonishing thing about our planet is its fabulous variety:

All things counter, original, spare, strange;
Whatever is fickle, freckled (who knows how?)
With swift, slow; sweet, sour; adazzle, dim;
He fathers-forth whose beauty is past change:
    Praise him.
         (from 'Pied Beauty' by Gerard Manley Hopkins)

The editor of any anthology of folk-tales naturally has responsibilities: to the cultures of the chosen tales; to language and craft; and to the book's audience. I have tried to discharge them. But the cornerstone of this anthology is my conviction that there is little now more important than the study of other nations and other cultures.

One crucial way of engaging with any civilization is through its artistic achievement—its music and literature and painting and sculpture and film. Out of study springs understanding; and out of understanding grows respect, and even love. This is joyful work we can begin as children, and that children can share with adults, through the telling and reading of folk-tales.

Kevin Crossley-Holland

Burnham Market
January 1998

To Tell the Truth

Parcels of fibs! Packets of moonshine! Tales so tall you couldn't see the top of them! The three brothers were incredible storytellers. Wherever they went, people flocked to hear them. First they laughed, then they scoffed and they hooted, and they never believed a single word.

One day, when the storytellers were on the road, they caught up with a young princess who was being carried on a palanquin by four sweating slaves. This princess wore her wealth on her sleeve; in fact, she wore it all over her. From manicured finger-nail to fingernail, and from elegant topknot to toe, she gleamed and sparkled and flashed.

'Which is worth more?' asked one brother. 'Her wealth or our words?'

'Let our tales talk,' said the second.

'Let them walk tall and count,' said the third.

So the three storytellers challenged the princess to a tale-contest.

'If we show we disbelieve a single word of your tale,' said the three brothers, 'we will become your slaves. If one of us so much as widens his eyes, or raises his eyebrows, or purses his lips, or even catches his breath, we will work for you for as long as we live. But, princess, if you say or show you disbelieve a single word of ours, then you must become our slave.'

Not that the three storytellers needed a slave. But the man who owns a slave owns everything to do with her: her freedom, her time, her energy, even the clothes she stands up in. And the three brothers could scarcely take their eyes off the young princess's gorgeous and valuable clothes.

'Who will be the judge?' the princess asked the storytellers.

'The first passer-by,' said one brother.

So the princess dismounted from her palanquin, and sat down with the brothers in the shade of a huge banyan tree. The storytellers felt quite sure they would win because the princess was just a princess whereas they, they were whoppers in a world of minnows, and no one ever believed a single word they said.

Before long, an old man came tottering down the dusty road. As soon as he had agreed to be their judge, the first brother stood up and began his story.

'I used to enjoy playing hide-and-seek when I was a boy. Most children do. Once, I remember, I hid from my two brothers near the top of an enormous banyan tree. The tallest tree in the wood. Ten times the size of this one!

'Up! Up! Then I lay along a grey branch, still as a sticking point, quiet as a cucumber, and that's where I stayed for most of the afternoon.

'While I hid, my brothers sought. They shouted my name, they even climbed into my tree, but they couldn't find me. At last the blue hour stole through the wood, so my brothers gave up, they went back home. I sat up, then. As stiff as an upper lip! Even though the crows were squawking, it was very quiet inside the tree.

'That was when I found out it's much more difficult to climb down than climb up. Worse, I could scarcely even see the branches below me. So I couldn't get down but I couldn't stay up. Not the whole night! Think what would have happened if I'd fallen asleep!

'What I did know was, with a rope, I'd be able to slide down. So to tell the truth, I nipped along to our neighbours, the ones who live close to the wood, and borrowed their rope—they were always lending us things and they didn't always get them back—and then I was able to slide down from the tree and run home. Whew!'

The first brother shook his head, and looked at the princess, but the princess had neither widened her eyes nor raised her eyebrows; she just nodded and half-smiled.

So then he sat down and the second brother stood up and began his story.

'Inside my brother's story is a second story. On the afternoon he hid from us at the top of the banyan tree, I criss-crossed the wood until I had covered every step of every track. In the green light I looked. In the stillness I listened. Then I saw something move and I thought it was him. I thought it was my brother. So I followed this something through the quaking bushes; but it was a tiger!

'This tiger snarled and opened its mouth—wide. As wide as I'm tall. So I hopped in. After all, there was no running away. I hopped in and, before the tiger could chew me into meatballs and bone-chips, I crawled headfirst into its stomach. Oh yes I did!

'So inside my brother's story is a second story of a second brother inside a tiger. I stretched and kicked and jumped around; I roared and I barked and yelled. The tiger thought there was a whole zoo inside him and he was afraid—afraid for the first time since he was a cub, and he stared up at the full moon as it turned blue-and-green.

'Then the tiger retched, and I turned head over heels. He retched again, and coughed, and spat me out. He spat me flying through the air. Over the trees! Out of the banyan wood! I landed right in the middle of our village.

'After that, the tiger decided there must be dozens of other villages with people more digestible than ours. So, young as I was, I saved my family and neighbours from danger. To tell the truth, I saved them from being eaten. And do you know what they call me?'

'Tiger!' said the princess. But that was all she said. She had neither pursed her lips nor caught her breath but just sat in the shade of the banyan tree, and nodded and half-smiled.

The three storytellers stared at each other. Was the young princess very clever or very stupid—so stupid she couldn't tell the difference between truth and make-believe? The third brother pursed his lips, and stood up, and began his story.

'Princess! Less than a day's walk from our village, there is a wide river. Not so long ago, I went there to net some fish, but the fishermen there all said they hadn't caught a tiddler between them—not for a week—and their wives and children and babies were half-starving.

'Now I know how to swim all right. I can swim all day long. So I told the fishermen I'd try to help them. I dived into the water, and turned myself into a fish. Yes, a fish!

'To begin with, I couldn't see much; the water was so murky. I nosed around in the shallows for a while; but then I swam right out into the thrust of the river.

'Lying on the sticky river bed was the most enormous fish. Much, much bigger than a pike! As large as a dolphin! There and then I realized what had happened. This monster was always hungry, painfully hungry. So he skulked in the middle of the river, beyond the reach of the fishermen's nets, and snapped up the fish as they swam by. He swallowed them all, and he swallowed them whole.

'That's why the fishermen had caught no fish. And the moment this horrible creature saw me, he grinned and lunged at me.

'At once I turned myself back into a man. Then I drove my sword through the water and straight into the fish's stomach. I slit it open, and a shoal of fish swam out. At least a thousand! And most of them were so glad to escape their prison they never even noticed the fishermen's nets. Not until they had swum right into them!

'I swam and then I staggered towards the river bank. And many of the fish that had escaped the monster and escaped the nets were so grateful they jumped on to the bank beside me. They wagged their tails! To tell the truth, there were far more fish than I could do with. More than enough for every fisherman there. They pelted me with little coins and then they sang me a song of friendship. So home I came, my head full of scales, my hands full of silver!'

The third brother opened his arms and looked at the young princess, but the princess had neither widened her eyes, nor raised her eyebrows, nor pursed her lips, nor even caught her breath; she just nodded and half-smiled. Then the three brothers stared at each other. Well! At least they knew that they were

storytellers whereas the princess was a princess, and that if they couldn't so much as make her shake her head, she certainly wouldn't be able to surprise them.

Then the princess stood tall under the banyan tree, gleaming and sparkling and flashing, and began her story.

'There is not much to say. As you see, I am a princess and a rich young woman. I own treasure, I own land, and I own slaves. The reason I'm on the road is that I am looking for three of my slaves who have run away.

'Each slave, as you know, is worth a very great deal—his clothes, his energy, his time, his freedom. So I have hunted high and low, and I must admit I was on the very point of giving up when I met you three. You three . . . brothers! You three . . . storytellers! So now my search is over, isn't it? You know who you really are: you're my three runaway slaves.'

When they heard this, the three brothers were shocked. What were they to do? If they said they believed the princess, they would be admitting they were her three runaway slaves; but if they said or showed they disbelieved her, they would have to become her slaves anyway.

The three brothers sat under the banyan tree, glum as lumps of dough. They whispered, they argued, they didn't know what to do. In fact, they dithered so long that the old man they had chosen as their judge pronounced that the tale-contest was at an end and that the winner was the young princess.

'I don't need any more slaves,' said the princess, smiling. 'But why do you three men tell nothing but tall tales? Parcels of fibs! Packets of moonshine! Canards! Claptrap! I will set you free on one condition. Go back to your village and tell people home truths as well. Tell them about themselves. Tell them hope and fear and bravery and love. Tell them their own stories!'

The Magic Brocade

Once upon a time, long, long ago, there lived in a small village in the southern part of China a mother and her three sons. Since the poor woman was a widow, she had to support her growing family as best she could. Fortunately she was very skilled at weaving fine brocade. This material was a speciality of the Chuang area where they lived and it was made of rich fabric with designs of silver, gold, and silk woven upon it. The widow was quite famous in the surrounding countryside for her brocades, as she had a special talent for making the birds and other animals and the flowers that she wove into her cloth appear lifelike. Some people even said that her flowers and animals and birds were even more beautiful than real ones.

One day the widow had to go into the market place to sell some cloth she had just finished. It took her no time at all to get rid of it, for everyone was anxious to buy her work. When she had completed her business she strolled among the stalls, looking at all the interesting objects for sale. Suddenly her glance was caught by a beautiful picture and she paused. In the painting was a marvellous white house surrounded by vast fields and grand walks which led to glorious gardens bursting with fruit and flowers. Between the stately trees in the background could be glimpsed some smaller buildings, and among the fluttering leaves flew rare brightly plumed birds of all kinds.

Instantly the widow fell in love with the picture and bought it. When she got home she showed it to her three sons, who also thought it was very beautiful.

'Oh,' sighed the widow, 'wouldn't it be wonderful if we lived in such a place!'

The two elder sons shook their heads and laughed.

'My dear mother, that's only an idle dream,' said the eldest.

'Perhaps it might happen in the next world,' agreed the second son, 'but not in this one.'

Only the youngest son comforted her.

'Why don't you weave a copy of the picture into a brocade?' he suggested. With a gentle smile on his face, he added, 'That will be nearly as good as living in it.'

This thought made the mother very happy. Right away she went out and bought all the coloured silk yarns she needed. Then she set up her loom and began to weave the design of the painting into the brocade.

Day and night, month after month, the mother sat at her loom weaving her silks. Though her back ached and her eyes grew strained from the exacting work, still she would not stop. She worked as if possessed. Gradually the two elder sons became annoyed.

One day the eldest one said with irritation, 'Mother, you weave all day but you never sell anything.'

'Yes!' grumbled the second. 'And we have to earn money for the rice you eat by chopping wood. We're tired of all this hard work.'

The youngest son didn't want his mother to be worried. He told his brothers not to complain and promised that he would look after everything. From then on, every morning he went up the mountain by himself and chopped enough wood to take care of the whole family.

Day after day the mother continued her weaving. At night she burned pine branches to make enough light. The branches smoked so much that her eyes became sore and bloodshot. But still she would not stop.

A year passed.

Tears from the mother's eyes began to drop upon the picture. She wove the crystal liquid into a bright clear river and also into a charming little fish pond.

Another year went by.

Now the tears from the mother's eyes turned into blood and dropped like red jewels upon the cloth. Quickly she wove them into a flaming sun and into brilliant red flowers.

Hour after hour, without a moment's stop, the widow went on weaving.

Finally, at the end of the third year, her brocade was done. The mother stepped away from her work and smiled with pride and with great happiness. There it all was: the beautiful house, the breathtaking gardens filled with exotic flowers and fruit, the brilliant birds, and beyond in the vast fields sheep and cattle grazing contentedly upon the grass.

Suddenly a great wind from the west howled through the house. Catching up the rare brocade it sped through the door and disappeared over the hill. Frantically the mother chased after her beautiful treasure, only to see it blown high into the sky, far beyond her reach. It flew straight towards the east and in a twinkling it had completely vanished.

The heartbroken mother, unable to bear such a calamity, fell into a deep faint. Carefully her three sons carried her into the house and laid her upon the bed. Hours later, after sipping some ginger broth, the widow slowly came to herself.

'My son,' she implored her eldest, 'go to the east and find my brocade for me. It means more to me than life.'

The boy nodded and quickly set out on his journey. After travelling eastward for more than a month, he came to a mountain pass where an old white-haired woman sat in front of a stone house. Beside her stood a handsome stone horse which looked as though it longed to eat the red fruit off the pretty tree that grew next to it. As the eldest boy passed by, the old lady stopped him.

'Where are you going, young man?' she asked.

'East,' he said, and told her the story of the brocade.

'Ah!' she said, 'the brocade your mother wove has been carried away by the fairies of the Sun Mountain because it was so beautifully made. They are going to copy it.'

'But, tell me, how can I recover it?' begged the boy.

'That will be very difficult,' said the old woman. 'First, you have to knock out two of your front teeth and put them into the mouth of my stone horse. Then he will be able to move and to eat the red fruit hanging from this tree. When he has eaten ten pieces, then you can mount him. He will take you directly to the Sun Mountain. But first you will have to pass through the Flame Mountain which burns with a continuous fierceness.'

Here the old lady offered a warning. 'You must not utter a word of complaint, for if you do you will instantly be burned to ashes. When you have arrived at the other side, you must then cross an icy sea.' With a grave nod she whispered, 'And if you give the slightest shudder, you will immediately sink to the bottom.'

After hearing all this, the eldest son felt his jaw and thought anxiously of the burning fire and lashing sea waves. He went white as a ghost.

The old woman looked at him and laughed.

'You won't be able to stand it, I can see,' she said. 'Don't go. I'll give you a small iron box full of gold. Take it and live comfortably.'

She fetched the box of gold from the stone house and gave it to the boy. He took it happily and went away. On his way home he began thinking about all the money he now had. 'This gold will enable me to live very well. If I take it home, I will have to share it. Spending it all on myself will be much more fun than spending it on four people.'

He decided right then and there not to go home and turned instead to the path which led to a big city.

At home the poor mother waited two months for her eldest son to return, but he did not come back. Gradually her illness got worse. At length she sent her second son to bring the brocade back.

When the boy reached the mountain pass he came upon the old woman at the stone house, who told him the same things she had told his older brother. As he learned all that he must do in order to obtain the brocade, he became frightened and his face paled. Laughing, the woman offered him a box of gold, just as she had his brother. Greatly relieved, the boy took it and went on his way, deciding also to head for the city instead of returning home.

After waiting and waiting for the second son to return home, the widow became desperately ill. At last she turned blind from weeping. Still neither of her sons ever came back.

The youngest son, beside himself with worry, begged his mother to let him go in search of the brocade.

'*I'll* bring it back to you, mother, I promise.'

Faint with exhaustion and despair, the widow nodded weakly.

Travelling swiftly, the youngest son took only half a month to arrive at the mountain pass. There he met the old woman in front of the stone house. She told him exactly the same things that she had told his two brothers, but added, 'My son, your brothers each went away with a box of gold. You may have one, too.'

With steady firmness the boy refused. 'I shall not let these difficulties stop me,' he declared. 'I am going to bring back the brocade that took my mother three years to weave.'

Instantly he knocked two teeth out of his mouth and put them into the mouth of the handsome stone horse. The stone horse came alive and went to the tall green tree and ate ten pieces of red fruit hanging from its branches. As soon as it had done this, the horse lifted its elegant head, tossed its silver mane, and neighed. Quickly the boy mounted its back, and together they galloped off towards the east.

After three days and nights the young son came to Flame Mountain. On every side fires spat forth wildly. The boy stared for a moment at the terrifying sight, then spurring his horse he dashed courageously up the flaming mountain, enduring the ferocious heat without once uttering a sound.

Once on the other side of the mountain, he came to a vast sea. Great waves frosted with chunks of ice crashed upon him as he made his way painfully across the freezing water. Though cold and aching, he held the horse's mane tightly, persisting in his journey without allowing himself to shudder.

Emerging on the opposite shore, he saw at once the Sun Mountain. Warm light flooded the air and flowers blossomed everywhere. On top of the mountain stood a marvellous palace and from it he could hear sounds of girlish laughter and singing.

Quickly the boy tapped his horse. It reared up and flew with great speed to the door of the palace. The boy got down and entered the front hall. There he found one hundred beautiful fairies, each sitting at a loom and weaving a copy of his mother's brocade.

The fairies were all very surprised to see him. One came forth at last and spoke.

'We shall finish our weaving tonight and you may have your mother's brocade tomorrow. Will it please you to wait here for the night?'

'Yes,' said the son. He sat down, prepared to wait forever if necessary for his mother's treasure. Several fairies graciously attended him, bringing delicious fruit to refresh him. Instantly all his fatigue disappeared.

When dusk fell, the fairies hung from the centre of the ceiling an enormous pearl which shone so brilliantly it lit the entire room. Then, while they went on weaving, the youngest son went to sleep.

One fairy finally finished her brocade, but it was not nearly as well done as the one the widow had made. The sad fairy felt she could not part with the widow's brocade and longed to live in that beautiful human world, so she embroidered a picture of herself on the original work.

When the young son woke up just before daylight, the fairies had all gone, leaving his mother's cloth under the shining pearl. Not waiting for daybreak the boy quickly clasped it to his chest and, mounting his horse, galloped off in the waning moonlight. Bending low upon the stallion's flowing mane and clamping his mouth tightly shut, he passed again through the icy sea and up and down the flaming mountain. Soon he reached the mountain pass where the old woman stood waiting for him in front of her stone house. Smiling warmly, she greeted him.

'Young man, I see you have come back.'

'Yes, old woman.' After he dismounted, the woman took his teeth from the horse and put them back into his mouth. Instantly the horse turned back to stone. Then she went inside the house and returned with a pair of deerskin shoes.

'Take these,' she said, 'they will help you get home.'

When the boy put them on he found he could move as though he had wings. In a moment he was back in his own house. He entered his mother's room and unrolled the brocade. It gleamed so brightly that the widow gasped and opened her eyes, finding her sight entirely restored.

Instantly cured of all illness, she rose from her bed. Together she and her son took the precious work outside to see it in the bright light. As they unrolled it, a strange, fragrant breeze sprang up and blew upon the brocade, drawing it out longer and longer and wider and wider until at last it covered all the land in sight. Suddenly the silken threads trembled and the picture burst into life. Scarlet flowers waved in the soft wind. Animals stirred and grazed upon the tender grasses of the vast fields. Golden birds darted in and out of the handsome trees and about the grand white house that commanded the landscape.

It was all exactly as the mother had woven it, except that now there was a beautiful girl in red standing by the fish pond. It was the fairy who had embroidered herself into the brocade.

The kind widow, thrilled with her good fortune, went out among her poor neighbours and asked them to come to live with her on her new land, and share the abundance of her fields and gardens.

It will not surprise you to learn that the youngest son married the beautiful fairy girl and that they lived together very happily for many, many years.

One day two beggars walked slowly down the road. They were the two elder sons of the widow, and it was clear from their appearance that they had long ago squandered all the gold they had. Astonished to see such a beautiful place, they decided to stop and beg something from the owner. But when they looked across the fields, they suddenly recognized that the people happily picnicking by the pretty stream were none other than their very own mother and brother—and a beautiful lady who must be their brother's wife. Blushing with shame, they quickly picked up their begging sticks and crept silently away.

The Tiger's Whisker

A young woman by the name of Yun Ok came one day to the house of a mountain hermit to seek his help. The hermit was a sage of great renown and a maker of charms and magic potions.

When Yun Ok entered his house, the hermit said, without raising his eyes from the fireplace into which he was looking: 'Why are you here?'

Yun Ok said, 'Oh, Famous Sage, I am in distress! Make me a potion!'

'Yes, yes, make a potion! Everyone needs potions! Can we cure a sick world with a potion?'

'Master,' Yun Ok replied, 'if you do not help me, I am truly lost!'

'Well, what is your story?' the hermit said, resigned at last to listen.

'It is my husband,' Yun Ok said. 'He is very dear to me. For the past three years he has been away fighting in the wars. Now that he has returned, he hardly speaks to me, or to anyone else. If I speak, he doesn't seem to hear. When he talks at all, it is roughly. If I serve him food not to his liking, he pushes it aside and angrily leaves the room. Sometimes when he should be working in the rice field, I see him sitting idly on top of the hill, looking towards the sea.'

'Yes, so it is sometimes when young men come back from the wars,' the hermit said. 'Go on.'

'There is no more to tell, Learned One. I want a potion to give my husband so that he will be loving and gentle, as he used to be.'

'Ha, so simple, is it?' the hermit said. 'A potion! Very well; come back in three days and I will tell you what we shall need for such a potion.'

Three days later Yun Ok returned to the home of the mountain sage. 'I have looked into it,' he told her. 'Your potion can be made. But the most essential ingredient is the whisker of a living tiger. Bring me this whisker and I will give you what you need.'

'The whisker of a living tiger!' Yun Ok said. 'How could I possibly get it?'

'If the potion is important enough, you will succeed,' the hermit said. He turned his head away, not wishing to talk any more.

Yun Ok went home. She thought a great deal about how she would get the tiger's whisker. Then one night when her husband was asleep, she crept from her house with a bowl of rice and meat sauce in her hand. She went to the place on the mountain-side where the tiger was known to live. Standing far off from the tiger's cave, she held out the bowl of food, calling the tiger to come and eat. The tiger did not come.

The next night Yun Ok went again, this time a little bit closer. Again she offered a bowl of food. Every night Yun Ok went to the mountain, each time a few steps nearer the tiger's cave than the night before. Little by little the tiger became accustomed to seeing her there.

One night Yun Ok approached to within a stone's throw of the tiger's cave. This time the tiger came a few steps towards her and stopped. The two of them stood looking at one another in the moonlight. It happened again the following night, and this time they were so close that Yun Ok could talk to the tiger in a soft, soothing voice. The next night, after looking carefully into Yun Ok's eyes, the tiger ate the food that she held out for him.

After that when Yun Ok came in the night, she found the tiger waiting for her on the trail. When the tiger had eaten, Yun Ok could gently rub his head with her hand. Nearly six months had passed since the night of her first visit. At last one night, after caressing the animal's head, Yun Ok said, 'Oh, Tiger, generous animal, I must have one of your whiskers. Do not be angry with me!'

And she snipped off one of the whiskers.

The tiger did not become angry, as she had feared he might. Yun Ok went down the trail, not walking but running, with the whisker clutched tightly in her hand.

The next morning she was at the mountain hermit's house just as the sun was rising from the sea. 'Oh, Famous One!' she cried. 'I have it! I have the tiger's whisker! Now you can make me the potion you promised so that my husband will be loving and gentle again!'

The hermit took the whisker and examined it. Satisfied that it had really come from a tiger, he leaned forward and dropped it into the fire that burned in his fireplace.

'Oh, sir!' the young woman called in anguish. 'What have you done with it?'

'Tell me how you obtained it,' the hermit said.

'Why, I went to the mountain each night with a little bowl of food. At first I stood afar, and I came a little closer each time, gaining the tiger's confidence. I spoke gently and soothingly to him, to make him understand I wished him only good. I was patient. Each night I brought him food, knowing that he would not eat. But I did not give up. I came again and again. I never spoke harshly. I never reproached him. And at last one night he took a few steps towards me. A time came when he would meet me on the trail and eat out of the bowl that I held in my hands. I rubbed his head, and he made happy sounds in his throat. Only after that did I take the whisker.'

'Yes, yes,' the hermit said, 'you tamed the tiger and won his confidence and love.'

'But you have thrown the whisker in the fire!' Yun Ok cried. 'It is all for nothing!'

'No, I do not think it is all for nothing,' the hermit said. 'The whisker is no longer needed. Yun Ok, let me ask you, is a man more vicious than a tiger? Is he less responsive to kindness and understanding? If you can win the love and confidence of a wild and bloodthirsty animal by gentleness and patience, surely you can do the same with your husband!'

Hearing this, Yun Ok stood speechless for a moment. Then she went down the trail, turning over in her mind the truth she had learned in the house of the mountain hermit.

Kotura,
Lord of the Winds

In a nomad camp there once lived an old man with his three daughters. The youngest was the kindest and cleverest of the three.

The old man was very poor. His *choom*, his tent of skins, was worn and full of holes. There was little warm clothing to wear. When the frost was very fierce the old man would huddle by the fire with his three daughters and try to keep warm. At night, before going to bed, they would put out the fire, and then they would shiver from the cold until morning.

Once, in the middle of winter, a terrible snow-storm came down on the tundra. The wind blew for a day, it blew for a second day, and it blew for a third day, and it seemed as if all the *chooms* would be blown quite away. The people dared not show their faces outside and sat in the *chooms*, hungry and cold.

So, too, the old man and his three daughters. They sat in the *choom* and listened to the storm raging, and the old man said, 'We'll never be able to sit out this blizzard. It was sent by Kotura, Lord of the Winds. He must be angry, he must be waiting for us to send him a good wife. You, my eldest daughter, must go to Kotura or else our whole people will perish. You must go and beg him to stop the blizzard.'

'How can I go?' the girl asked. 'I don't know the way.'

'I will give you a little sledge. Place it so that it faces the wind, give it a push and follow it. The wind will untie the strings on your coat, but you must not stop to tie them. The snow will get into your shoes, but you must not stop to shake it out. Never pause till you reach a tall mountain. Climb it, and when you get to the top, then only can you stop to shake out the snow from your shoes and tie the strings on your coat. By and by a little bird will fly up to you and perch on your shoulder. Do not chase it away, be kind to it and fondle it gently. Then get into your sledge and coast down the mountain. The sledge will bring you straight to the door of Kotura's *choom*. Enter the *choom*, but touch nothing, just sit there and wait. When Kotura comes, do all he tells you to do.'

Eldest Daughter donned her furs, placed the sledge her father gave her so that it faced the wind, and with a push sent it gliding along.

She walked after it a little way, and the strings on her coat came undone, the snow got into her shoes and she was very, very cold. She did not do as her father bade her to do, but stopped and began to tie the strings on her coat and to shake the snow out of her shoes. After that she moved on, in the face of the wind. She walked a long time till at last she saw a tall mountain. No sooner had she climbed it than a little bird flew up to her and was about to perch on her shoulder. But Eldest Daughter waved her hands to chase it off, and the bird circled over her for a little while and then flew away. Eldest Daughter got into her sledge and coasted down the mountainside, and the sledge stopped by a large *choom*.

The girl went inside, and looked about her, and the first thing she saw was a large piece of roasted venison. She made up a fire, warmed herself and began to tear pieces of fat off the meat. She would tear off a piece and eat it, and then tear off another and eat it too, and she had eaten her fill when all of a sudden she heard someone coming up to the *choom*. The skin that hung over the entrance was lifted, and a young giant entered. This was Kotura himself. He looked at Eldest Daughter and said, 'Where do you come from, woman, and what do you want here?'

'My father sent me to you,' answered Eldest Daughter.

'Why did he send you?'

'So that you would take me to wife.'

'I was out hunting and I have brought back some meat. Stand up now and cook it for me,' Kotura said.

Eldest Daughter did as she was told, and when the meat was ready, Kotura told her to take it out of the pot and divide it in two parts.

'You and I will eat one half of the meat,' he said. 'Put the other in a wooden dish and take it to the neighbouring *choom*. Do not go into the *choom* yourself, but wait at the entrance. An old woman will come out to you. Give her the meat and wait till she brings back the empty dish.'

Eldest Daughter took the meat and went outside. The wind was howling, and the snow falling, and it was quite dark. How could one find anything in such a storm! . . . Eldest Daughter walked off a little way, stopped, thought a while and then threw the meat in the snow. After that she came back to Kotura with the empty dish.

Kotura glanced at her and said, 'Have you given the neighbours the meat?'

'Yes, I have,' Eldest Daughter replied.

'Show me the dish; I want to see what they gave you in return for the meat,' he told her.

Eldest Daughter showed him the empty dish, but Kotura said nothing. He ate his share of the meat and went to bed.

In the morning he rose, brought some untanned deerskins into the *choom* and said, 'While I am out hunting, dress these skins and make me a new coat from them, new shoes and new mittens. I will put them on when I come back and see if you are clever with your hands or not.'

And with these words, Kotura went off to hunt in the tundra, and Eldest Daughter set to work. Suddenly the hanging of skin over the entrance lifted, and a grey-haired old woman came in.

'Something has got into my eye, child,' said she. 'See if you can take it out.'

'I have no time to bother with you,' answered Eldest Daughter, 'I am busy working.'

The old woman said nothing but turned away and left the *choom*. Eldest Daughter was left alone. She dressed the skins hastily and began cutting them with a knife, hurrying to get her work done by evening. Indeed, in such a hurry was she that she did not try to make the clothes nicely, but only to get them finished as quickly as possible. She had no needle to sew with, and only one day to do the work in, and it was all she could do to get anything done at all.

In the evening Kotura came back from his hunting.

'Are my new clothes ready?' he asked her.

'They are,' replied Eldest Daughter.

Kotura took the clothes, and he ran his hands over them, and the skins felt rough to his touch, so badly were they dressed. He looked, and he saw that the garments were poorly cut, sewn together carelessly and much too small for him.

At this he became very angry, and he threw Eldest Daughter out of the *choom*. He threw her far, far out, and she fell into a drift of snow and lay there till she froze to death.

And the howling of the wind became fiercer than ever.

The old man sat in his *choom* and he listened to the wind howling and the storm raging day in and day out, and said, 'Eldest Daughter did not heed my words, she did not do as I bade her. That is why the wind does not stop howling. Kotura is angry. You must go to him, Second Daughter.'

The old man made a little sledge, he told Second Daughter just what he had told Eldest Daughter, and he sent her off to Kotura. And himself he remained in the *choom* with his youngest daughter, and waited for the blizzard to stop.

Second Daughter placed the sledge so that it faced the wind, and giving it a push, went along after it. The strings of her coat came undone as she walked and the snow got into her shoes. She was very cold, and forgetting her father's behest, shook the snow out of her shoes and tied the strings of her coat sooner than he had told her to.

She came to the mountain and climbed it, and seeing the little bird, waved her hands and chased it away. Then she got into her

sledge and coasted down the mountainside straight up to
Kotura's *choom*.

She entered the *choom*, made up a fire, had her fill of venison
and sat down to wait for Kotura.

Kotura came back from his hunting, he saw Second Daughter
and asked her, 'Why have you come to me?'

'My father sent me to you,' replied Second Daughter.

'Why did he send you?'

'So that you would take me to wife.'

'Why do you sit there then? I am hungry, be quick and cook
me some meat.'

When the meat was ready, Kotura ordered Second Daughter
to take it out of the pot and cut it in two parts.

'You and I will eat one half of the meat,' Kotura said. 'As for
the other, put it in that wooden dish yonder and take it to the
neighbouring *choom*. Do not enter the *choom* yourself, but
stand near it and wait for your dish to be brought out to you.'

Second Daughter took the meat and went outside. The wind
was howling and the snow whirling and it was hard to make out
anything. So, not liking to go any further, she threw the meat in
the snow, stood there a while and then went back to Kotura.

'Have you given them the meat?' Kotura asked.

'Yes, I have,' Second Daughter replied.

'You have come back very soon. Show me the dish, I want to
see what they gave you in return for the meat.'

Second Daughter did as she was told, and Kotura glanced at
the empty dish, but said not a word and went to bed. In the
morning he brought in some untanned deerskins and told
Second Daughter, just as he had her sister, to make him some
new clothes by evening.

'Set to work,' he said. 'In the evening I will see how well you
can sew.'

With these words Kotura went off to hunt and Second
Daughter set to work. She was in a great hurry, for somehow
she had to get everything done by evening. Suddenly a grey-
haired old woman came into the *choom*.

'A mote has got into my eye, child,' she said. 'Take it out, do.
I cannot manage it myself.'

'I am too busy to bother with your old mote!' Second
Daughter replied. 'Go away and let me work.'

And the old woman made no reply and went away without another word.

When night fell Kotura came back from his hunting.

'Are my new clothes ready?' he asked.

'Yes, they are,' Second Daughter replied.

'Let me try them on then.'

Kotura put on the clothes, and he saw that they were badly cut and much too small, and the seams ran all askew. Kotura flew into a rage, he threw Second Daughter where he had thrown her sister, and she too froze to death.

And the old man sat in his *choom* with his youngest daughter and waited in vain for the storm to calm down. The wind was fiercer than ever, and it seemed as if the *choom* would be blown away any minute.

'My daughters did not heed my words,' the old man said. 'They have made things worse, they have angered Kotura. You are my last remaining daughter, but still I must send you to Kotura in the hope that he will take you to wife. If I don't, our whole people will perish from hunger. So get ready, daughter, and go.'

And he told her where to go and what to do.

Youngest Daughter came out of the *choom*, she placed the sledge so that it faced the wind and, with a push, sent it gliding along. The wind was howling and roaring, trying to throw Youngest Daughter off her feet, and the snow blinded her eyes so that she could see nothing.

But Youngest Daughter plodded on through the blizzard, never forgetting a word of her father's behest and doing everything just as he had bade her. The strings of her coat came undone, but she did not stop to tie them. The snow got into her shoes, but she did not stop to shake it out. It was very cold, and the wind was very strong, but she did not pause and went on and on.

It was only when she came to the mountain and climbed it that she stopped and began shaking the snow from her shoes and tying the strings of her coat. Then a little bird flew up to her and perched on her shoulder. But Youngest Daughter did not chase the bird away. Instead, she fondled and stroked it tenderly. When the bird flew away Youngest Daughter got into her sledge and coasted down the mountainside straight up to Kotura's *choom*.

She went into the *choom* and waited. Suddenly the skin over the entrance was lifted and the young giant came in. When he saw Youngest Daughter he laughed and said, 'Why have you come to me?'

'My father sent me,' answered Youngest Daughter.

'Why did he send you?'

'To beg you to stop the storm, for if you don't, all our people will perish.'

'Why do you sit there? Why don't you make up a fire and cook some meat?' Kotura said. 'I am hungry, and so must you be too, for I see you have eaten nothing since you came.'

Youngest Daughter cooked the meat quickly, took it out of the pot and gave it to Kotura, and Kotura ate some of it and then told her to take one half of the meat to the neighbouring *choom*.

Youngest Daughter took the dish of meat and went outside. The wind was roaring loudly and the snow whirling and spinning. Where was she to go? Where was the *choom* of the neighbours to be found? She stood there a while, thinking, and then she started out through the storm, not knowing herself where she was going.

Suddenly there appeared before her the very same little bird that had flown up to her on the mountain. Now it began darting about near her face. Youngest Daughter decided to follow the bird's lead. Whichever way the bird flew, there she went.

On and on she walked, and at last, off to one side, a little distance away, she saw what looked like a spark flashing. Youngest Daughter was overjoyed, and she went in that direction, thinking that the *choom* was there. But when she drew near, she found that what she had thought to be a *choom* was a large mound with smoke curling up from it. Youngest Daughter walked round the mound and she prodded it with her foot, and suddenly there was a door before her. A grey-haired old woman looked out of the door and said, 'Who are you? Why have you come?'

'I have brought you some meat, grandmother,' Youngest Daughter replied. 'Kotura asked me to give it to you.'

'Kotura, you say? Very well, then, let me have it. And you wait here, outside.'

Youngest Daughter stood by the mound and waited. She waited a long time. At last the door opened again, the old woman looked out and handed her the wooden dish. There was something heaped on it, but the girl could not make out what it was. She took the dish and returned with it to Kotura.

'Why were you away so long?' Kotura asked. 'Did you find the *choom*?'

'Yes, I did.'

'Did you give them the meat?'

'Yes.'

'Let me have the dish, I want to see what is in it.'

Kotura looked, and he saw that there were several knives in the dish and steel needles and scrapers and brakes for dressing skins. Kotura laughed aloud and said, 'You have received many fine things that will be very useful to you.'

In the morning Kotura rose and he brought some deerskins into the *choom* and ordered Youngest Daughter to make him a new coat, shoes, and mittens by evening.

'If you make them well,' he said, 'I will take you to wife.'

Kotura went away, and Youngest Daughter set to work. The old woman's present proved very useful. Youngest Daughter had everything she needed to make the clothes with. But how much could one do in a single day? . . . Youngest Daughter spent no time thinking about it, but tried to do as much as she could. She dressed the skins and she scraped them, she cut and she sewed. All of a sudden the skin over the entrance lifted, and a grey-haired old woman came in. Youngest Daughter knew her at once: it was the same old woman to whom she had taken the meat.

'Help me, my child,' the old woman said. 'There's a mote in my eye. Please take it out for me, I cannot do it myself.'

Youngest Daughter did not refuse. She put aside her work and soon had the mote out of the old woman's eye.

'Good,' said the old woman, 'my eye does not hurt any more. Now look in my right ear.'

Youngest Daughter looked in the old woman's ear and started.

'What do you see there?' the old woman asked.

'There is a girl sitting in your ear,' Youngest Daughter replied.

'Why don't you call her? She will help you to make Kotura's clothes for him.'

Youngest Daughter was overjoyed, and she called to the girl. At her call, not one, but four young girls jumped out of the old woman's ear, and all four set to work. They dressed the skins and they scraped them, they cut and they sewed. The garments were soon ready. After that the old woman hid the four girls in her ear again and went away.

In the evening Kotura returned from his hunting.

'Have you done all that I told you to do?' he asked.

'Yes, I have,' Youngest Daughter replied.

'Let me see my new clothes, I will try them on.'

Youngest Daughter gave him the clothes, and Kotura took them and passed his hand over them: the skins were soft and pleasant to the touch. He put on the garments, and they were neither too small nor too large, but fitted him well and were made to last.

Kotura smiled and said, 'I like you, Youngest Daughter, and my mother and four sisters like you too. You work well, and you have courage. You braved a terrible storm in order that your people might not perish. Be my wife, stay with me in my *choom*.'

No sooner were the words out of his mouth than the storm in the tundra was stilled. No longer did the people try to hide from the wind, no longer did they freeze. One and all, they came out of their *chooms* into the light of day!

Why the Fish
Laughed

As a fisherwoman passed by the palace hawking her fish, the queen appeared at one of the windows and beckoned her to come near and show her what she had. At that moment a very big fish jumped about in the bottom of the basket.

'Is it a male or a female?' asked the queen. 'I'd like to buy a female fish.'

On hearing this, the fish laughed aloud.

'It's a male,' replied the fisherwoman, and continued on her rounds.

The queen returned to her room in a great rage. When the king came to see her that evening, he could tell that something was wrong.

'What's the matter?' he asked. 'Are you not well?'

'I'm quite well, thank you. But I'm very much annoyed at the strange behaviour of a fish. A woman showed me one today, and when I asked whether it was male or female, the fish laughed most rudely.'

'A fish laugh? Impossible! You must be dreaming.'

'I'm not a fool. I saw it with my own eyes and heard it laugh with my own ears.'

'That's very strange. All right, I'll make the necessary enquiries.'

The next morning, the king told his wazir what his wife had told him and ordered the wazir to investigate the matter and be ready with a satisfactory answer within six months, on pain of death.

The wazir promised to do his best, though he didn't know where to begin. For the next five months he laboured tirelessly to find a reason for the laughter of the fish. He went everywhere and consulted everyone—the wise and the learned, the people skilled in magic and trickery, they were all consulted. Nobody could explain the mystery of the laughing fish. So he returned brokenhearted to his house and began to arrange his affairs, sure now that he was going to die. He was well enough acquainted with the king's ways to know that His Majesty would not go back on his threat. Among other things, he advised his son to travel for a time, until the king's anger had cooled off somewhat.

The young fellow, who was both clever and handsome, started off and went wherever his legs and his kismet would take him. After a few days, he fell in with an old farmer who was on his way back to his village from a journey. The young man found him pleasant and asked if he might go with him. The old farmer agreed, and they walked along together. The day was hot, and the way was long and weary.

'Don't you think it would be much more pleasant if we could carry one another sometimes?' said the young man.

What a fool this man is! thought the old man.

A little later, they passed through a field of grain ready for the sickle and waving in the breeze, looking like a sea of gold.

'Is this eaten or not?' asked the young man.

The old man didn't know what to say, and said, 'I don't know.'

After a little while, the two travellers came to a big village, where the young man handed his companion a pocket knife, and said, 'Take this, friend, and get two horses with it. But please bring it back. It's very precious.'

The old man was half amused and half angry. He pushed away the knife, muttering that his friend was either mad or trying to play the fool. The young man pretended not to notice his reply and remained silent for a long time, till they reached a city a short distance from the old farmer's village. They walked about the bazaar and went to the mosque, but nobody greeted them or invited them to come in and rest.

'What a large cemetery!' exclaimed the young man.

What does the fellow mean, thought the old farmer, calling this city full of people a cemetery?

On leaving the city their way led through a cemetery where some people were praying beside a grave and distributing *chapatis* to passers-by in the name of their beloved dead. They gave some of the bread to the two travellers also, as much as they could eat.

'What a splendid city this is!' said the young man.

Now the man is surely crazy! thought the old farmer. I wonder what he'll do next. He'll be calling the land water, the water land. He'll be speaking of light when it's dark, and of darkness when it's light. But he kept his thoughts to himself.

Presently they had to wade through a stream. The water was rather deep, so the old farmer took off his shoes and *pajamas* and crossed over. But the young man waded through it with his shoes and *pajamas* on.

'Well, I've never seen such a perfect idiot, in word and deed,' said the old man to himself.

Yet he liked the fellow. He seemed cultivated and aristocratic. He would certainly amuse his wife and daughter. So he invited him home for a visit.

The young man thanked him and then asked, 'But let me ask, if you please, if the beam of your house is strong.'

The old farmer mumbled something and went home to tell his family, laughing to himself. When he was alone with them, he said, 'This young man has come with me a long way, and I've asked him to stay with us. But the fellow is such a fool that I can't make anything of what he says or does. He wants to know if the beam of this house is all right. The man must be mad!'

Now, the farmer's daughter was a very sharp and wise girl. She said to him, 'This man, whoever he is, is no fool. He only wishes to know if you can afford to entertain him.'

'Oh, of course,' said the farmer, 'I see. Well, perhaps you can help me to solve some of his other mysteries. While we were walking together, he asked whether we should not carry one another. He thought it would be a pleasanter mode of travel.'

'Certainly,' said the girl. 'He meant that one of you should tell the other a story to pass the time.'

'Oh yes. Then, when we were passing through a wheatfield, he asked me whether it was eaten or not.'

'And didn't you know what he meant, father? He simply wished to know if the owner of the field was in debt or not. If he was in debt, then the produce of the field was as good as eaten. That is, it would all go to his creditors.'

'Yes, yes, of course. Then, on entering a village, he asked me to take his pocket knife and get two horses with it, and bring back the knife to him.'

'Are not two stout sticks as good as two horses for helping one along the road? He only asked you to cut a couple of sticks and be careful not to lose the knife.'

'I see,' said the farmer. 'While we were walking through the city, we did not see anyone we knew, and not a soul gave us a scrap of anything to eat, till we reached the cemetery. There, some people called us and thrust *chapatis* into our hands. So my friend called the city a cemetery and the cemetery a city.'

'Look, father, inhospitable people are worse than the dead, and a city full of them is a dead place. But in the cemetery, which is crowded with the dead, you were greeted by kind people who gave you bread.'

'True, quite true,' said the astonished farmer. 'But then, just now, when we were crossing the stream, he waded across without taking off even his shoes.'

'I admire his wisdom,' said the daughter. 'I've often thought how stupid people were to get into that swiftly flowing stream and walk over those sharp stones with bare feet. The slightest stumble and they would fall and get wet from head to foot. This friend of yours is a very wise man. I would like to see him and talk to him.'

'Very well, I'll go and find him and bring him in.'

'Tell him, father, that our beams are strong enough, and then he will come in. I'll send on ahead a present for the man, to show that we can afford a guest.'

Then she called a servant and sent him to the young man with a present of a dish of porridge, twelve *chapatis*, and a jar of milk with the following message: 'Friend, the moon is full, twelve months make a year, and the sea is overflowing with water.'

On his way, the bearer of this present and message met his little son who, seeing what was in the basket, begged his father to give him some of the food. The foolish man gave him a lot of the porridge, a *chapati*, and some milk. When he saw the young man, he gave him the present and the message.

'Give your mistress my greetings,' he replied. 'And tell her that the moon is new, that I can find only eleven months in the year, and that the sea is by no means full.'

Not understanding the meaning of these words, the servant repeated them word for word to his mistress; and thus his theft was discovered, and he was punished. After a little while, the young man appeared with the old farmer. He was treated royally, as if he were the son of a great man, though the farmer knew nothing of his origins. In the course of the conversation, he told them everything—about the fish's laughter, his father's threatened execution, and his own exile—and asked their advice about what he should do.

'The laughter of the fish,' said the girl, 'which seems to have been the cause of all this trouble, indicates that there is a man in the women's quarters of the palace, and the king doesn't know anything about it.'

'Great! That's great!' exclaimed the wazir's son. 'There's yet time for me to return and to save my father from a shameful and unjust death.'

The following day he rushed back to his own country, taking with him the farmer's daughter. When he arrived, he ran to the palace and told his father what he had heard. The poor wazir, now almost dead from the expectation of death, was carried at once to the king in a palanquin. He repeated to the king what his son had said.

'A man in the queen's quarters! Never!' said the king.

'But it must be so, Your Majesty,' replied the wazir, 'and to prove the truth of what I've just heard, I propose a test. Please call together all the female attendants in your palace and order them to jump over a large pit, specially dug for this purpose. The man will at once betray his sex by the way he jumps.'

The king had the pit dug and ordered all the female servants of the palace to try to jump over it. All of them tried, but only one succeeded. That one was found to be a man!

Thus was the queen satisfied and the faithful old wazir saved.

Soon after that, the wazir's son married the old farmer's daughter. And it was a most happy marriage.

The Tongue-cut Sparrow

It was autumn, and the dawn was breaking. The forest was afire with the red of the maple trees; the cranes glided down to the watery rice-fields to dab for their morning meal; the croaks of the bull-frogs rumbled from the river banks; and Mount Fuji, wreathed in clouds, breathed idly and contentedly on the distant skyline.

It was a season and a morning dear to the old woodcutter's heart, and neither his poverty nor the sharp tongue of his irascible wife disturbed his tranquillity and happiness as slowly, with bent back and grasping a stout staff in his hand, he tramped through the forest to cut the day's fuel.

The birds knew him as a loving and gentle friend and chirruped in time to his walk, or flew from branch to branch along his path, waiting for him to scatter the millet grains which he always carried for them in a small bag tucked in his kimono sash. He had just stopped to throw the millet on the ground, when above the twittering he heard a plaintive cry of 'Chi! chi! chi! Chi! chi! chi!'

It seemed to come from a nearby bush though there was nothing to be seen. The woodcutter, sensing that a bird was in distress, went quickly to where the cry appeared to come from, and parting the bush, saw a small sparrow lying in the grass panting with fright and unable to move. Picking it up gently in both hands, he examined it and found that one of its legs was wounded. He tucked the sparrow into his kimono against the warmth of his breast and returned home at once to attend to the little sick creature.

His wife stormed bitterly at him when she learned the reason for his return and showered ill-natured complaints on him at the prospect of another mouth to feed, even though it was such a small one. The woodcutter, long resigned to her harsh tongue, went about quietly and unconcernedly tending to the sparrow. He laid it on an old cloth in a corner and fed it with warm rice-water and soft grains of millet. Day after day he cared for the little bird and with such unfailing devotion that, when the first snows came, its leg had already mended and its body was well and strong.

While it was ill the sparrow rarely ventured from the cage the woodcutter had fashioned for it, but as it became stronger, it became more venturesome. It took to hopping about the straw mat room and the wooden veranda outside, but ever with a watchful eye on the woodcutter's wife, who loathed it and lost no opportunity for attacking it with her broom and heaping on its head the wrath of the seven gods of thunder.

With the woodcutter it was different. The sparrow adored his gentle rescuer and the old woodcutter in turn loved the sparrow with all the warmth of his tender heart. Each evening it perched on the thatched roof to await his return from the forest. As he emerged from the darkening trees, it would set up an excited welcoming cry of 'Chun, chun, chun!' and fly round his head, sit on his shoulder, and pour its twitterings into his ear.

In the mornings it was a different story. As soon as the sparrow saw the old man preparing to leave, it huddled for-lornly in the corner of its cage and sang its plaintive 'Chi! chi! chi! Chi! chi! chi!' The woodcutter, equally sad at parting from his pet, would take the little bird gently in his hands, and stroking the soft feathers, say, 'Well, well, now! Do you think I am leaving you for ever? Content yourself, my friend. I shall be back before the last light leaves the trees.'

One morning the old man went off as usual, having first told his wife to take good care of the sparrow and give it something to eat during the day. The old woman merely grunted, muttered a curse, and proceeded with her preparations for washing out their spring kimonos. She drew water from the well and filled the great wooden pail, and in this she placed the fine cotton kimonos to steep. Then the long bamboo poles had to be wiped clean and slung from branch to branch of the trees. On these the kimonos would be threaded from sleeve to sleeve, so that they would dry quickly in the light breeze that fanned the trees.

Next she put some of her precious store of rice-flour into a deep earthenware bowl and mixed it with a little of the water into a glistening white paste. Today she took especial care to mix it fine and smooth, for she was preparing her own and her husband's best kimonos for the ceremonious advent of spring, and it was her custom to soak them in the rice-paste to give them a fine glossy sheen. Their supply of food was scanty enough, but she always managed to save enough of the flour for this yearly ritual.

Leaving the bowl of paste on the veranda, she squatted down by the wooden tub and began the long task of rubbing and steeping, steeping and rubbing, until the kimonos were clean and fresh as young bamboo shoots.

It was long past midday before she finished, and the poor sparrow, now ravenous, was singing its best to win the old woman's heart and her millet grains. But to no avail. She continued with her washing as if the bird did not exist, and the sour lines on her face told it that she had no intention of giving it anything. Dejected, it flew to the veranda, and seeing the bowl, perched on its rim. Whatever the white paste was inside, it looked good, smelt good, and, 'It tastes delicious, chun! chun!' cried the sparrow as it withdrew its beak and the rich rice-paste passed over its tongue.

'Oh! Oh! Oh! What a dish! What a find!' it chirruped in delight, and down went its beak again and did not reappear until the bottom of the bowl gleamed bare and clear in the midday winter sun. The sparrow hopped from the bowl on to the veranda and was preening itself in the sunshine when the old woman returned with the kimonos to dip them in the paste. When she saw the empty bowl, her whole body began shaking with hatred and anger, and seizing the sparrow before it had time to dodge out of her reach, she yelled, 'You did it! You did it! You gluttonous, grasping scavenger! Now I'll put an end to that pretty song of yours for good. Do you hear? For good! For good!'

As her voice rose to a screech, she pulled a pair of scissors from her pocket and forcing the sparrow's beak apart, slit its tongue with the sharp blades and flung the poor creature to the ground. The sparrow turned and churned the dust and its wings beat the earth in agony. Cries of pain formed in its throat, but no sounds came from its beak. Several times it tried to lift itself from the earth, but its sufferings seemed to anchor it. Round and round it struggled and fluttered. Then, with one last effort of its little pain-filled body, it rose in the air and disappeared over the tree-tops of the forest.

Returning home that evening, the woodcutter was greatly surprised not to hear his usual welcome as he approached the hut. His pet was nowhere to be seen. And no glad 'Chun, chun, chun!' broke the evening stillness. Perturbed and uneasy, he went straight to its cage but found it empty. Turning to his wife he asked, 'Where is our little Chunko?'

'The nasty creature ate every morsel of my rice-paste: so I slit its tongue and drove it away. Wherever it is now, it is better than being here; for I could stand the wretch no longer,' his wife replied in anger.

'Oh, how pitiful! How pitiful!' cried the woodcutter in anguish, as if his own tongue had suffered the fate of his little sparrow. 'What a cruel, what a wicked thing to do! You will suffer for this evil, indeed! Where is my little friend now? Where can it have gone?'

'The further the better for my part,' snapped back his wife, untouched by her husband's distress. 'And a good riddance into the bargain!'

That night the woodcutter could not sleep. He turned and tossed in wakeful anxiety for his little bird, calling out from time to time in the hope that it might answer. When at last light came, he rose and dressed quickly and went to the forest in search of it. For a long time he wandered calling out, 'Tongue-cut sparrow, where are you? Where are you? Come to me, my little Chunko!'

But only the croaks of the bull-frogs, the cries of the cranes high overhead, and the chirrupings of the forest birds answered; the gay, glad song of 'Chun, chun, chun!' was nowhere to be heard. All the morning he searched and far into the afternoon, forgetful of food or weariness and with thought only for his little friend. As the evening light settled over the forest, turning the shadowy trees to the shapes of menacing giants and ferocious beasts, he sat down at the foot of a tree, exhausted and desolate, but still calling out, 'My little tongue-cut Chunko, where are you? Where are you?'

Overcome by the sadness in the woodcutter's voice, some sparrows, perched above him in the tree-tops, flew down to greet and to talk to him. The old man was overjoyed to see them and begged them for news of his friend. The birds were deeply moved by the woodcutter's grief, and twittering among themselves, they finally said, 'Grandpapa San, we know your Chunko well and where it lives. Follow us and we shall lead you to its home.'

The woodcutter, all thought of his weariness gone, sprang up and started out after the sparrows. He followed in the darkness for a long time, till at last they came to a clearing and there, in the midst of a moss-covered patch, surrounded by bamboo saplings, was a house gaily lit with lanterns hanging from the thatched eaves.

Immediately a throng of sparrows came out to welcome him. They lined up before him and bowed deeply until their beaks touched the ground. They showed him into the house with every courtesy, helping him to remove his straw-bound clogs and putting soft slippers on his feet. They led him along a corridor of shining cedar wood to a room of newly-laid straw matting. Here he courteously knocked off the soft slippers and entered in his cloth socks. The sparrows pulled back the decorated sliding screens of an inner room to reveal little Chunko surrounded by a flock of attendants, sitting on the floor awaiting his arrival.

'Oh! little friend, I have found you at last! I have looked in every tree in the forest to bring you back and comfort you and ask your forgiveness for the wickedness of my wife. And your tongue? Is it healed? How I grieved for you! I am overjoyed to see you again,' the woodcutter cried with the tears trickling down his cheeks.

'Thank you, thank you, Grandpapa! I am completely healed. Thank you! I, too, am overjoyed to see you,' wept the little sparrow and flew to the shoulder of the old man, who stroked it gently and tenderly.

'But, now, you must meet my parents,' said Chunko.

So saying, the sparrow led him into another room and presented him to its parents, who knew already of their child's rescue from death and the great kindness bestowed upon it during the long days of its illness by the old woodcutter. Bowing low, the parent birds expressed their grateful thanks to the old man, murmuring with deep gratitude that their obligation to him could never be repaid. They summoned the serving birds and instructed them to prepare a feast.

As an honoured guest, they seated the old man nearest to the alcove in which a silk scroll inscribed with a poem hung. The old woodcutter was lost in wonder at the great beauty of the table and its furnishings. The chopsticks were of pure ivory, the soup-bowls of gilded lacquer, and the serving dishes were from the finest kilns in the land. Exquisite dish followed exquisite dish and all was served with delicacy and taste.

After the feast a group of elegant and gaily-kimonoed young sparrows entered, and to the accompaniment of two older birds—one who plucked the strings of the samisen and the other who chanted the words of the song—they performed the famous classical dance, 'The Wind among the Bamboo Leaves'. At that moment a light wind rose in the bamboo grove outside, shaking the branches and rustling the leaves in harmony with the sweet voices of the dancers as they joined in the words of the song.

As the dance finished and the wind among the leaves died away, the dancers bowed gracefully before disappearing into the inner room. Almost immediately they were followed by a second group, all carrying many-coloured paper parasols. The music of the samisen became sparkling and gay; the parasols twirled and spun; the dancers' feet beat 'tom, tom, tom'; and the lanterns hanging from the eaves swayed in rhythm with the dance. The woodcutter's eyes sparkled, he beat time with his chopsticks, and he was lost to all but the merriment of the wonderful scene.

The music faded and the dancers bowed and pattered out. Thoughts of his wife began to trouble the old man and reluctantly he told his hosts that he must return home. The sparrows were deeply disappointed and tried hard to dissuade him, but the woodcutter said that it would be unkind to leave his wife alone any longer and that he must return. Never before had he known that life could be so good, so gay, and so gracious; never would he forget this evening and the rare kindness of his honourable hosts. But now he must leave. They pressed him no further.

Then the father bird spoke, 'Honourable and gentle wood-cutter, we are deeply conscious of your greatness of heart and the loving care you bestowed upon our only child. You came to love Chunko as your own, and Chunko loved you as a father. We want you to remember that our humble home will always be yours, our unworthy food will be your food, and all we possess we shall always share with you. But tonight we wish you to accept a gift from us as a token of our unbounded gratitude.'

At this, two wicker baskets were brought before the old man by the serving birds and placed on the floor.

'Here are two baskets,' continued the father bird. 'One is large and heavy; the other is small and light. Whichever you choose, my honourable friend, is yours, and is given with the heartfelt wishes of us all.'

The woodcutter was deeply moved and tears filled his eyes. He looked at the parent birds for a long time unable to speak. At last he said, 'I have no wish for many possessions in this world. I am old and frail and my time on earth will not be much longer. My needs are very small. So I shall accept most gratefully the smaller basket.'

The serving birds carried the basket to the entrance hall and there they tied it on the old man's back and helped him on with his clogs. All the sparrows gathered at the door to wish him farewell.

'Goodbye, my little friends. Goodbye, little Chunko! Look after yourself! It was a wonderful evening and I shall never forget it,' said the old man and bowed courteously many times. With a final wave of his hand, he left the grove and disappeared into the blackness of the forest with a flock of sparrows flying in front to put him on his way.

When he reached home the clouds were already glowing with the morning sun. He found his wife as angry as a November storm because of his long absence and her fury was unleashed over the poor woodcutter's head. Suddenly catching sight of the basket on his back, her tirade stopped.

'What's that you've got on your back?' she said in a voice filled with curiosity.

'It is a gift from the parents of little Chunko,' replied her husband.

'Well, why do you stupidly stand there and not tell me? What is it? What have the creatures given you? Don't stand there like someone dead! Off with it from your back and see what's inside!' carped her greedy voice, and grasping the straps, she trailed the basket from his shoulders and tore open the lid.

A burst of dazzling brightness momentarily blinded her avaricious eyes, for inside lay kimonos soft as the morning dew and dyed with the petals of wild flowers, rolls of silk spun from the plumes of cranes, branches of coral from the seas of heaven, and ornaments sparkling brighter than the eyes of lovers. They both gazed in silence, dazed and bewildered; these were riches beyond even the world of their imagination. 'A poet's dreamings,' murmured the old man, and fell into silence again. The old woman drove in her hands and let the ornaments trickle through her trembling fingers.

'We are rich! We are rich! We are rich!' she repeated over and over.

Later that day the old man recounted the story of his adventure from the beginning. When his wife heard that he had chosen the small basket when he might have had the larger one, she burst out in anger.

'What sort of a stupid husband have I? You bring home a small basket when with a little more trouble you could have brought home twice the quantity of treasures. We would have been doubly rich. This very day I will go myself and pay the birds a visit. I shall not be so senseless as you. I will see to it that I return with the big basket.'

The old woodcutter argued and pleaded with her to be content with what they had. They were rich beyond the wealth of kings—enough for them and all the generations of their relatives. But her ears were stopped by the thoughts of her clutching, covetous mind, and grasping her outer wrap, she rushed out in a fever of anticipation.

As she had a good idea of the whereabouts of the sparrow's house from her husband's description, she reached the bamboo grove before midday.

'Tongue-cut sparrow, where are you? Where are you, little Chunko? Come to me!' she cried.

But her voice was harsh and even her smooth pleadings could not conceal the cantankerousness of her nature. It was a long time before any bird appeared. At last two sparrows flew from the house and curtly asked her what was her business.

'I have come to see my friend, little Chunko,' she answered.

Without saying another word, the sparrows led her to the house, where she was met by the serving birds, who, also quiet and reserved, led her along the corridor to the inner room. She was in so much hurry that she refused to stop to remove her wooden clogs and the sparrows were horrified at such insolent bad manners. When little Chunko saw her, it flew terrified to a roof beam.

'Ah! I see that you are quite recovered, my little pet. I knew I had not really hurt you!' she said in a honeyed voice. Then forgetting all womanly modesty and oblivious of the cold atmosphere about her, she blurted out, 'I am in a hurry. Please do not bother to dance for me. And I have no time to eat anything either. But I have come a long way, so please give me a souvenir of my visit quickly, as I must return at once.'

In silence the serving birds brought in two baskets, one large and heavy and one small and light, and placed them before her.

'As a parting gift from us, please accept one of these baskets,' said the father bird. 'As you see, one is large and heavy and the other is small and light. Whichever you choose is yours.'

Barely waiting for the parent bird to finish speaking, the old woman pointed eagerly to the large basket.

'It is yours,' said the bird gravely.

In the hall, with many shoves and heaves, the sparrows hoisted the basket on to the old woman's back and bowed her in silence out of the door. She wasted no time in bows in return but hastened off into the cover of the forest, staggering under the weight of the basket.

No sooner was she out of sight of the bamboo grove than she dragged the basket from her back and flung open the lid. Horrified she fell back as monsters and devils poured out with eyes shooting flames, mouths belching smoke, and ears emitting sulphurous clouds. Some had seven horned heads that lolloped and rolled on their slithery bodies, some had arms that writhed and coiled like snakes waving and searching blindly through the sulphurous air. Bodies, tenuous and billowing and spiked with the horns of great sea-shells, floated upwards and outwards; among them one in the semblance of a young girl with floating black hair whose sole feature was a single eyeball set in the centre of a blank, white face. All these rose and bent and drifted over the horror-stricken body of the old woman.

'Where is this grasping, greedy, wicked woman?' they screamed, and the snaky arms groped and twisted round her. Suddenly all the monsters shrieked with one searing, ear-splitting voice, 'There she is! There is the evil-minded hag! Let us blow sulphur in her eyes and they'll be greedy no longer. Let us embrace her to our shell-spiked breasts and destroy the wickedness in her flesh. Let us peck and nibble her with our forked tongues until she dies, dies, dies.'

Panic-stricken the old woman fled, all feeling frozen out of her body. Through bush and bramble and water she sped with the swiftness of the wind, the monsters in mad pursuit behind.

'Peck her, nibble her, blow sulphur in her eyes; puncture her flesh with our spiked breasts,' they screeched.

'Oh! Buddha! Help me! Save me from these devils!' the old woman screamed.

Their bodies floated over her, their blindly groping arms stretched out to enfold her. Suddenly there was a burst of light among the trees. It was the setting sun showering the sky with rose and gold. As the golden radiance flooded the forest the monsters huddled back with yells of dismay, and turning in panic, they vanished into the darkness of the trees and were seen no more.

The old woman stopped, breathless and trembling, her body sick in every pore. The radiance in the forest was now dying, and dreading the monsters' return, she started off again, exhausted and trembling at every step.

When she reached home, her husband, shocked at her pitiful state, ran out and helped her to the veranda, where she sat panting for some time before she was able to speak.

'What has happened to you? What has happened to you? Do please tell me!' pleaded the old man.

His wife, after telling him her story, said, 'I have been ill-natured, evil-minded, and greedy all my life. This is the retribution I have deserved. I have had my lesson, a bitter one, but not perhaps so bitter as the life I have led you. Now I know how evil I have been. From this hour onwards, I will mend my ways. I will try to be a kinder, gentler woman and a better wife to you, my dear husband.'

He placed his hand on her shoulder and they both knew that the bad days were gone for ever. For the years that were left to them they knew no want and never a harsh word passed the old woman's lips. The sparrows became their closest friends and each paid regular visits to the other's home. Long after the old couple died, the sparrows commemorated the story of the old man and the old woman in a song, and for all I know they sing it to their children still.

The Son of
Seven Queens

Once upon a time there lived a king who had seven queens, but no children. This was a great grief to him, especially when he remembered that on his death there would be no heir to inherit the kingdom.

Now it happened one day that a poor old fakir came to the king, and said, 'Your prayers are heard, your desire shall be accomplished, and one of your seven queens shall bear a son.'

The king's delight at this promise knew no bounds, and he gave orders for appropriate festivities to be prepared against the coming event throughout the length and breadth of the land.

Meanwhile the seven queens lived luxuriously in a splendid palace, attended by hundreds of female slaves, and fed to their hearts' content on sweetmeats and confectionery.

Now the king was very fond of hunting, and one day, before he started, the seven queens sent him a message saying, 'May it please our dearest lord not to hunt towards the north today, for we have dreamt bad dreams, and fear lest evil should befall you.'

The king, to allay their anxiety, promised regard for their wishes, and set out towards the south; but as luck would have it, although he hunted diligently, he found no game. Nor had he more success to the east or west, so that, being a keen sportsman, and determined not to go home empty-handed, he forgot all about his promise, and turned to the north.

Here also he was at first unsuccessful, but just as he made up his mind to give up for that day, a white hind with golden horns and silver hoofs flashed past him into a thicket. So quickly did it pass that he scarcely saw it; nevertheless a burning desire to capture and possess the beautiful strange creature filled his breast. He instantly ordered his attendants to form a ring round the thicket, and so encircle the hind; then, gradually narrowing the circle, he pressed forward till he could distinctly see the white hind panting in the midst. Nearer and nearer he advanced, till, just as he thought to lay hold of the beautiful strange creature, it gave one mighty bound, leapt clean over the king's head, and fled towards the mountains.

Forgetful of all else, the king, setting spurs to his horse, followed at full speed. On, on he galloped, leaving his retinue far behind, keeping the white hind in view, never drawing bridle, until, finding himself in a narrow ravine with no outlet, he reined in his steed. Before him stood a miserable hovel, into which, being tired after his long, unsuccessful chase, he entered to ask for a drink of water. An old woman, seated in the hut at a spinning-wheel, answered his request by calling to her daughter, and immediately from an inner room came a maiden so lovely and charming, so white-skinned and golden-haired, that the king was transfixed by astonishment at seeing so beautiful a sight in the wretched hovel.

She held the vessel of water to the king's lips, and as he drank he looked into her eyes, and then it became clear to him that the girl was none other than the white hind with the golden horns and silver feet he had chased so far.

Her beauty bewitched him, so he fell on his knees, begging her to return with him as his bride; but she only laughed, saying seven queens were quite enough even for a king to manage. However, when he would take no refusal, but implored her to have pity on him, promising everything she could desire, she replied, 'Give me the eyes of your seven queens, and then perhaps I may believe you mean what you say.'

The king was so carried away by the glamour of the white hind's magical beauty, that he went home at once, had the eyes of his seven queens taken out, and, after throwing the poor blind creatures into a noisome dungeon whence they could not escape, set off once more for the hovel in the ravine, bearing with him his horrible offering. But the white hind only laughed cruelly when she saw the fourteen eyes, and threading them as a necklace, flung it round her mother's neck saying, 'Wear that, little mother, as a keepsake, whilst I am away in the king's palace.'

Then she went back with the bewitched monarch, as his bride, and he gave her the seven queens' rich clothes and jewels to wear, the seven queens' palace to live in, and the seven queens' slaves to wait upon her; so that she really had everything a witch could desire.

Now, very soon after the seven wretched hapless queens had their eyes torn out, and were cast into prison, a baby was born to the youngest of the queens. It was a handsome boy, but the other queens were very jealous that the youngest amongst them should be so fortunate. But though at first they disliked the handsome little boy, he soon proved so useful to them, that ere long they all looked on him as their son. Almost as soon as he could walk about he began scraping at the mud wall of their dungeon, and in an incredibly short space of time had made a hole big enough for him to crawl through. Through this he disappeared, returning in an hour or so laden with sweetmeats, which he divided equally amongst the seven blind queens.

As he grew older he enlarged the hole, and slipped out two or three times every day to play with the little nobles in the town. No one knew who the tiny boy was, but everybody liked him, and he was so full of funny tricks and antics, so merry and bright, that he was sure to be rewarded by some girdle-cakes, a handful of parched grain, or some sweetmeats. All these things he brought home to his seven mothers, as he loved to call the seven blind queens, who by his help lived on in their dungeon when all the world thought they had starved to death ages before.

At last, when he was quite a big lad, he one day took his bow and arrow, and went out to seek for game. Coming by chance past the palace where the white hind lived in wicked splendour and magnificence, he saw some pigeons fluttering round the white marble turrets, and, taking good aim, shot one dead. It came tumbling past the very window where the white queen was sitting; she rose to see what was the matter, and looked out. At the first glance of the handsome young lad standing there bow in hand, she knew by witchcraft that it was the king's son.

She nearly died of envy and spite, determining to destroy the lad without delay; therefore, sending a servant to bring him to her presence, she asked him if he would sell her the pigeon he had just shot.

'No,' replied the sturdy lad, 'the pigeon is for my seven blind mothers, who live in the noisome dungeon, and who would die if I did not bring them food.'

'Poor souls!' cried the cunning white witch. 'Would you not like to bring them their eyes again? Give me the pigeon, my dear, and I faithfully promise to show you where to find them.'

Hearing this, the lad was delighted beyond measure, and gave up the pigeon at once. Whereupon the white queen told him to seek her mother without delay, and ask for the eyes which she wore as a necklace.

'She will not fail to give them,' said the cruel queen, 'if you show her this token on which I have written what I want done.'

So saying, she gave the lad a piece of broken potsherd, with these words inscribed on it—'Kill the bearer at once, and sprinkle his blood like water!'

Now, as the son of seven queens could not read, he took the fatal message cheerfully, and set off to find the white queen's mother.

Whilst he was journeying he passed through a town, where every one of the inhabitants looked so sad, that he could not help asking what was the matter. They told him it was because the king's only daughter refused to marry; so when her father died there would be no heir to the throne. They greatly feared she must be out of her mind, for though every good-looking young man in the kingdom had been shown to her, she declared she would only marry one who was the son of seven mothers, and who ever heard of such a thing? The king, in despair, had

ordered every man who entered the city gates to be led before the princess; so, much to the lad's impatience, for he was in an immense hurry to find his mother's eyes, he was dragged into the presence chamber.

No sooner did the princess catch sight of him than she blushed, and, turning to the king, said, 'Dear father, this is my choice!'

Never were such rejoicings as these few words produced. The inhabitants nearly went wild with joy, but the son of seven queens said he would not marry the princess unless they first let him recover his mothers' eyes. When the beautiful bride heard his story, she asked to see the potsherd, for she was very learned and clever. Seeing the treacherous words, she said nothing, but taking another similar-shaped bit of potsherd, she wrote on it these words—'Take care of this lad, giving him all he desires,' and returned it to the son of seven queens, who, none the wiser, set off on his quest.

Ere long he arrived at the hovel in the ravine where the white witch's mother, a hideous old creature, grumbled dreadfully on reading the message, especially when the lad asked for the necklace of eyes. Nevertheless she took it off, and gave it to him, saying, 'There are only thirteen of 'em now, for I lost one last week.'

The lad, however, was only too glad to get any at all, so he hurried home as fast as he could to his seven mothers, and gave two eyes apiece to the six elder queens; but to the youngest he gave one, saying, 'Dearest little mother! I will be your other eye always!'

After this he set off to marry the princess, as he had promised, but when passing by the white queen's palace he saw some pigeons on the roof. Drawing his bow, he shot one, and it came fluttering past the window. The white hind looked out, and lo! there was the king's son alive and well.

She cried with hatred and disgust, but sending for the lad, asked him how he had returned so soon, and when she heard how he had brought home the thirteen eyes, and given them to the seven blind queens, she could hardly restrain her rage. Nevertheless she pretended to be charmed with his success, and told him that if he would give her this pigeon also, she would reward him with the Jogi's wonderful cow, whose milk flows all day long, and makes a pond as big as a kingdom. The lad, nothing loath, gave her the pigeon; whereupon, as before, she bade him go and ask her mother for the cow, and gave him a potsherd whereupon was written—'Kill this lad without fail, and sprinkle his blood like water!'

But on the way the son of seven queens looked in on the princess, just to tell her how he came to be delayed, and she, after reading the message on the potsherd, gave him another in its stead; so that when the lad reached the old hag's hut and asked her for the Jogi's cow, she could not refuse, but told the boy how to find it; and, bidding him of all things not to be afraid of the eighteen thousand demons who kept watch and ward over the treasure, told him to be off before she became too angry at her daughter's foolishness in thus giving away so many good things.

Then the lad did as he had been told bravely. He journeyed on and on till he came to a milk-white pond, guarded by the eighteen thousand demons. They were really frightful to behold, but, plucking up courage, he whistled a tune as he walked through them, looking neither to the right nor the left. By and by he came upon the Jogi's cow, tall, white and beautiful, while the Jogi himself, who was king of all the demons, sat milking her day and night, and the milk streamed from her udder, filling the milk-white tank.

The Jogi, seeing the lad, called out fiercely, 'What do you want here?'

Then the lad answered, according to the old hag's bidding, 'I want your skin, for King Idra is making a new kettle-drum, and says your skin is nice and tough.'

Upon this the Jogi began to shiver and shake (for no Jinn or Jogi dares disobey King Idra's command), and, falling at the lad's feet, cried, 'If you will spare me I will give you anything I possess, even my beautiful white cow!'

To this the son of seven queens, after a little pretended hesitation, agreed, saying that after all it would not be difficult to find a nice tough skin like Jogi's elsewhere; so, driving the wonderful cow before him, he set off homewards. The seven queens were delighted to possess so marvellous an animal, and though they toiled from morning till night making curds and whey, besides selling milk to the confectioners, they could not use half the cow gave, and became richer and richer by the day.

Seeing them so comfortably off, the son of seven queens started off with a light heart to marry the princess; but when passing the white hind's palace he could not resist sending a bolt at some pigeons which were cooing on the parapet. One fell dead just beneath the window where the white queen was sitting. Looking out, she saw the lad hale and hearty standing before her, and grew whiter than ever with rage and spite.

She sent for him to ask how he had returned so soon, and when she heard how kindly her mother had received him, she nearly had a fit; however, she dissembled her feelings as well as she could, and, smiling sweetly, said she was glad to have been able to fulfil her promise, and that if he would give her this third pigeon, she would do yet more for him than she had done before, by giving him the million-fold rice, which ripens in one night.

The lad was of course delighted at the very idea, and, giving up the pigeon, set off on his quest, armed as before with a potsherd, on which was written, 'Do not fail this time. Kill the lad, and sprinkle his blood like water!'

But when he looked in on his princess, just to prevent her becoming anxious about him, she asked to see the potsherd as usual, and substituted another, on which was written, 'Yet again give this lad all he requires, for his blood shall be as your blood!'

Now when the old hag saw this, and heard how the lad wanted the million-fold rice which ripens in a single night, she fell into the most furious rage, but being terribly afraid of her daughter, she controlled herself, and bade the boy go and find the field guarded by eighteen million demons, warning him on no account to look back after having plucked the tallest spike of rice, which grew in the centre.

So the son of seven queens set off, and soon came to the field where, guarded by eighteen million demons, the million-fold rice grew. He walked on bravely, looking neither to the right or left, till he reached the centre and plucked the tallest ear, but as he turned homewards a thousand sweet voices rose behind him, crying in tenderest accents, 'Pluck me too! Oh, please pluck me too!' He looked back, and lo! there was nothing left of him but a little heap of ashes!

Now as time passed by and the lad did not return, the old hag grew uneasy, remembering the message 'his blood shall be as your blood'; so she set off to see what had happened.

Soon she came to the heap of ashes, and knowing by her arts what it was, she took a little water, and kneading the ashes into a paste, formed it into the likeness of a man; then, putting a drop of blood from her little finger into its mouth, she blew on it, and instantly the son of seven queens started up as well as ever.

'Don't you disobey orders again!' grumbled the old hag. 'Or next time I'll leave you alone. Now be off, before I repent my kindness!'

So the son of seven queens returned joyfully to his seven mothers, who, by the aid of the million-fold rice, soon became the richest people in the kingdom. Then they celebrated their son's marriage to the clever princess with all imaginable pomp; but the bride was so clever, she would not rest until she had made known her husband to his father, and punished the wicked white witch. So she made her husband build a palace exactly like the one in which the seven queens had lived, and in which the white witch now dwelt in splendour. Then, when all was prepared, she bade her husband give a grand feast for the king.

Now the king had heard much of the mysterious son of seven queens, and his marvellous wealth, so he gladly accepted the invitation; but what was his astonishment when on entering the palace he found it was a facsimile of his own in every particular! And when his host, richly attired, led him straight to the private hall, where on royal thrones sat the seven queens, dressed as he had last seen them, he was speechless with surprise, until the princess, coming forward, threw herself at his feet, and told him the whole story.

Then the king awoke from his enchantment, and his anger rose against the wicked white hind who had bewitched him so long, until he could not contain himself. So she was put to death, and her grave ploughed over, and after that the seven queens returned to their own splendid palace, and everybody lived happily.

The Power of Love

A young man was intending to get married, when suddenly Death appeared and stood in front of him.

'You shall die on your wedding day,' he said.

Petrified with fear, the young man could not utter a single word. He wandered sadly off until he came to the foot of Mount Biledjan. He looked up and saw an old man with a white beard seated upon an aery throne, a staff in his hand. The old man's face shone with a bright light.

'Why are you so pale, boy?' asked the old man. 'Where are you going?'

'I'm running away from Death,' replied the young man. 'I'm in grave trouble, that's for sure!'

The old man smiled grimly, nodded his head and stroked his beard.

'Nobody has ever yet managed to escape from that mangy bag-o'-bones, sure enough!' he said. 'But I'll tell you something: his beard is firmly in *my* grasp, and *I* tell him when to take the soul of such and such a man, or shorten the life of such and such another, or lengthen that of such and such another.'

'Who are you then, grandfather?'

'They call me Time.'

'If you have such power, let me fall at your feet and beg you to save me! You can see that I'm still very young, and full of vigour. Why does he encompass my downfall? What have I done to him?'

The old man was moved.

'For so long as you remain terrified of Death, you will flee him, and remain for ever homeless,' he said. 'So walk one hundred paces to my right until you come to a wild plum tree. There you will find a well with water as limpid as the eye of a crane. Drink of that water, and the taste shall rid you of your fear, and the spirit of fortitude shall rise within you. Then go your way, and God be with you.'

The young man kissed the old man's hand, thanked him, found the well, drank the magic water which rid him of his fear and inspired him with fortitude, and went on his way. He marched on and on, until he came to a city built at the edge of a great sea. Here he settled for a few years, earned himself a small fortune, and then made his way back home to his mother and father. No sooner had he crossed the threshold, however, when, hey presto! there stood Death in front of him!

'So you thought you'd escape me, did you?' said Death. 'Who can extricate himself from my clutches, pray? It's all up with you now! Come on, hand over your soul!'

The young man's mother darted in between them.

'Why do you kill my young son?' she cried. 'If you must have someone's soul, take mine!'

Death started to tug at her soul, till it began to leave her feet and move up through her windpipe. The old woman could not stand it for long. 'Help, Death is ravishing my soul!' she cried.

Death relaxed his grip.

The young man's father darted forward.

'Do not kill my only son, the pillar and light of my house!' he cried. 'If you must have someone's soul, take mine!'

Death started to draw his soul till it left his legs and moved up past his tongue. The old man could not stand it for long.

'Help me, son! Death is robbing me of my soul to save your life!' he cried.

Death relaxed his grip.

'I cannot blame them,' said the young man. 'There is no need for them to suffer for my sake. But since you are here, let us go to the house of my betrothed. If she is not prepared to sacrifice up her soul for me, then most gladly will I surrender my own!'

So Death and the young man went to the house of his intended bride. As soon as the girl saw the young man, Death had no time to set to work before she ran up, threw her arms round the young man's neck, and kissed him warmly. So close was their embrace, it seemed they were but one body and soul.

'Ho there!' shouted Death. 'That's enough! I've no more time to waste. Tell me what you wish to do!'

'What do *you* want?' asked the girl.

'I am here to take your young man's soul!' said Death.

'If you must take someone's soul, take mine!' said the girl.

Death began to tug at her soul, till it slowly came away at the tips of her toes and the roots of her hair.

'Why are you torturing me so?' cried the girl. 'If you want my soul, take it at one go! Let me only first kiss my betrothed, as I yearn to do, and then do as you will!'

Death snatched away the girl's soul with one sharp tug. No sooner had he done so, however, than he began to marvel at her great love and devotion, and being unable to dismiss the young man and the young woman from his mind, he relented, and he gave her back her soul, and left them together, and went on his way. The young man and his betrothed returned home in great joy. For three days and three nights the wedding festivities continued, and they achieved their hearts' desire.

Three apples fell from Heaven: one for the bride, one for the bridegroom, and one for the white-bearded old man, who was, is, and ever shall be, until the End of Time. Amen.

The Forty Thieves

In a town in Persia there dwelt two brothers, one named Cassim, the other Ali Baba. Cassim was married to a rich wife and lived in plenty, while Ali Baba had to maintain his wife and children by cutting wood in a neighbouring forest and selling it in the town. One day, when Ali Baba was in the forest, he saw a troop of men on horseback, coming towards him. He was afraid they were robbers, and climbed into a tree for safety. When they came up to him and dismounted, he counted forty of them.

The finest man among them, whom Ali Baba took to be their captain, went a little way among some bushes, and said, 'Open, Sesame!' so plainly that Ali Baba heard him. A door opened in the rocks, and having made the troop go in, he followed them, and the door shut again of itself. Ali Baba, fearing they might come out and catch him, was forced to sit patiently in the tree. At last the door opened again, and the Forty Thieves came out.

The captain then closed the door, saying, 'Shut, Sesame!' Every man mounted, the captain put himself at their head, and they returned as they came.

Then Ali Baba climbed down and went to the door concealed among the bushes, and said, 'Open, Sesame!' and it flew open. Ali Baba, who expected a dull, dismal place, was greatly surprised to find it large and well lighted. He saw rich bales of merchandise—silk, stuff-brocades all piled together, and gold and silver in heaps, and money in leather purses.

He went in and the door shut behind him. He did not look at the silver, but brought out as many bags of gold as he thought his asses could carry, loaded them with the bags, and hid it all with faggots. Using the words, 'Shut, Sesame!' he closed the door and went home.

Then he drove his asses into the yard, carried the money bags to his wife, and emptied them out before her. He bade her keep the secret, and he would go and bury the gold. 'Let me first measure it,' said his wife. 'I will go and borrow a measure from someone, while you dig the hole.' So she ran to the wife of Cassim and borrowed a measure. Knowing Ali Baba's poverty, the sister was curious to find out what sort of grain his wife wished to measure, and artfully put some suet at the bottom of the measure.

Ali Baba's wife went home and set the measure on the heap of gold, and filled it and emptied it often, to her great content. She then carried it back to her sister, without noticing that a piece of gold was sticking to it, which Cassim's wife perceived directly her back was turned.

She grew very curious, and said to Cassim, 'Cassim, your brother is richer than you. He does not count his money, he measures it.' He begged her to explain this riddle, which she did by showing him the piece of money and telling him where she found it.

Cassim grew envious and went to his brother in the morning before sunrise. 'Ali Baba,' he said, showing him the gold piece, 'you pretend to be poor and yet you measure gold.'

By this Ali Baba perceived that through his wife's folly Cassim and his wife knew their secret, so he confessed all and offered Cassim a share.

'That I expect,' said Cassim, 'but I must know where to find the treasure, otherwise I will discover all, and you will lose all.'

Ali Baba, more out of kindness than fear, told him of the cave, and the very words to use.

Cassim left Ali Baba, meaning to get the treasure for himself. He rose early next morning, and set out with ten mules loaded with great chests. He soon found the place, and the door in the rock. He said, 'Open, Sesame!' and the door opened and shut behind him.

He hastened to gather together as much of the treasure as possible, but when he was ready to go he could not remember what to say for thinking of his great riches. Instead of 'Sesame,' he said, 'Open, Barley!' and the door remained fast. He named several different sorts of grain, all but the right one, and the door still stuck fast. He was so frightened at the danger he was in that he had as much forgotten the word as if he had never heard it.

About noon the robbers returned to their cave, and saw Cassim's mules roving about with great chests on their backs. This gave them the alarm: they drew their sabres, and went to the door, which opened on their captain's saying: 'Open, Sesame!'

Cassim, who had heard the trampling of their horses' feet, resolved to sell his life dearly, so when the door opened he leaped out and threw the captain down. In vain, however, for the robbers with their sabres soon killed him. On entering the cave they saw all the bags laid ready, and could not imagine how anyone had got in without knowing their secret. They cut Cassim's body into four quarters, and nailed them up inside the cave, in order to frighten anyone who should venture in, and went away in search of more treasure.

As night drew on Cassim's wife grew very uneasy, and ran to her brother-in-law, and told him where her husband had gone. Ali Baba did his best to comfort her, and set out to the forest in search of Cassim. The first thing he saw on entering the cave was his dead brother. Full of horror, he put the body on one of his asses, and bags of gold on the other two, and, covering all with some faggots, returned home. He drove the two asses laden with gold into his own yard, and led the other to Cassim's house. The door was opened by the slave Morgiana, whom he knew to be both brave and cunning.

Unloading the ass, he said to her, 'This is the body of your master, who has been murdered, but whom we must bury as though he had died in his bed. I will speak with you again, but now tell your mistress I am come.'

The wife of Cassim, on learning the fate of her husband, broke out into cries and tears, but Ali Baba offered to take her to live with him and his wife if she would promise to keep his counsel and leave everything to Morgiana; whereupon she agreed, and dried her eyes.

Morgiana, meanwhile, sought an apothecary and asked him for some lozenges. 'My poor master,' she said, 'can neither eat nor speak, and no one knows what his distemper is.' She carried home the lozenges and returned next day weeping, and asked for an essence only given to those just about to die. Thus, in the evening, no one was surprised to hear the wretched shrieks and cries of Cassim's wife and Morgiana, telling everyone that Cassim was dead.

The day after Morgiana went to an old cobbler near the gates of the town, put a piece of gold in his hand, and bade him follow her with his needle and thread. Having bound his eyes with a handkerchief, she took him to the room where the body lay, pulled off the bandage, and bade him sew the quarters together, after which she covered his eyes again and led him home. Then they buried Cassim, and Morgiana his slave followed him to the grave, weeping and tearing her hair, while Cassim's wife stayed at home uttering lamentable cries. Next day she went to live with Ali Baba, who gave Cassim's shop to his eldest son.

The Forty Thieves, on their return to the cave, were much astonished to find Cassim's body gone and some of their money bags. 'We are certainly discovered,' said the captain, 'and shall be undone if we cannot find out who it is that knows our secret. Two men must have known it; we have killed one, we must now find the other. To this end one of you must go into the city and discover whom we have killed, and whether men talk of the strange manner of his death. If the messenger fails he must lose his life, lest we be betrayed.'

One of the thieves offered to do this, disguised himself, and happened to enter the town at daybreak, just by Baba Mustapha's stall. The thief bade him good day, saying, 'Honest man, how can you possibly see to stitch at your age?'

'Old as I am,' replied the cobbler, 'I have very good eyes, and you will believe me when I tell you that I sewed a dead body together in a place where I had less light than I have now.'

The robber was overjoyed at his good fortune, and, giving him a piece of gold, desired to be shown the house where he stitched up the dead body.

At first Mustapha refused, saying that he had been blindfolded; but when the robber gave him another piece of gold he began to think he might remember the turnings if blindfolded as before. This plan succeeded; the robber partly led him, and was partly guided by him, right in front of Cassim's house, the door of which the robber marked with a piece of chalk. Then, well pleased, he bade farewell to Baba Mustapha and returned to the forest.

By-and-by Morgiana, going out, saw the mark the robber had made, quickly guessed that some mischief was brewing, and fetching a piece of chalk marked two or three doors on each side, without saying anything to her master or mistress.

The thief, meantime, told his comrades of his discovery. The captain thanked him, and bade him show him the house he had marked. But when they came to it they saw that five or six of the houses were chalked in the same manner. The guide was at once beheaded for having failed. Another robber was despatched, and, having won over Baba Mustapha, marked the house in red chalk; but Morgiana being again too clever for them, the second messenger was put to death also.

The captain now resolved to go himself, but, wiser than the others, he did not mark the house, but looked at it so closely that he could not fail to remember it. He ordered his men to go into the neighbouring villages and buy nineteen mules, and thirty-eight leather jars, all empty, except one which was full of oil. The captain put one of his men, fully armed, into each, rubbing the outside of the jars with oil from the full vessel. Then the nineteen mules were loaded with thirty-seven robbers in jars, and the jar of oil, and reached the town by dusk.

The captain stopped his mules in front of Ali Baba's house, and said to Ali Baba, who was sitting outside for coolness, 'I have brought some oil from a distance to sell at tomorrow's market, but it is now so late that I know not where to pass the night, unless you will take me in.'

Though Ali Baba had seen the captain of the robbers in the forest, he did not recognize him in the disguise of an oil merchant. He bade him welcome and went to Morgiana to bid her prepare a bed and supper for his guest. After they had supped he went again to speak to Morgiana in the kitchen, while the captain went into the yard to tell his men what to do.

Beginning at the first jar he said to each man, 'As soon as I throw some stones from the window of the chamber where I lie, cut the jars open with your knives and come out and I will be with you in a trice.' He returned to the house, and Morgiana led him to his chamber.

She then told Abdallah, her fellow-slave, to set on the pot to make some broth for her master, who had gone to bed. Meanwhile her lamp went out, and she had no more oil in the house.

'Do not be uneasy,' said Abdallah, 'go into the yard and take some out of one of those jars.'

Morgiana took the oil pot, and went into the yard. When she came to the first jar the robber inside said softly, 'Is it time?'

Any other slave but Morgiana, on finding a man in the jar instead of the oil she wanted, would have screamed and made a noise; but she, knowing the danger her master was in, bethought herself of a plan, and answered quietly, 'Not yet, but presently.' She went to all the jars, giving the same answer, till she came to the jar of oil. She now saw that her master, thinking to entertain an oil merchant, had let thirty-eight robbers into his house.

She filled her oil pot, went back to the kitchen and, having lit her lamp, went again to the oil jar and filled a large kettle full of oil. When it boiled she went and poured enough oil into every jar to stifle and kill the robber inside. When this brave deed was done she went back to the kitchen and waited to see what would happen.

In a quarter of an hour the captain of the robbers awoke, got up, and opened the window. As all seemed quiet he threw down some little pebbles which hit the jars. He listened, and as none of his men seemed to stir he grew uneasy, and went down into the yard. On going to the first jar and saying, 'Are you asleep?' he smelt the hot boiled oil, and knew at once that his plot to murder Ali Baba and his household had been discovered. He found all the gang were dead, and, missing the oil out of the last jar, became aware of the manner of their death. He then forced the lock of a door leading into a garden and made his escape. Morgiana heard and saw all this, and, rejoicing at her success, went to bed and fell asleep.

At daybreak Ali Baba arose, and, seeing the oil jars there still, asked why the merchant had not gone with his mules. Morgiana bade him look in the first jar and see if there was any oil. Seeing a man, he started back in terror. 'Have no fear,' said Morgiana, 'the man cannot harm you: he is dead.'

Ali Baba, when he had recovered somewhat from his astonishment, asked what had become of the merchant. 'Merchant!' said she. 'He is no more a merchant than I am!' And she told him the whole story, assuring him that it was a plot of the robbers of whom only three were left, and that the white and red chalk marks had something to do with it. Ali Baba at once gave Morgiana her freedom, saying that he owed her his life. They then buried the bodies in Ali Baba's garden, while the mules were sold in the market.

The captain returned to his lonely cave and firmly resolved to avenge his companions by killing Ali Baba. He dressed himself carefully, and went into the town, where he took lodgings in an inn. In the course of a great many journeys to the forest he carried away many rich stuffs and much fine linen, and set up a shop opposite that of Ali Baba's son. He called himself Cogia Hassan, and as he was both civil and well dressed he soon made friends with Ali Baba's son, and through him with Ali Baba, whom he was continually asking to sup with him.

Ali Baba, wishing to return his kindness, invited him into his house, thanking him for his kindness to his son. When the merchant was about to take his leave Ali Baba stopped him, saying, 'Where are you going, sir, in such haste? Will you not stay and sup with me?'

The merchant refused, saying that he had a reason; and, on Ali Baba's asking him what that was, he replied, 'It is, sir, that I can eat no victuals that have any salt in them.'

'If that is all,' said Ali Baba, 'let me tell you that there shall be no salt in either the meat or the bread that we eat tonight.'

He went to give this order to Morgiana, who was much surprised. 'Who is this man,' she said, 'who eats no salt with his meat?'

'He is an honest man, Morgiana,' returned her master, 'therefore do as I bid you.'

But she desired to see this strange man, so she helped Abdallah to carry up the dishes, and saw in a moment that Cogia Hassan was the robber captain and carried a dagger under his garment. 'I am not surprised,' she said to herself, 'that this wicked man, who intends to kill my master, will eat no salt with him; but I will hinder his plans.'

She sent up the supper by Abdallah, while she made ready. When the dessert had been served, Cogia Hassan was left alone with Ali Baba and his son, whom he thought to make drunk and then to murder them. Morgiana, meanwhile, put on a head-dress like a dancing-girl's, and clasped a girdle round her waist, from which hung a dagger with a silver hilt, and said to

Abdallah, 'Take your tabor, and let us go and divert our master and his guest.'

Abdallah took his tabor and played before Morgiana until they came to the door, where Abdallah stopped playing and Morgiana made a low curtsy. 'Come in, Morgiana,' said Ali Baba, 'and let Cogia Hassan see what you can do.' Turning to Cogia Hassan, he said, 'She's my slave and my housekeeper.'

Cogia Hassan was by no means pleased, for he feared that his chance of killing Ali Baba was gone for the present; but he pretended great eagerness to see Morgiana. After she had performed several dances she drew her dagger and made passes with it, as if it were part of the dance. Suddenly, out of breath, she snatched the tabor from Abdallah with her left hand, and, holding the dagger in her right, held out the tabor to her master. Ali Baba and his son put a piece of gold into it, and Cogia Hassan, seeing that she was coming to him, pulled out his purse to make her a present, but while he was putting his hand into it Morgiana plunged the dagger into his heart.

'Unhappy girl!' cried Ali Baba and his son. 'What have you done to ruin us?'

'It was to preserve you, master, not to ruin you,' answered Morgiana. 'See here,' opening the false merchant's garment and showing the dagger. 'See what an enemy you have entertained! Remember, he would eat no salt with you, and what more would you have? Look at him! He is both the false oil merchant and the captain of the Forty Thieves.'

Ali Baba was so grateful to Morgiana for thus saving his life that he offered her to his son in marriage, who readily consented, and a few days after the wedding was celebrated with great splendour.

At the end of a year Ali Baba, hearing nothing of the two remaining robbers, judged they were dead, and set out to the cave. The door opened on his saying, 'Open, Sesame!' He went in, and saw that nobody had been there since the captain left it. He brought away as much gold as he could carry, and returned to town. He told his son the secret of the cave, which his son handed down in his turn, so the children and grandchildren of Ali Baba were rich to the end of their lives.

Trousers Mehmet
and the Sultan's Daughter

Once there was and twice there wasn't a clever village boy named Mehmet. When his old father died, leaving him nothing but a pair of baggy trousers and his blessing, Mehmet stored the blessing in his heart. Then, putting the trousers over his shoulder, he set one foot before the other till he came to Istanbul.

No work, no bread, thought he. Though I can read, I've learned no trade, so I shall carry burdens to earn my keep. And since I have neither basket nor rope, these trousers must serve as my sack.

A kind old tailor sewed the trouser legs shut. Then, 'Hamal! Porter!' he shouted. 'Let Trousers Mehmet carry your bundles!'

'Trousers Mehmet, here's a package!' Soon Mehmet's cheerful face appeared in shops and markets throughout the city, and he had work a-plenty.

One day just as he left Sirkeci Station carrying a heavy load, he saw a splendid procession on its way from Topkapi Palace to the Covered Bazaar. In a golden litter sat the sultan's daughter, with her merry brown eyes smiling at him above her veil.

'Ah, how I could love that lady!' sighed Mehmet as he watched. 'But she's far too fine to love a poor hamal like me.'

As for the princess, the handsome hamal had touched her heart. 'There is a young man who truly pleases me,' she murmured. 'But what can bring a princess and a porter together?'

Amid the bustle and the chatter of the Covered Bazaar, the princess thought long and longer about Trousers Mehmet. Suddenly she had an idea.

The next morning, she went before the sultan. 'Father, is it not time for me to be married?' she asked.

'Married!' he exclaimed. 'For two years, young men have come seeking your hand. But would you choose one? Not at all!'

'Father, none of them was half as clever as you,' she said, 'and therefore none of them would do.'

'And how am I to find such a clever young man?' asked the sultan, pleased by his daughter's compliment.

'You could set a task so difficult that only the cleverest of men could complete it,' she suggested.

The sultan considered the matter. Then, 'Yes, my daughter,' he decided. 'I shall send envoys to every kingdom inviting princes to compete for my daughter's hand.'

'Only princes, father?' she asked. 'It is not only princes who are clever.'

'You are right, my daughter,' he agreed.

And, true enough, criers were sent out immediately shouting, 'Come! Come! Whoever seeks to wed the princess must come to Topkapi Palace!'

Within three or five days, young men of every shape and size and station had gathered at the palace. Even Trousers Mehmet joined the throng. He loved the princess already, and no one had said that hamals could not try for her hand.

Looking directly at the suitors, the sultan himself announced, 'The man who wins my daughter must bring to me one who hunts, who throws away what he catches, and who carries with him what he cannot find.'

The suitors stared at one another. Who could make sense of such a task as that? Clearly, the sultan had lost his wits. One by one, they turned away, except for Trousers Mehmet. He stood there, thinking. The sultan was said to be a clever man. Perhaps this was a riddle . . . not one to be found in books, but on the lips of the people.

As Mehmet went out slowly into the busy street, the muezzin called from a minaret of Sultan Ahmet mosque. 'It is time for noonday prayer,' said Mehmet. 'After that, I shall think about the sultan's task.'

He hurried to Ablutions Fountain in the mosque yard. There he washed himself three times. Then, leaving his shoes at the mosque door, he went inside to pray.

As Mehmet passed a public fountain after the holy service, he saw a wretched peasant making himself clean. His washing done, the peasant set about that unpleasant bit of business known to the poor the world over.

Mehmet smiled. Then suddenly his heart pounded, tum tum tum. Was this by any chance the kind of hunter the sultan meant? He went to the peasant. 'Brother,' he said, 'if you will come with me for half an hour, I shall buy your bread and cheese for three or five days.'

The peasant stared at Mehmet. 'Empty words do not fill an empty stomach,' he grumbled. Then, as Mehmet still stood there, he said, 'First I must finish what I am doing, son. Then I shall come.'

'If you wish the bread and cheese, you must come now,' said Mehmet. 'You may finish what you are doing when we reach Topkapi Palace.'

'The sultan's palace!' exclaimed the peasant. 'Indeed not! My life is worth more to me than bread and cheese. Still, my father used to say that it's better to die on a full stomach than to live on an empty one . . .'

'Fear not,' said Mehmet. 'Only trust me, and you will see. Come.' And he and the peasant went directly to the palace.

Immediately, they were taken to the sultan. The ruler stared at Mehmet curiously. A hamal . . . with an old pair of trousers for a basket! And he had a ragged peasant with him, itching and scratching. 'Well,' said the sultan, 'what is your business here?'

'This morning, sire,' said Mehmet, 'you set a task for the man who wished to wed your daughter. I have brought the hunter you described.' Then, turning to the peasant, Mehmet said, 'Now, brother, you may finish that business you began at the fountain.'

Obediently, the peasant began to search among his tattered clothes for lice. As he found a louse, he would flatten it on his thumbnail and then throw it away. One, two, three, four, five—and still he scratched.

'Enough!' said the sultan, smiling a little despite himself.

'Well, sire,' asked Mehmet, 'have I not brought to you one who hunts, who throws away what he catches, and who carries with him what he cannot find?'

'You have,' agreed the sultan.

'Praise be to Allah!' said Mehmet happily. And from his worn purse, he gave the peasant a handful of coins. 'Eat with a hearty appetite, brother,' he said, 'and thank you. May your way be open.' The peasant left, pleased with this strange bargain.

'Now,' said Mehmet eagerly, 'when may I marry your daughter?'

The sultan's eyes glittered coldly. 'Not so fast,' he warned. 'I do not intend to have my daughter marry a hamal.'

'But, sire,' Mehmet said, 'you promised . . .'

'I know,' interrupted the sultan angrily. 'But how could I guess that a porter would seek her hand? Naturally, a hamal would be well acquainted with lice! No, you cannot have my daughter, unless . . . unless you succeed in a second task, and then a third. Then you may have my daughter.'

Mehmet swallowed his anger and disappointment. 'Very well, sire,' he said. 'What is the second task?'

The sultan thought for a moment. Then he replied, 'You must bring me life which enters an empty box alone, yet comes out bringing death with it.'

Mehmet's shoulders sagged, but he bowed and left the sultan's presence. 'Fair or unfair, he is none the less the sultan,' the hamal murmured, 'and the father of the lovely princess. Thorns and roses surely grow on the same tree! Still, Allah willing, I shall win the sultan's daughter.'

He straightened his shoulders and went directly to the Covered Bazaar. 'At least,' he decided, 'I can buy a box while I am thinking.'

He searched among the stalls until he found a small wooden box with a snug cover. Paying the shopkeeper, he tucked the box into his sash.

As he was leaving the Bazaar, he heard the boom-boom-boom of a drum and the mellow piping of a zurna. 'Come and see!' a showman sang, and the crowd hurried to his stall. 'Wonders from India.' 'Wonders from China.' 'See something you have never seen before—a miracle!' Mehmet read the bold signs above the stall.

For a moment forgetting his own problem, Mehmet smiled. 'Man is truly as old as his head, not his years. Just see the crowd scramble!'

Suddenly he noticed something special. 'From Egypt,' the sign said. As he reached out to touch what he saw, the showman shouted, 'Take your hands off that cage. There's trouble inside.'

'I'll pay you well for just half of that trouble,' said Mehmet quietly, and reached into his sash for his box and his purse.

'Do you know what you are buying?' asked the showman.

'I know what I am buying,' answered Mehmet. Carefully, carefully . . . in a moment, Mehmet had a small something in his box. And the showman had a large sum in his purse.

With his joy shortening his journey, Mehmet was soon at the palace. 'Well,' asked the sultan, 'have you brought life in a box?'

'Yes, sire, and it brings death with it when it leaves the box,' replied Trousers Mehmet. 'Here it is.'

The sultan turned the box over and over. Then he laughed. 'You are bold, young man, but how can you prove what you say? There is no way of seeing into that box of yours. Open it.'

'As you say, sire,' said Mehmet politely, and he lifted the cover just enough so that the sultan could see the gleaming eyes of a deadly asp.

'Shut it!' the sultan cried. And Mehmet shut the box.

'Well, sire,' said Mehmet, smiling, 'I have accomplished the second task. What is the third task to be?'

The sultan stared at the young hamal. Then slowly he drew forth his own silken handkerchief. Holding it out to Mehmet, he said, 'Bring me a thousand forests in this handkerchief.'

Mehmet took the handkerchief and slipped it safely into his sash. He studied the sultan's face, but it gave no hint of the answer. Had he come within a hair of winning his princess only to lose her on this puzzling task? Still, he kept the small bird of hope alive within his breast.

'This may be another riddle,' he mused as he left the palace and walked along the winding streets and through the main gate into Gülhane Park. As he wandered along a shady path, he murmured, 'I begin with the name of Allah. A thousand forests . . .' Suddenly there was a snapping sound beneath his foot. He moved his shoe, and—Allah be praised!—there lay an answer to the puzzle.

He picked up another just like the one he had crushed. Rolling the treasure inside the sultan's handkerchief, he tucked it gently into his sash. Then he hurried back to the palace.

'Well,' said the ruler, 'have you hidden the forests somewhere? I cannot see even the handkerchief.'

'Here, sire,' answered Trousers Mehmet, drawing it carefully from his sash. The sultan stared curiously as Mehmet unrolled the handkerchief and took out a single acorn.

A broad smile spread across the sultan's face. Who could deny that Allah proposed a thousand forests from that one acorn? And, indeed, who could doubt that Allah proposed this clever young man as a husband fit for the sultan's daughter?

Thus it was that Trousers Mehmet came to marry the sultan's daughter, in a wedding that lasted forty days and forty nights. May we all have a share in their happiness!

The Nightingale
that Shrieked

This happened, or maybe it did not.
The time is long past, and much is forgot.

Aking once sent his crier through the kingdom to inform
the people that for three successive nights they must
light neither lamp nor fire—that their houses must
show no spark or glimmer of light or they would suffer terrible
punishment. Then the king said to his minister, 'Now we shall
judge for ourselves who obeys the sultan's word and who is
careless of his command.'

Night fell, and the king and his minister disguised themselves
to look like two wandering dervishes. Together they roamed the
streets of the city, from which every straying foot had with-
drawn, since the night was black as blindness. There was not a
light to be seen. But on turning a corner, the two noticed a faint

glow coming from a hut that stood by itself. They peeped through the window and saw three girls busily spinning wool in the light of a lamp which they had dimmed with an upturned sieve.

One girl was saying to the others, 'How I wish I were married to the sultan's baker! Then I should have bread to eat as often as I wanted.'

Another said, 'If only I were the wife of the sultan's cook! Then I should dine off meat every day of my life.'

But the youngest said, 'I would never consent to marry any lesser man than the sultan himself. If he made me his queen, within the year I should bear him twins—a boy with locks of silver and gold, and a girl for whom the sun shines when she smiles and the rain falls when she weeps.'

In the morning a messenger came from the palace to summon the three girls to the king's presence. The first two sisters sank on the doorstone and trembled, saying, 'Allah protect us as we stand between two fires. If we obey the king's command and do not work at night we die of hunger, and if we disobey we die of punishment.'

But the youngest sister told the messenger, 'Let the king send us fine robes to wear, for we are poor and have no clothes in which to enter a royal court.' And when the three girls stood before the king they wore gowns of velvet striped red and black.

They say, 'the talk of the evening is covered with butter and melts in the morning,' but the king married the eldest girl to his baker as she had wished and the next to his cook. The youngest girl who had said, 'I shall bear the sultan twins before the year is out, a boy with locks of silver and gold, and a girl for whom the sun shines when she smiles and the rain falls when she cries' —this girl he kept for himself. As soon as the necessary preparations were made, he married her according to the tradition of the prophet.

Who grew jealous of her? The king's old wife. As one before our time has said, 'When have women loved a fair-skinned girl or men loved a hero?' What did the old queen do? For a long time she did nothing, biding her time. She saw the new queen's belly rising, and she waited. She heard the midwife sitting at the new queen's pillow, chanting:

O great father Noah,
Who saved our souls,
Save this child in her hour of woe!

and she waited. But when the new queen gave birth to a pair of twins—as golden and as radiant as she had promised—the old queen said to the midwife, 'Take the newborn infants from their mother's side, and in their place put this little dog and this clay jar.'

Does not gold achieve all things? The midwife did the old queen's bidding and threw the two princelings into the palace garden.

Now the women began to wail and beat their cheeks. 'A calamity and a scandal! The king's new queen has given birth to a puppy dog and a water jug!' The king, ashamed, sent his queen away to live the life of a discarded wife.

What of the twins? Our God is praiseworthy indeed, for they were found by the king's gardener, whose wife was barren and had grown old childless. She pressed the babies to her breast, resting one on her right shoulder and one on her left, and nurtured them as if they had been the fruit of her own body.

The child in a tale grows fast. So it was with these two. In time the gardener built them a little house to live in. The fair brother with the locks of silver and gold, and his sister for whose smile the sun shone and for whose tears the rain fell, were such as fill the eye and set the tongue wagging. News of them reached the old queen, and once again she sent for the midwife to instruct her what to do.

The midwife waited until the brother had gone hunting and the girl was sitting in the house by herself. Then she knocked at the door and paid a visit. 'How perfect is this house!' she said. 'You lack nothing but the Tree of Apples that Dance and Apricots that Sing growing before your door. Then it would be complete.'

When the brother returned, he found his sister weeping. 'Why such tears?' he asked. And she told him of the midwife's visit, confessing that now she could not be truly happy until she had the magic fruit tree growing by her door. 'Gather up provisions for a journey; I shall set out tomorrow morning in search of your tree,' said her brother.

Next day the boy began to walk, trusting his fate to the All-Merciful. From place to place he travelled asking where he should seek the magic tree, but none knew how to advise him. At last he reached the foot of a high mountain. He climbed to its top, and there stood a Ghoul with one foot pointing to the east and one foot pointing to the west. The hair of his head was matted and covered his brow. The hair of his brow was thick and covered his eyes. 'Peace, O father Ghoul,' said the boy.

> *Had not your greeting*
> *Preceded your speaking,*
> *I should have torn you limb from limb*
> *And snapped your bones and picked them clean!*

the monster replied.

The boy went up to the Ghoul and cut the knotted hair on his head and shaved the bushy hair of his brows. The monster sighed with pleasure and said, 'You have brought back the light into my face, so may Allah light up your path before you. Tell me: what are you seeking and what have you come for?' The boy explained his search, and the Ghoul said, 'If you follow this road you will come to the land of Ghouls. The tree that you seek grows in the garden of the king. Its leaves are so broad that you could swaddle two infants in each. But first go to my brother. He is older than I am by one day and wiser by one year. Ask him to help you.'

The boy journeyed onward until ahead he saw the Ghoul's brother sitting in the middle of the path with his legs stretched out before him. 'Peace, O father Ghoul,' said the boy, and the monster replied as his brother had done,

> *Had not your greeting*
> *Preceded your speaking,*
> *I should have torn you limb from limb*
> *And snapped your bones and picked them clean!*

The boy did as he had done with the first Ghoul, snipping the hair that covered his forehead and trimming his eyebrows. Then the Ghoul asked, 'What has brought you from the land of men to the land of spirits and Djinn?'

'Allah brought me and I came,' the boy said. And he told the Ghoul how he was looking for the Tree of Apples that Dance and Apricots that Sing to give to his sister.

The Ghoul said, 'Continue along this road, and you will see my sister sitting at her handmill grinding salt or fine white sugar. If you find her grinding salt, stop where you stand and do not let her see you. But if she should be grinding sugar, run to her as quickly as you can and nurse at each of her breasts. For once you have tasted her milk, she will do you no harm but help you as a mother helps her son.'

The boy did as the Ghoul had told him. Finding the Ghoul's sister milling sugar, he pounced on her right breast before she could look up and see who was coming. She said,

> *Whoever suckles the breast on my right*
> *Is dear to my heart and a son in my sight.*

When he turned to the other breast, she said,

> *Whoever suckles the breast on my left*
> *Is dear as the son whom I love the best.*

'What is the cause of your coming?' she asked the boy, 'and for what reason will you be going?' When he had told her about the Tree of Apples that Dance and Apricots that Sing, she said, 'Wait till my seven sons come home in the evening; they will help you. But for your protection I must hide you.' And she turned him into an onion like the other onions in her basket.

When it was dark the seven young Ghouls came home, saying, 'Mother, mother, there is about you a smell of men!'

She said, 'How can that be, when I have been sitting in this place all day long. It is you who have gone abroad and mingled with the humans in their towns, and their smell has clung to the tails of your gowns.'

Despite her words, the young Ghouls said, 'If you are hiding a woman we shall guard her like a sister, and if you are hiding a man we shall help him like a brother. May God protect him and visit a traitor's punishment on his betrayer.'

At that, their mother returned the boy to his own shape and told her sons how he was searching for the Tree of Apples that Dance and Apricots that Sing. 'I know the place, and I can take him there in a month,' said the oldest son.

'I can lead him to it in a week,' said another.

And the youngest said, 'Climb on to my back, and I shall carry you there in the twinkling of an eye.'

So the boy flew on the youngest Ghoul's back to the garden of the king of Ghouls. With a monster's strength the young spirit uprooted the Tree of Apples that Dance and Apricots that Sing. And the boy took it to his sister to plant by the door of their house.

What did the king's old wife say when she saw that the boy with the locks of silver and gold had returned from his journey, whole and unharmed? She sent the midwife to visit his sister again. 'How cool it is in the shade of your tree, and how merry to see the apples dancing and hear the apricots sing!' the midwife said. 'Now indeed you own everything there is to own ... except Bulbul Assiah, the Nightingale who Shrieks.'

'How can I find Bulbul Assiah?' the girl asked.

'He who brought you the tree of the dancing apples and singing apricots will surely bring you Bulbul Assiah,' the old woman said.

The sister told her brother about the nightingale and admitted that she could not live happily until she possessed it. The boy loved his sister, and to make her content, he set out once more. This time he took the shortest road to the home of the Ghouls, his adopted brothers. And the youngest flew with him to the aviary of the king of the Ghouls and showed him the cage that held Bulbul Assiah. The boy lifted it from its hook and brought it home to his sister.

Now the gardener, seeing the wonders that his children had collected—the tree with the dancing and singing fruits and the golden cage of Bulbul Assiah—went to the king and said, 'For forty years I have worked in your garden, yet you have never visited my house. Now I wish you to come and eat my food.'

'If Allah wills it, I shall come tomorrow,' said the king. Next day when the king entered the gardener's yard, the apples danced and the apricots sang on the tree in front of his children's house. And Bulbul Assiah began to shriek from his perch.

> *Who but a she-dog*
> *Born of a she-dog*
> *Knows how to whelp pups?*
> *A queen can only bear*
> *Noble lords and ladies fair.*
> *Our sultan's wife bore no pup or jug of water*
> *But a golden son and a comely daughter.*
> *A boy with shining locks of gold and silver*
> *A girl—why, the sun shines at her laughter.*

So the king discovered that the brother and sister were his own twin son and daughter. He called their mother back from her seclusion and ordered a feast to last forty days and forty nights to celebrate her return.

> *As for the wicked old midwife,*
> *May torments hound her all her life!*

Zlateh the Goat

At Hanukkah time the road from the village to the town is usually covered with snow, but this year the winter had been a mild one. Hanukkah had almost come, yet little snow had fallen. The sun shone most of the time. The peasants complained that because of the dry weather there would be a poor harvest of winter grain. New grass sprouted, and the peasants sent their cattle out to pasture.

For Reuven the furrier it was a bad year, and after long hesitation he decided to sell Zlateh the goat. She was old and gave little milk. Feyvel the town butcher had offered eight gulden for her. Such a sum would buy Hanukkah candles, potatoes and oil for pancakes, gifts for the children, and other holiday necessaries for the house. Reuven told his oldest boy Aaron to take the goat to town.

Aaron understood what taking the goat to Feyvel meant, but he had to obey his father. Leah, his mother, wiped the tears from her eyes when she heard the news. Aaron's younger sisters, Anna and Miriam, cried loudly. Aaron put on his quilted jacket and a cap with earmuffs, bound a rope around Zlateh's neck, and took along two slices of bread with cheese to eat on the road. Aaron was supposed to deliver the goat by evening, spend the night at the butcher's, and return the next day with the money.

While the family said goodbye to the goat, and Aaron placed the rope around her neck, Zlateh stood as patiently and good-naturedly as ever. She licked Reuven's hand. She shook her small white beard. Zlateh trusted human beings. She knew that they always fed her and never did her any harm.

When Aaron brought her out on the road to town, she seemed somewhat astonished. She'd never been led in that direction before. She looked back at him questioningly, as if to say, 'Where are you taking me?' But after a while she seemed to come to the conclusion that a goat shouldn't ask questions. Still, the road was different. They passed new fields, pastures, and huts with thatched roofs. Here and there a dog barked and came running after them, but Aaron chased it away with his stick.

The sun was shining when Aaron left the village. Suddenly the weather changed. A large black cloud with a bluish centre appeared in the east and spread itself rapidly over the sky. A cold wind blew in with it. The crows flew low, croaking. At first it looked as if it would rain, but instead it began to hail as in summer. It was early in the day, but it became dark as dusk. After a while the hail turned to snow.

In his twelve years Aaron had seen all kinds of weather, but he had never experienced a snow like this one. It was so dense it shut out the light of the day. In a short time their path was completely covered. The wind became as cold as ice. The road to town was narrow and winding. Aaron no longer knew where he was. He could not see through the snow. The cold soon penetrated his quilted jacket.

At first Zlateh didn't seem to mind the change in weather. She too was twelve years old and knew what winter meant. But when her legs sank deeper and deeper into the snow, she began to turn her head and look at Aaron in wonderment. Her mild eyes seemed to ask, 'Why are we out in such a storm?' Aaron hoped that a peasant would come along with his cart, but no one passed by.

The snow grew thicker, falling to the ground in large, whirling flakes. Beneath it Aaron's boots touched the softness of a ploughed field. He realized that he was no longer on the road. He had gone astray. He could no longer make out which was east or west, which way was the village, the town. The wind whistled, howled, whirled the snow about in eddies. It looked as if white imps were playing tag on the fields. A white dust rose above the ground. Zlateh stopped. She could walk no longer.

Stubbornly she anchored her cleft hooves in the earth and bleated as if pleading to be taken home. Icicles hung from her white beard, and her horns were glazed with frost.

Aaron did not want to admit the danger, but he knew just the same that if they did not find shelter they would freeze to death. This was no ordinary storm. It was a mighty blizzard. The snowfall had reached his knees. His hands were numb, and he could no longer feel his toes. He choked when he breathed. His nose felt like wood, and he rubbed it with snow. Zlateh's bleating began to sound like crying. Those humans in whom she had so much confidence had dragged her into a trap. Aaron began to pray to God for himself and for the innocent animal.

Suddenly he made out the shape of a hill. He wondered what it could be. Who had piled snow into such a huge heap? He moved towards it, dragging Zlateh after him. When he came near it, he realized that it was a large haystack which the snow had blanketed.

Aaron saw immediately that they were saved. With great effort he dug his way through the snow. He was a village boy and knew what to do. When he reached the hay, he hollowed out a nest for himself and the goat. No matter how cold it may be outside, in the hay it is always warm. And hay was food for Zlateh. The moment she smelt it she became contented and began to eat. Outside the snow continued to fall. It quickly covered the passageway Aaron had dug. But a boy and an animal need to breathe, and there was hardly any air in their hideout. Aaron bored a kind of window through the hay and snow and carefully kept the passage clear.

Zlateh, having eaten her fill, sat down on her hind legs and seemed to have regained her confidence in man. Aaron ate his two slices of bread and cheese, but after the difficult journey he was still hungry. He looked at Zlateh and noticed her udders were full. He lay down next to her, placing himself so that when he milked her he could squirt the milk into his mouth. It was rich and sweet. Zlateh was not accustomed to being milked that way, but she did not resist. On the contrary, she seemed eager to reward Aaron for bringing her to a shelter whose very walls, floor, and ceiling were made of food.

Through the window Aaron could catch a glimpse of the chaos outside. The wind carried before it whole drifts of snow.

It was completely dark, and he did not know whether night had already come or whether it was the darkness of the storm. Thank God that in the hay it was not cold. The dried grass and field flowers exuded the warmth of the summer sun. Zlateh ate frequently; she nibbled from above, below, from the left and right. Her body gave forth an animal warmth, and Aaron cuddled up to her. He had always loved Zlateh, but now she was like a sister. He was alone, cut off from his family, and wanted to talk.

He began to talk to Zlateh. 'Zlateh, what do you think about what has happened to us?' he asked.

'Maaaa,' Zlateh answered.

'If we hadn't found this stack of hay, we would both be frozen stiff by now,' Aaron said.

'Maaaa,' was the goat's reply.

'If the snow keeps on falling like this, we may have to stay here for days,' Aaron explained.

'Maaaa,' Zlateh bleated.

'What does "maaaa" mean?' Aaron asked. 'You'd better speak up clearly.'

'Maaaa. Maaaa,' Zlateh tried.

'Well, let it be "maaaa" then,' Aaron said patiently. 'You can't speak, but I know you understand. I need you and you need me. Isn't that right?'

'Maaaa.'

Aaron became sleepy. He made a pillow out of some hay, leaned his head on it, and dozed off. Zlateh too fell asleep.

When Aaron opened his eyes, he didn't know whether it was morning or night. The snow had blocked up his window. He tried to clear it, but when he had bored through to the length of his arm, he still hadn't reached the outside. Luckily he had his stick with him and was able to break through to the open air. It was still dark outside. The snow continued to fall and the wind wailed, first with one voice and then with many. Sometimes it had the sound of devilish laughter.

Zlateh too awoke, and when Aaron greeted her, she answered, 'Maaaa.' Yes, Zlateh's language consisted of only one word, but it meant many things. Now she was saying, 'We must accept all that God gives us—heat, cold, hunger, satisfaction, light, and darkness.'

Aaron had awakened hungry. He had eaten up his food, but Zlateh had plenty of milk.

For three days Aaron and Zlateh stayed in the haystack. Aaron had always loved Zlateh, but in these three days he loved her more and more. She fed him with her milk and helped him keep warm. She comforted him with her patience. He told her many stories, and she always cocked her ears and listened. When he patted her, she licked his hand and his face. Then she said, 'Maaaa,' and he knew it meant, I love you too.

The snow fell for three days, though after the first day it was not as thick and the wind quieted down. Sometimes Aaron felt that there could never have been a summer, that the snow had always fallen, ever since he could remember. He, Aaron, never had a father or mother or sisters.

He was a snow child, born of the snow, and so was Zlateh. It was so quiet in the hay that his ears rang in the stillness. Aaron and Zlateh slept all night and a good part of the day. As for Aaron's dreams, they were all about warm weather. He dreamed of green fields, trees covered with blossoms, clear brooks, and singing birds.

By the third night the snow had stopped, but Aaron did not dare to find his way home in the darkness. The sky became clear and the moon shone, casting silvery nets on the snow. Aaron dug his way out and looked at the world. It was all white, quiet, dreaming dreams of heavenly splendour. The stars were large and close. The moon swam in the sky as in a sea.

On the morning of the fourth day Aaron heard the ringing of sleigh bells. The haystack was not far from the road. The peasant who drove the sleigh pointed out the way to him—not to the town and Feyvel the butcher, but home to the village. Aaron had decided in the haystack that he would never part with Zlateh.

Aaron's family and their neighbours had searched for the boy and the goat but had found no trace of them during the storm. They feared they were lost. Aaron's mother and sisters cried for him; his father remained silent and gloomy. Suddenly one of the neighbours came running to their house with the news that Aaron and Zlateh were coming up the road.

There was great joy in the family. Aaron told them how he had found the stack of hay and how Zlateh had fed him with her milk. Aaron's sisters kissed and hugged Zlateh and gave her a special treat of chopped carrots and potato peel, which Zlateh gobbled up hungrily.

Nobody ever again thought of selling Zlateh, and now that the cold weather had finally set in, the villagers needed the services of Reuven the furrier once more. When Hanukkah came, Aaron's mother was able to fry pancakes every evening, and Zlateh got her portion too. Even though Zlateh had her own pen, she often came to the kitchen, knocking on the door with her horns to indicate that she was ready to visit, and she was always admitted. In the evening Aaron, Miriam, and Anna played dreidel. Zlateh sat near the stove watching the children and the flickering of the Hanukkah candles.

Once in a while Aaron would ask her, 'Zlateh, do you remember the three days we spent together?'

And Zlateh would scratch her neck with a horn, shake her white bearded head and come out with the single sound which expressed all her thoughts, and all her love.

The Pied Piper of Hamelin

ats! There was a ruin of rats. A rat-attack! A plague of rats. Sidling along streets; scavenging in shops; high-tailing around houses. No one in Hamelin knew what to do about them.

To begin with, there were only a few more than usual. As if the town-rats had simply invited their friends from upriver and downriver to come and have a look round Hamelin.

But then there were a lot more than usual, as if all those friends had decided to stay on, and before long invited their friends.

People began to complain. They didn't like the sight of them, always scurrying round corners, or the smell of them, so sour and strong. And they didn't like the sound of them, squeaking and scritching-and-scratching in every single house.

How fast they were on their feet! They bit the hind-legs of dogs ten times their size; they buried their teeth in the throats of cats; and they actually nipped babies in their cradles.

From the corners of kitchens, they grinned at cooks and then sprang up and licked their soup-ladles; they nose-dived under larder doors, and gnawed their way into the casks of salted sprat and salted herring; they chewed the rims of cheeses; then they curled up their tails, and nested inside men's Sunday hats. Rats! There was a ruin of rats. A rat-attack! A plague of rats.

At last the people of Hamelin marched to the Town Hall. They were shouting. They were chanting. They were carrying banners with words painted on them: RATS OUT! and I SMELL A RAT; and also, more worryingly for the mayor, I SMELL A MAYOR.

The mayor wasn't a rat. He was such a knickerbockered dumpling he couldn't have scampered anywhere to save his life; and his eyes weren't small or beady but large and grey and somehow faded; but he did have a fur coat—a brown velvet gown lined with white ermine. And so did all the councillors.

'We paid for those gowns,' shouted one man.

'And we'll have them off your backs,' called another.

'Rats! What are you going to do about them?'

'Get rid of them!'

'You're useless!'

'Disgraceful!'

The mayor and the councillors could see that, unless they got rid of the rats, they would never be elected again. But what were they to do? The town ratcatcher had laid traps and sprinkled poison and, true, he had caught a few dozen rats. But you can't catch a whole army any more than you can catch a rainstorm in a pail. So what were they to do?

For more than an hour the mayor and councillors sat in council.

They sat in silence and rocked to and fro and racked their brains.

'Oh! My head aches,' said the mayor. 'It's all very well. All very well!'

At noon, the mayor's stomach invited him to stop thinking about rats. It told him it was time to think about a large bowl of thick green turtle soup.

'Good idea!' murmured the mayor, and his eyes brightened.

At that moment, there was a gentle but firm rat-a-tat-tat at the great oak door of the council chamber.

The mayor gave a start. 'Oh dear!' he said, and he fanned himself with his right hand. 'Anything like that and—and I think it's a rat.' Using his elbows, the mayor levered himself upright in his carved mayoral chair. 'Come in!' he cried.

In came the strangest-looking figure. In and straight up to the mayor. He was wrapped in a gown so long he could have trapped its hem under his heels, and this gown was half yellow and half red: a marvel, a swaying jigsaw of crescents and diamonds, full-moons and coffins and zigzags and squares.

The man himself was tall and thin, with green and blue eyes. He had one of those seamless, hairless, almost ageless faces, and might have been thirty or fifty or even seventy years old.

The man smiled at the mayor and, so it seemed to them, at each of the councillors—little, quick elfin smiles.

'Please, your honours,' said the man. 'Please and listen.'

'Go on!' said the mayor.

'And hurry up about it, man!' said the mayor's stomach.

'I may be able to help you,' said the man. 'I have a special skill! I can make every creature under the sun follow me.'

'Follow you?' said the mayor.

'Every creature that creeps or runs or swims or flies. I've led away armies of moles and toads and vipers. Do you understand?'

'I follow you,' said the mayor.

'And people call me the Pied Piper,' said the man, holding up his hands and trilling his fingers.

Then for the first time the mayor and councillors of Hamelin noticed that the man was wearing a red-and-yellow sash round his neck, with a little reed pipe dangling from it.

'You see!' said the man, smiling. 'Now please and listen! Last June I saved the Cham of Tartary from a terrible swarm of gnats.'

'You did?' said the councillors.

'They were whining around his whiskers,' said the Piper.

'Pickled pepper!' said the mayor.

'And in Asia,' said the Piper, 'I rescued the Nizam from a brood of vampire-bats. So as you see: I can rid Hamelin of your plague of rats.'

'You can?' said the mayor. 'How much? I mean: how much?'
'One thousand guilders.'

'One thousand!' exclaimed the mayor. 'One! We'll give you fifty thousand—and cheap at the price.'

The Piper smiled another little, quick smile and bowed. Then he sailed out of the Town Hall, followed by the mayor and the councillors. Down in the street, the Piper waited until quite a crowd had gathered around him, curious to see what he would do. Then he raised his reed pipe and pursed his lips; his blue-green eyes were dancing.

As soon as the Piper began to play, there was a far-off sound, like a sound at the back of your mind, or the sound of the distant sea. But this hum became a mutter, and the mutter a grumble, and the grumble a rumble, as rats jumped down from barrels and ran along rafters and drummed over floorboards and tumbled downstairs, hundreds of rats, thousands of them, all eager to join the dance.

There were black rats and brown rats and some black-and-tans. Mothers and fathers and squeaking friskers. Grey-faced grandparents. Thick-waisted uncles and stern aunts with whiskers!

The Piper advanced from street to street, and he never stopped piping, not for one moment. He danced the rats all the way round Hamelin and then he led them down to the river. The Piper walked straight into the water and the rats followed him. They all dived in and drowned in the River Weser—all except one.

This one rat swam right across the river. He ran back to Ratland, and when he got there, he told the other rats: 'That music! What music! When the Piper started to play, I heard a sigh of bread rising in the oven and the hiss of fresh milk squirting into the pail; I heard the seething of damson jam; I heard corks popping and bacon crackling; I heard bubble-and-squeak! I heard a sweet, sweet voice telling me to eat and drink and eat—and at that moment, I found myself up to my neck in cold water.'

Then all the people of Hamelin began to gather in the market-place and the church bells rang. They rang and rang until the steeple rocked.

The mayor was purple in the face with pleasure. 'Get sticks!' he shouted. 'Get long poles! Poke out their holy nests! Block up their poky holes! I don't want a trace of them left in Hamelin.'

Then the Piper sauntered into the market-place. 'But first, your honour,' he said, 'please and pay me my one thousand guilders.'

'One thousand guilders!' exclaimed the mayor, and he turned from purple to blue.

'One thousand!' murmured the councillors. 'We can't afford a thousand. What about our council dinners?'

'Mmm!' murmured the mayor. 'We could buy a butt of Rhine wine for half that amount.'

'And then there's the claret and the Graves and the Moselle.'

'Exactly!' said the mayor. He rubbed his nose and then he winked at the councillors. 'Well!' he said. 'The rats are drowned and dead, and the dead can't come back to life, can they!' The mayor wagged a finger at the Piper. 'A thousand indeed! We were only joking, and you know it. But fair's fair: we'll give you a decent bottle, and here—take fifty guilders!'

'Don't you play around with me!' said the Piper, and his eyes shone blue and green, like candle-flames sprinkled with salt. 'I'm in a hurry. I've promised to be in Baghdad in time for supper.'

'Baghdad!' cried the mayor.

'The caliph's cook is making me a bowl of his best stew. I rid his kitchen of a nest of scorpions, and that's all he can afford.'

The mayor turned puce. He began to fan himself with his right hand.

'I didn't drive a hard bargain with him,' said the Piper, 'but I won't let you off—not one penny. And I'll tell you this: if you anger me, I'll pipe another kind of tune.'

'Are you telling me you've charged that cook a bowl of stew, and you're asking us for a thousand guilders?' demanded the mayor. 'I'm not going to be insulted by you—you piebald gypsy! How dare you threaten me? You can blow on your pipe until you balloon! Blow until you burst!'

The Piper raised his reed pipe and pursed his lips; and before he had blown three notes, there was a far-off sound, like the sound of wind in the high tree-tops. But this rustling became a bustling, and the bustling a hustling, as dozens and dozens of children burst into the market-place. Scampering and skipping and shouting and laughing, they thronged around the Piper, all of them eager to join the dance.

There were boys. There were girls. Brothers, half-brothers, sisters, step-sisters. There were little tiny creatures, who had only just learned to walk. And last, a moon-faced boy, whose right leg was all crooked.

Then the Piper stepped out of the market-place, and he never stopped piping, not for one moment. Hopping and clapping, quickstepping, chattering, the children of Hamelin followed him. Their clogs clattered on the cobblestones.

But the mayor and the councillors: they were spellbound. The magical music that made the children dance and sing silenced them and rooted them to the spot. They couldn't move; they couldn't even shout warnings.

The Pied Piper danced the children all the way round Hamelin and then, to the terror of the mayor and councillors, he led them down to the river.

The Weser slipped and slapped against its banks. It sang happy and sad, it echoed the death-songs of all the drowned rats.

Right at the water's edge, the Piper turned aside. He set off down the path along the river-bank, and all the children danced after him. They left Hamelin behind, and crossed the July meadows, and reached the foot of basking Koppelberg.

The hill was steep, the path was steep. But just as it seemed the Piper and children could climb no further, a green door swung open in the side of the hill. The Piper didn't pause. No! With a little, quick smile he walked straight in, and all the children of Hamelin stepped in after him.

All? All except one. The boy with the crooked leg couldn't dance. He was still way below, calling out to his friends, dragging himself up the stony path.

Then the green door swung shut again, and the moon-faced boy was left on the hillside. He stared and stared; then he folded on to his hands and knees.

The spluttering mayor and councillors sent town messengers north and south and east and west, with instructions to offer the Piper as much silver and gold as he wanted, if only he would bring the children back to Hamelin. But where had he gone? Where were the children? Time passed.

The men and women of Hamelin wept for their sons and daughters. They named the track that runs along the river-bank Pied Piper Street. They cut a story in stone. They painted a church window. Time passed.

Time passed and the moon-faced boy pressed his palms to the earth and stood up on Koppelberg.

'That music!' he said. 'What music! When the Piper started to play, I heard him promise and promise me: a happy land, right next to the town, where rainbows dance in waterfalls and horses have eagles' wings and nothing is not strange. The pear-trees and plum-trees are always in fruit! The roses never fade! And I promise and promise you: your foot will soon be cured.'

The boy's mouth tightened. His friends! His sharings and secret dreams and games and laughter! High on the hill, he left behind his childhood, and began to make his way back to Hamelin.

Stan Bolovan

Once upon a time what happened did happen, and if it
had not happened this story would never have been
told.

On the outskirts of a village just where the oxen were turned
out to pasture, and the pigs roamed about burrowing with their
noses among the roots of the trees, there stood a small house. In
the house lived a man who had a wife, and the wife was sad all
day long.

'Dear wife, what is wrong with you that you hang your head
like a drooping rosebud?' asked her husband one morning. 'You
have everything you want; why cannot you be merry like other
women?'

'Leave me alone, and do not seek to know the reason,' replied
she, bursting into tears, and the man thought that it was no time
to question her, and went away to his work.

He could not, however, forget all about it, and a few days after he enquired again the reason of her sadness, but only got the same reply. At length he felt he could bear it no longer, and tried a third time, and then his wife turned and answered him.

'Good gracious!' cried she. 'Why cannot you let things be as they are? If I were to tell you, you would become just as wretched as myself. If you would only believe, it is far better for you to know nothing.'

But no man yet was ever content with such an answer. The more you beg him not to enquire, the greater is his curiosity to learn the whole.

'Well, if you must know,' said the wife at last, 'I will tell you. There is no luck in this house—no luck at all!'

'Is not your cow the best milker in all the village? Are not your trees as full of fruit as your hives are full of bees? Has anyone cornfields like ours? Really, you talk nonsense when you say things like that!'

'Yes, all that you say is true, but we have no children.'

Then Stan understood, and when a man once understands and has his eyes opened it is no longer well with him. From that day the little house in the outskirts contained an unhappy man as well as an unhappy woman. And at the sight of her husband's misery the woman became more wretched than ever.

And so matters went on for some time.

Some weeks had passed, and Stan thought he would consult a wise man who lived a day's journey from his own house. The wise man was sitting before his door when he came up, and Stan fell on his knees before him. 'Give me children, my lord, give me children.'

'Take care what you are asking,' replied the wise man. 'Will not children be a burden to you? Are you rich enough to feed and clothe them?'

'Only give them to me, my lord, and I will manage somehow!' and at a sign from the wise man Stan went his way.

He reached home that evening tired and dusty, but with hope in his heart. As he drew near his house a sound of voices struck upon his ear, and he looked up to see the whole place full of children. Children in the garden, children in the yard, children looking out of every window—it seemed to the man as if all the children in the world must be gathered there. And none was bigger than the other, but each was smaller than the other, and every one was more noisy and more impudent and more daring than the rest, and Stan gazed and grew cold with horror as he realized that they all belonged to him.

'Good gracious! How many there are! How many!' he muttered to himself.

'Oh, but not one too many,' smiled his wife, coming up with a crowd more children clinging to her skirts.

But even she found that it was not so easy to look after a hundred children, and when a few days had passed and they had eaten up all the food there was in the house, they began to cry, 'Father! I am hungry—I am hungry,' till Stan scratched his head and wondered what he was to do next. It was not that he thought there were too many children, for his life had seemed more full of joy since they appeared, but now it came to the point he did not know how he was to feed them. The cow had ceased to give milk, and it was too early for the fruit trees to ripen.

'Do you know, old woman,' said he one day to his wife, 'I must go out into the world and try to bring back food somehow, though I cannot tell where it is to come from.'

To the hungry man any road is long, and then there was always the thought that he had to satisfy a hundred greedy children as well as himself.

Stan wandered, and wandered, and wandered, till he reached to the end of the world, where that which is, is mingled with that which is not, and there he saw, a little way off, a sheepfold, with seven sheep in it. In the shadow of some trees lay the rest of the flock.

Stan crept up, hoping that he might manage to decoy some of them away quietly, and drive them home for food for his family, but he soon found this could not be. For at midnight he heard a rushing noise, and through the air flew a dragon, who drove apart a ram, a sheep, and a lamb, and three fine cattle that were lying down close by. And besides these he took the milk of seventy-seven sheep, and carried it home to his old mother, that she might bathe in it and grow young again. And this happened every night.

The shepherd bewailed himself in vain: the dragon only laughed, and Stan saw that this was not the place to get food for his family.

But though he quite understood that it was almost hopeless to fight against such a powerful monster, yet the thought of the hungry children at home clung to him like a burr, and would not be shaken off, and at last he said to the shepherd, 'What will you give me if I rid you of the dragon?'

'One of every three rams, one of every three sheep, one of every three lambs,' answered the herd.

'It is a bargain,' replied Stan, though at the moment he did not know how, supposing he *did* come off the victor, he would ever be able to drive so large a flock home.

However, that matter could be settled later. At present night was not far off, and he must consider how best to fight with the dragon.

Just at midnight, a horrible feeling that was new and strange to him came over Stan—a feeling that he could not put into words even to himself, but which almost forced him to give up the battle and take the shortest road home again. He half turned; then he remembered the children, and turned back.

'You or I,' said Stan to himself, and took up his position on the edge of the flock. 'Stop!' he suddenly cried, as the air was filled with a rushing noise, and the dragon came dashing past.

'Dear me!' exclaimed the dragon, looking round. 'Who are you, and where do you come from?'

'I am Stan Bolovan, who eats rocks all night, and in the day feeds on the flowers of the mountain; and if you meddle with those sheep I will carve a cross on your back.'

When the dragon heard these words he stood quite still in the middle of the road, for he knew he had met with his match.

'But you will have to fight me first,' he said in a trembling voice, for when you faced him properly he was not brave at all.

'I fight you?' replied Stan. 'Why, I could slay you with one breath!' Then, stooping to pick up a large cheese which lay at his feet, he added, 'Go and get a stone like this out of the river, so that we may lose no time in seeing who is the best man.'

The dragon did as Stan bade him, and brought back a stone out of the brook.

'Can you get buttermilk out of your stone?' asked Stan.

The dragon picked up his stone with one hand, and squeezed it till it fell into powder, but no buttermilk flowed from it. 'Of course I can't!' he said, half angrily.

'Well, if you can't, I can,' answered Stan, and he pressed the cheese till buttermilk flowed through his fingers.

When the dragon saw that, he thought it was time he made the best of his way home again, but Stan stood in his path.

'We have still some accounts to settle,' said he, 'about what you have been doing here,' and the poor dragon was too frightened to stir, lest Stan should slay him at one breath and bury him among the flowers in the mountain pastures.

'Listen to me,' he said at last. 'I see you are a very useful person, and my mother has need of a fellow like you. Suppose you enter her service for three days, which are as long as one of your years, and she will pay you each day seven sacks full of ducats.'

Three times seven sacks full of ducats! The offer was very tempting, and Stan could not resist it. He did not waste words, but nodded to the dragon, and they started along the road.

It was a long, long way, but when they came to the end they found the dragon's mother, who was as old as time itself, expecting them. Stan saw her eyes shining like lamps from afar, and when they entered the house they beheld a huge kettle standing on the fire, filled with milk. When the old mother found that her son had arrived empty-handed she grew very angry, and fire and flame darted from her nostrils, but before she could speak the dragon turned to Stan.

'Stay here,' said he, 'and wait for me; I am going to explain things to my mother.'

Stan was already repenting bitterly that he had ever come to such a place, but, since he was there, there was nothing for it but to take everything quietly, and not show that he was afraid.

'Listen, mother,' said the dragon as soon as they were alone, 'I have brought this man in order to get rid of him. He is a terrific fellow who eats rocks, and can press buttermilk out of a stone,' and he told her all that had happened the night before.

'Oh, just leave him to me!' she said. 'I have never yet let a man slip through my fingers.' So Stan had to stay and do the old mother service.

The next day she told him that he and her son should try which was the strongest, and she took down a huge club, bound seven times with iron.

The dragon picked it up as if it had been a feather, and, after whirling it round his head, flung it lightly three miles away, telling Stan to beat that if he could.

They walked to the spot where the club lay. Stan stooped and felt it; then a great fear came over him, for he knew that he and all his children together would never lift that club from the ground.

'What are you doing?' asked the dragon.

'I was thinking what a beautiful club it was, and what a pity it is that it should cause your death.'

'How do you mean—my death?' asked the dragon.

'Only that I am afraid that if I throw it you will never see another dawn. You don't know how strong I am!'

'Oh, never mind that—be quick and throw.'

'If you are really in earnest, let us go and feast for three days: that will at any rate give you three extra days of life.'

Stan spoke so calmly that this time the dragon began to get a little frightened, though he did not quite believe that things would be as bad as Stan said.

They returned to the house, took all the food that could be found in the old mother's larder, and carried it back to the place where the club was lying. Then Stan seated himself on the sack of provisions, and remained quietly watching the setting moon.

'What are you doing?' asked the dragon.

'Waiting till the moon gets out of my way.'

'What do you mean? I don't understand.'

'Don't you see that the moon is exactly in my way? But of course, if you like, I will throw the club into the moon.'

At these words the dragon grew uncomfortable for the second time. He prized the club, which had been left him by his grandfather, very highly, and had no desire that it should be lost in the moon.

'I'll tell you what,' he said, after thinking a little. 'Don't throw the club at all. I will throw it a second time, and that will do just as well.'

'No, certainly not!' replied Stan. 'Just wait till the moon sets.'

But the dragon, in dread lest Stan should fulfil his threats, tried what bribes could do, and in the end had to promise Stan seven sacks of ducats before he was suffered to throw back the club himself.

'Oh, dear me, that is indeed a strong man,' said the dragon, turning to his mother. 'Would you believe that I have had the greatest difficulty in preventing him from throwing the club into the moon?'

Then the old woman grew uncomfortable too! Only to think of it! It was no joke to throw things into the moon! So no more was heard of the club, and the next day they had all something else to think about.

'Go and fetch me water!' said the mother, when the morning broke, and gave them twelve buffalo skins with the order to keep filling them till night.

They set out at once for the brook, and in the twinkling of an eye the dragon had filled the whole twelve, carried them into the house, and brought them back to Stan. Stan was tired: he could scarcely lift the buckets when they were empty, and he shuddered to think of what would happen when they were full. But he only took an old knife out of his pocket and began to scratch up the earth near the brook.

'What are you doing there? How are you going to carry the water into the house?' asked the dragon.

'How? Dear me, that is easy enough! I shall just take the brook!'

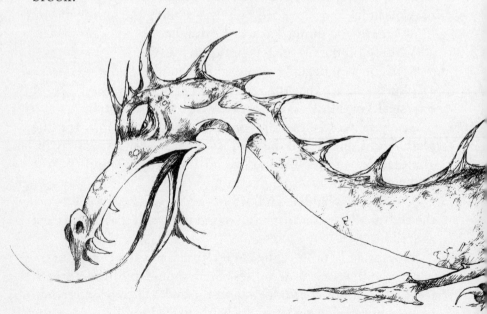

At these words the dragon's jaw dropped. This was the last thing that had ever entered his head, for the brook had been as it was since the days of his grandfather.

'I'll tell you what!' he said. 'Let me carry your skins for you.'

'Most certainly not,' answered Stan, going on with his digging, and the dragon, in dread lest he should fulfil his threat, tried what bribes would do, and in the end had again to promise seven sacks of ducats before Stan would agree to leave the brook alone and let him carry the water into the house.

On the third day the old mother sent Stan into the forest for wood, and, as usual, the dragon went with him.

Before you could count three he had pulled up more trees than Stan could have cut down in a lifetime, and had arranged them neatly in rows. When the dragon had finished, Stan began to look about him, and, choosing the biggest of the trees, he climbed up it, and, breaking off a long rope of wild vine, bound the top of the tree to the one next it. And so he did to a whole line of trees.

'What are you doing there?' asked the dragon.

'You can see for yourself,' answered Stan, going quietly on with his work.

'Why are you tying the trees together?'

'Not to give myself unnecessary work; when I pull up one, all the others will come up too.'

'But how will you carry them home?'

'Dear me! Don't you understand that I am going to take the whole forest back with me?' said Stan, tying two other trees as he spoke.

'I'll tell you what,' cried the dragon, trembling with fear at the thought of such a thing, 'let me carry the wood for you, and you shall have seven times seven sacks full of ducats.'

'You are a good fellow, and I agree to your proposal,' answered Stan, and the dragon carried the wood.

Now the three days' service which were to be reckoned as a year were over, and the only thing that disturbed Stan was, how to get all those ducats back to his home!

In the evening the dragon and his mother had a long talk, but Stan heard every word through a crack in the ceiling.

'Woe be to us, mother,' said the dragon, 'this man will soon get us into his power. Give him his money, and let us be rid of him.'

But the old mother was fond of money, and did not like this.

'Listen to me,' she said. 'You must murder him this very night.'

'I am afraid,' answered he.

'There is nothing to fear,' replied the old mother. 'When he is asleep take the club, and hit him on the head with it. It is easily done.'

And so it would have been, had not Stan heard all about it. And when the dragon and his mother had put out their lights, he took the pigs' trough and filled it with earth, and placed it in his bed, and covered it with clothes. Then he hid himself underneath, and began to snore loudly.

Very soon the dragon stole softly into the room, and gave a tremendous blow on the spot where Stan's head should have been. Stan groaned loudly from under the bed, and the dragon went away as softly as he had come. Directly he had closed the door, Stan lifted out the pigs' trough, and lay down himself, after making everything clean and tidy, but he was wise enough not to shut his eyes that night.

The next morning he came into the room when the dragon and his mother were having their breakfast.

'Good morning,' said he.

'Good morning. How did you sleep?'

'Oh, very well, but I dreamed that a flea had bitten me, and I seem to feel it still.'

The dragon and his mother looked at each other. 'Do you hear that?' whispered he. 'He talks of a flea. I broke my club on his head.'

This time the mother grew as frightened as her son. There was nothing to be done with a man like this, and she made all haste to fill the sacks with ducats, so as to get rid of Stan as soon as possible. But on his side Stan was trembling like an aspen, as he could not lift even one sack from the ground. So he stood still and looked at them.

'What are you standing there for?' asked the dragon.

'Oh, I was standing here because it has just occurred to me that I should like to stay in your service for another year. I am ashamed that when I get home they should see I have brought back so little. I know that they will cry out, "Just look at Stan Bolovan, who in one year has grown as weak as a dragon."'

Here a shriek of dismay was heard both from the dragon and his mother, who declared they would give him seven or even seven times seven the number of sacks if he would only go away.

'I'll tell you what!' said Stan at last. 'I see you don't want me to stay, and I should be very sorry to make myself disagreeable. I will go at once, but only on condition that you shall carry the money home yourself, so that I may not be put to shame before my friends.'

The words were hardly out of his mouth before the dragon had snatched up the sacks and piled them on his back. Then he and Stan set forth.

The way, though really not far, was yet too long for Stan, but at length he heard his children's voices, and stopped short. He did not wish the dragon to know where he lived, lest some day he should come to take back his treasure. Was there nothing he could say to get rid of the monster? Suddenly an idea came into Stan's head, and he turned round.

'I hardly know what to do,' said he. 'I have a hundred children, and I am afraid they may do you harm, as they are always ready for a fight. However, I will do my best to protect you.'

A hundred children! That was indeed no joke! The dragon let fall the sacks from terror, and then picked them up again. But the children, who had had nothing to eat since their father had left them, came rushing towards him, waving knives in their right hands and forks in their left, and crying, 'Give us dragon's flesh; we will have dragon's flesh.'

At this dreadful sight the dragon waited no longer: he flung down his sacks where he stood and took flight as fast as he could, so terrified at the fate that awaited him that from that day he has never dared to show his face in the world again.

The Dead Man's Nightcap

On a farm beside a church there lived, among others, a young boy and a girl. The boy made a habit of scaring the girl, but she had got so used to it that she was never frightened of anything, for if she did see something she thought it was the boy trying to scare her.

One day it so happened that the washing had been done, and that among the things there were many white nightcaps, such as were in fashion then. In the evening the girl was told to fetch in the washing, which was out in the churchyard. She runs out, and begins to pick up the washing. When she has almost finished, she sees a white spectre sitting on one of the graves. She thinks to herself that the lad is planning to scare her, so she runs up and snatches the spectre's cap off (for she thought the boy had taken one of the nightcaps) and says: 'Now don't you start trying to scare me this time!'

So she went indoors with the washing; the boy had been indoors the whole time. They started sorting out the washing; there was one nightcap too many now, and it was earthy on the inside. Then the girl was scared.

Next morning the spectre was still sitting on the grave, and people did not know what to do about it, as nobody dared take the cap back, and so they sent word all round the district, asking for advice. There was one old man in the district who declared that it would be impossible to stop something bad coming of it, unless the girl herself took the cap back to the spectre and placed it on its head in silence, and that there ought to be many people there to watch.

The girl was forced to go with the cap and place it on the spectre's head, and so she went, though her heart was not much in it, and she placed the cap on the head of the spectre, and when she had done so she said, 'Are you satisfied now?'

But at this the dead man started to his feet, struck her, and said, 'Yes! And you, are you satisfied?'

And with these words he plunged down into the grave. The girl fell down at the blow, and when men ran to pick her up, she was already dead. The boy was punished because he used to scare her, for it was considered that the whole unfortunate affair had been his fault, and he gave up scaring people. And that is the end of this tale.

Vasilissa the Fair

A merchant and his wife living in a certain country had an only daughter, the beautiful Vasilissa. When the child was eight years old the mother was seized with a fatal illness, but before she died she called Vasilissa to her side and, giving her a little doll, said, 'Listen, dear daughter. Remember my last words. I am dying, and bequeath to you now, together with a parent's blessing, this doll. Keep it always beside you, but show it to nobody; if at any time you are in trouble, give the doll some food and ask its advice.' Then the mother kissed her daughter, sighed deeply and died.

After his wife's death the merchant grieved for a long time, and next began to think whether he should not wed again. He was handsome and would have no difficulty in finding a bride; moreover, he was especially pleased with a certain little widow, no longer young, who possessed two daughters of about the same age as Vasilissa.

The widow was famous as both a good housekeeper and a good mother to her daughters, but when the merchant married her he quickly found she was unkind to his daughter. Vasilissa, being the chief beauty in the village, was on that account envied by her stepmother and stepsisters. They found fault with her on every occasion, and tormented her with impossible tasks; thus, the poor girl suffered from the severity of her work and grew dark from exposure to wind and sun.

Vasilissa endured all and became every day more beautiful; but the stepmother and her daughters who sat idle with folded hands, grew thin and almost lost their minds from spite. What supported Vasilissa? This. She received assistance from her doll; otherwise she could not have surmounted her daily difficulties.

Vasilissa, as a rule, kept a dainty morsel for her doll, and in the evening when everyone had gone to bed she would steal to her closet and regale her doll and say, 'Now, dear, eat and listen to my grief! Though I am living in my father's house, my life is joyless; a wicked stepmother makes me wretched; please direct my life and tell me what to do.'

The doll tasted the food, and gave advice to the sorrowing child, and in the morning performed her work, so that Vasilissa could rest in the shade or pluck flowers; already the beds had been weeded, and the cabbages watered, and the water carried, and the stove heated. It was nice for Vasilissa to live with her doll.

Several years passed. Vasilissa grew up, and the young men in the town sought her hand in marriage; but they never looked at the stepsisters. Growing more angry than ever, the stepmother answered Vasilissa's suitors thus: 'I will not let you have my youngest daughter before her sisters.' She dismissed the suitors and vented her spite on Vasilissa with harsh words and blows.

But it happened that the merchant was obliged to visit a neighbouring country, where he had business; and in the meanwhile the stepmother went to live in a house situated close to a thick forest. In the forest was a glade, in which stood a cottage, and in the cottage lived Baba-Yaga, who admitted nobody to her cottage, and devoured people as if they were chickens.

Having moved to the new house, the merchant's wife continually, on some pretext or other, sent the hated Vasilissa into the forest, but the girl always returned home safe and unharmed, because the doll directed her and took care she did not enter Baba-Yaga's cottage.

Spring arrived, and the stepmother assigned to each of the three girls an evening task; thus, she set one to make lace, a second to knit stockings, and Vasilissa to spin. One evening, having extinguished all the lights in the house except one candle in the room where the girls sat at work, the stepmother went to bed. In a little while the candle needed attention, and one of the stepmother's daughters took the snuffers and, beginning to cut the wick, as if by accident, put out the light.

'What are we to do now?' said the girls. 'There is no light in the whole house, and our tasks are unfinished; someone must run for a light to Baba-Yaga.'

'I can see my pins,' said the daughter who was making lace. 'I shall not go.'

'Neither shall I,' said the daughter who was knitting stockings. 'My needles are bright.'

'You must run for a light. Go to Baba-Yaga's,' they both cried, pushing Vasilissa from the room.

Vasilissa went to her closet, placed some supper ready for the doll, and said, 'Now, little doll, have something to eat and hear my trouble. They have sent me to Baba-Yaga's for a light, and she will eat me.'

'Do not be afraid!' answered the doll. 'Go on your errand, but take me with you. No harm will befall you while I am present.' Vasilissa placed the doll in her pocket, crossed herself and entered the thick forest, but she trembled.

Suddenly a horseman galloped past; he was white and dressed in white, his steed was white and had a white saddle and bridle. The morning light was appearing.

The girl went further and another horseman rode past; he was red and dressed in red and his steed was red. The sun rose.

Vasilissa walked all night and all day, but on the following evening she came out in a glade, where stood Baba-Yaga's cottage. The fence around the cottage was made of human bones, and on the fence there were fixed human skulls with eyes. Instead of doorposts at the gates there were human legs; instead of bolts there were hands, instead of a lock there was a mouth with sharp teeth. Vasilissa grew pale from terror and stood as if transfixed.

Suddenly another horseman rode up; he was black and dressed in black and upon a black horse; he sprang through Baba-Yaga's gates and vanished, as if he had been hurled into the earth. Night came on. But the darkness did not last long; the eyes in all the skulls on the fence lighted up, and at once it

became as light throughout the glade as if it were midday. Vasilissa trembled from fear, and not knowing whither to run, she remained motionless.

Suddenly she heard a terrible noise. The trees cracked, the dry leaves rustled, and out of the forest Baba-Yaga appeared, riding in a mortar which she drove with a pestle, while she swept away traces of her progress with a broom. She came up to the gates and stopped; then sniffing about her, cried, 'Phoo, phoo, I smell a Russian! Who is here?'

Vasilissa approached the old woman timidly and gave her a low bow; then she said, 'It is I, granny! My stepsisters have sent me to you for a light.'

'Very well,' said Baba-Yaga, 'I know them. If you first of all live with me and do some work, then I will give you a light. If you refuse, I will eat you.' Then she turned to the gates and exclaimed, 'Strong bolts, unlock; wide gates, open!' The gates opened, and Baba-Yaga went in whistling. Vasilissa followed, and all again closed.

Having entered the room, the witch stretched herself and said to Vasilissa, 'Hand me everything in the oven; I am hungry.' Vasilissa lit a torch from the skulls upon the fence and, drawing the food from the oven, handed it to the witch. The meal would have been sufficient for ten men. Moreover, Vasilissa brought up from the cellar kvass, and honey, and beer and wine. The old woman ate and drank almost everything. She left nothing for Vasilissa but some fragments, end-crusts of bread and tiny morsels of sucking pig.

Baba-Yaga lay down to sleep and said, 'When I go away tomorrow, take care that you clean the yard, sweep out the cottage, cook the dinner and get ready the linen. Then go to the cornbin, take a quarter of the wheat and cleanse it from impurities. See that all is done, otherwise I shall eat you.'

After giving these injunctions Baba-Yaga began to snore. But Vasilissa placed the remains of the old woman's meal before her doll and, bursting into tears, said, 'Now, little doll, take some food and hear my grief. Baba-Yaga has set me a terrible task, and has threatened to eat me if I fail in any way; help me!'

The doll answered, 'Have no fear, beautiful Vasilissa! Eat your supper, say your prayers and lie down to sleep; morning is wiser than evening.'

It was early when Vasilissa woke, but Baba-Yaga, who had already risen, was looking out of the window. Suddenly the light from the eyes in the skulls was extinguished; then a pale horseman flashed by, and it was altogether daylight. Baba-Yaga went out and whistled; a mortar appeared before her with a pestle and a hearth broom. A red horseman flashed by, and the sun rose. Then Baba-Yaga took her place in the mortar and went forth, driving herself with the pestle and sweeping away traces of her progress with the broom.

Vasilissa remained alone and, eyeing Baba-Yaga's house, wondered at her wealth. The girl did not know which task to begin with. But when she looked she found that the work was already done: the doll had separated from the wheat the last grains of impurity.

'Oh, my dear liberator,' said Vasilissa to the doll, 'you have rescued me from misfortune!'

'You have only to cook the dinner,' said the doll, climbing into Vasilissa's pocket. 'God help you to prepare it; then rest in peace!'

Towards evening Vasilissa laid the table and awaited Baba-Yaga's return. It became dusk, and a black horseman flashed by the gates; it had grown altogether dark. But the eyes in the skulls shone and the trees cracked and the leaves rustled. Baba-Yaga came. Vasilissa met her. 'Is all done?' asked the witch.

'Look for yourself, granny!'

Baba-Yaga examined everything and, vexed that she had no cause for anger, said, 'My true servants, my bosom friends, grind my wheat!' Three pairs of hands appeared, seized the wheat and bore it from sight.

Baba-Yaga ate to repletion, prepared for sleep, and again gave an order to Vasilissa. 'Tomorrow repeat your task of today; in addition remove the poppies from the cornbin and cleanse them from earth, seed by seed; you see, someone has maliciously mixed earth with them!' Having spoken, the old woman turned to the wall and snored.

Vasilissa began to feed her doll, who said, as on the previous day, 'Pray to God and go to sleep; morning is wiser than evening; all will be done, dear Vasilissa!'

In the morning Baba-Yaga departed again in her mortar, and immediately Vasilissa and the doll set to work at their tasks. The old woman returned, observed everything and cried out, 'My faithful servants, my close friends, squeeze the oil from the poppies!' Three pairs of hands seized the poppies and bore them from sight. Baba-Yaga sat down to dine, and Vasilissa stood silent.

'Why do you say nothing?' remarked the witch. 'You stand as if you were dumb.'

Timidly Vasilissa replied, 'If you would permit me, I should like to ask you a question.'

'Ask, but remember, not every question leads to good. You will learn much; you will soon grow old.'

'I only wish to ask you,' said the girl, 'about what I have seen. When I came to you a pale horseman dressed in white on a white horse overtook me. Who was he?'

'He is my clear day,' answered Baba-Yaga.

'Then another horseman, who was red and dressed in red, and who rode a red horse, overtook me. Who was he?'

'He was my little red sun!' was the answer.

'But who was the black horseman who passed me at the gate, granny?'

'He was my dark night; all three are my faithful servants.'

Vasilissa recalled the three pairs of hands, but was silent.

'Have you nothing more to ask?' said Baba-Yaga.

'I have, but you said, granny, that I shall learn much as I grow older.'

'It is well,' answered the witch, 'that you have enquired only about things outside and not about anything here! I do not like my rubbish to be carried away, and I eat over-inquisitive people! Now I will ask you something. How did you succeed in performing the tasks which I set you?'

'My mother's blessing assisted me,' answered Vasilissa.

'Depart, favoured daughter! I do not require people who have been blessed.' Baba-Yaga dragged Vasilissa out of the room and pushed her beyond the gate, took down from the fence a skull with burning eyes and, putting it on a stick, gave it to the girl and said, 'Take this light to your stepsisters; they sent you here for it.'

Vasilissa ran off, the skull giving her light, which only went out in the morning; and at last, on the evening of the second day, she reached home. As she approached the gates, she was on the point of throwing away the skull, for she thought that there would no longer be any need for a light at home. Then suddenly a hollow voice from the skull was heard to say, 'Do not cast me aside, but carry me to your stepmother.' Glancing at the house, and not seeing a light in any of the windows, she decided to enter with the skull.

At first her stepmother and stepsisters met her with caresses, telling her that they had been without a light from the moment of her departure; they could not strike a light in any way, and if anybody brought one from the neighbours, it went out directly it was carried into the room. 'Perhaps your light will last,' said the stepmother. When they carried the skull into the room its eyes shone brightly and looked continually at the stepmother and her daughters. All their efforts to hide themselves were vain; wherever they rushed they were ceaselessly pursued by the eyes, and before dawn had been burnt to ashes, though Vasilissa was unharmed.

In the morning the girl buried the skull in the ground, locked up the house and visited the town, where she asked admission into the home of a certain old woman who was without kindred. Here she lived quietly and awaited her father. But one day she said to the old woman, 'It tires me to sit idle, granny! Go off and buy me some of the best flax; I will busy myself with spinning.'

The old woman purchased the flax and Vasilissa sat down to spin. The work proceeded rapidly, and the thread when spun was as smooth and fine as a small hair. The thread lay in heaps, and it was time to begin weaving, but a weaver's comb could not be found to suit Vasilissa's thread, and nobody would undertake to make one. Then the girl had recourse to her doll, who said, 'Bring me an old comb that has belonged to a weaver, and an old shuttle, and a horse's mane, and I will do everything for you.'

Vasilissa obtained everything necessary, and lay down to sleep. The doll, in a single night, made a first-rate loom. Towards the end of winter linen had been woven of so fine a texture that it could be drawn through the needle where the thread should pass.

In spring the linen was bleached, and Vasilissa said to the old woman, 'Sell this linen, granny, and keep the money for yourself.'

The old woman glanced at the work and said with a sigh, 'Ah! my child, nobody but a tsar would wear such linen. I will take it to the palace.'

She went to the royal dwelling, and walked up and down in front of the windows. When the tsar saw her he said, 'What do you desire, old woman?'

'Your Majesty,' she answered, 'I have brought some wonderful material, and will show it to nobody but yourself.'

The tsar ordered that she should be admitted, and marvelled when he saw the linen. 'How much do you ask for it?' he enquired.

'It is not for sale, Tsar and Father! I have brought it as a gift.' The tsar thanked her, and sent her away with some presents.

Some shirts for the tsar were cut out from this linen, but a seamstress could nowhere be found to complete them. At last the tsar summoned the old woman and said to her, 'You were able to spin and weave this linen, so you will be able to sew together some shirts from it.'

'Tsar, it was not I who spun and wove the linen; it is the work of a beautiful maiden.'

'Well, let her sew them!'

The old woman returned home and related everything to Vasilissa. The girl said in reply, 'I knew that this work would not pass out of my hands.' She shut herself in her room and began the undertaking; soon, without resting her hands, she had completed a dozen shirts.

The old woman bore them to the tsar, while Vasilissa washed herself and combed her hair, dressed and then took a seat at the window, and there awaited events. She saw a royal servant come to the old woman's house. He entered the room and said, 'The Tsar-Emperor desires to see the skilful worker who made his shirts, and to reward her out of his royal hands.'

Vasilissa presented herself before the tsar. So much did she please him that he said, 'I cannot bear to separate from you; become my wife!' The tsar took her by her white hands, placed her beside himself, and the wedding was celebrated.

Vasilissa's father quickly returned to rejoice at his daughter's good fortune and to live with her. Vasilissa took the old woman into the palace, and never separated from the little doll, which she kept in her pocket.

The Three Blows

Their stone farmhouse seemed to grow out of the grey-green skirt of the mountain. The walls were lichenous, one part of the roof was covered with slate and the other part with turf. The whole building was so low slung it seemed to be crouching.

It wasn't alone. Megan could stand at their door (you had to stoop to get in or out) and see three other small-holdings within reach, almost within shouting distance. And no more than a mile away, along the track north and west, huddled and patient, was the little village of Llanddeusant.

But when the wind opened its throat and rain swept across the slopes; when the lean seasons came to Black Mountain; when wolves circled the pens and small birds left their sanskrit in the snow: the farm seemed alone then, alone in the world— and all the more so to Megan since her husband had died leaving her to bring up their baby son and run the farm on her own.

But Megan was a hard-working woman. As the years passed, her holding of cattle and sheep and goats so increased that they strayed far and wide over Black Mountain. And all the while her son grew and grew until he became a big-boned young man: rather awkward, very strong-willed, and shy and affectionate. Yet sometimes, when she looked at him sitting by the fire, lost in his own sliding dreams, it seemed to Megan that she didn't really quite know her son. He's like his father, she thought. Something hidden. What is he thinking?

Gwyn spent most of his time up on Black Mountain, herding the cattle and sheep and goats. More often than not he followed them up to a remote place in a fold of the mountain: it was a secret eye, a dark pupil that watched the sun and moon and stars: the little lake of Llyn y Fan Fach.

One spring morning, Gwyn was poking along the edge of the lake, on his way to the flat rock where he sometimes sat and spread out his provisions—barley-bread, maybe, and a chump of cheese, a wooden bottle seething with ale. Gwyn clambered on to the rock and stared out across the lake, silver and obsidian. And there, sitting on the glassy surface of the water, combing her hair, he saw a young woman. She was using the water as a mirror, charming her hair into ringlets, arranging them so that they covered her shoulders; and only when she had finished did she look up and see Gwyn, awkward on the rock, open-mouthed, arms stretched out, offering her bread . . .

Slowly, so slowly she scarcely seemed to move at all, the young woman glided over the surface of the water towards Gwyn and, entranced, he stepped down to meet her.

And then Gwyn heard her voice. It was like a bell, heard long ago and remembered: very sweet and very low. 'Your bread's baked and hard,' she said. 'It's not easy to catch me.'

Which is just what Gwyn tried to do. He lunged into the lake, and at once the girl sank from sight; she left her smile behind, playing on the smooth surface of the water.

For a while Gwyn stood and stared. A stray cloud passed in front of the sun; the water shivered. Gwyn felt as if he had found the one thing in this world that mattered only to lose it. And he resolved to come back, to find the girl and catch her, whatever the cost.

Gwyn turned away from the lake. He set off down the string-thin sheep-runs, the network that covered the steep shoulders of the mountain. At first he walked slowly, but by the time he reached the doors of his farmhouse he was almost running, so eager was he to tell his mother about the bewitching girl he had seen up at Llyn y Fan Fach.

'Stuff!' said Megan. 'You and your dreams.' But as she listened to Gwyn, she did not doubt that he was telling the truth. Perhaps she saw in the young man at her hearth another young man at the same hearth long before, shining and stammering. But then she quailed as she thought of what might become of Gwyn if he was caught up with the fairy folk.

'I won't be put off,' said Gwyn. 'I won't be put off if that's what you're thinking.'

'Leave her alone, Gwyn,' said Megan. 'Take a girl from the valley.'

'I won't be put off,' said Gwyn.

'You won't catch her,' Megan said, 'not unless you listen to me.'

'What do you mean?' said Gwyn.

'"Your bread's baked and hard." Isn't that what she said?'

Gwyn nodded.

'Well, then. Take up some toes. Take up some toes. Stands to reason.'

'Toes?' said Gwyn.

'Pieces of dough. Unbaked and just as they are.'

Gwyn followed his mother's advice. As night began to lose its thickness, yet before you could say it was dawn, he filled one pocket with dough, and quietly let himself out of the farmhouse without waking his mother. He sniffed the cool air and began to climb the dun and misty mountain.

She was not there. Shape-changing mist that plays tricks with the eyes dipped and rose and dipped over the dark water until the sun came down from the peaks and burned it away. Birds arrived in boating parties, little fish made circles, and she was not there.

Not long before dusk, Gwyn saw that two of his cows were lumbering straight towards the top of the dangerous escarpment on the far side of the lake. He stood up at once and began to run round the lake after them. 'Stupids!' he bawled. 'You'll lose your footing.'

Then she was there. She was there, sitting on the shimmer of the water, smiling, just as she had done on the day before.

Gwyn stopped. He reached out his arms and, as the beautiful young woman drifted towards him, he gazed at her: the blue-black sheen of her hair, her long fingers, the green water-silk of her dress, and her little ankles and sandals tied with thongs. Then Gwyn dug into his pockets and offered her the unbaked dough and not only that but his hand too and his heart for ever.

'Your bread is unbaked,' said the young woman. 'I will not have you.' Then she raised her arms and sank under the surface of the water.

Gwyn cried out, and the rockface heard and answered him, all hollow and disembodied. But even as he looked at the lake and listened to the sounds, each as mournful as the other, Gwyn thought of the girl's smile and was half-comforted. 'I'll catch you,' he said.

'You caught the cows,' said Megan later that evening. 'That's what matters.'

Gwyn grinned.

'Anyhow,' said Megan, 'you're not going up there again, are you?'

'You know I am,' said Gwyn.

'In that case,' said his mother, 'listen to me. I'd take some partly baked bread up with you.'

Gwyn reached Llyn y Fan Fach again as day dawned. He kept a watch on the lake and his whole face glowed—his cheeks and chin and ears and eyes, above all his eyes—as if he had just turned away from a leaping fire. He felt strong and he felt weak.

This time it was the sheep and goats that strayed towards the rockface and scree at the far end of the lake. But Gwyn knew how nimble-footed they were. Even when they loosened and dislodged a rock that bumped and bundled down the escarpment and splashed into the lake, they were in no danger.

All morning, wayward April shook sheets of sunlight and rain over the lake and then, in the afternoon, the clouds piling in from the west closed over the mountain. For hour after hour, Gwyn crouched on the smooth rock or padded round the rim of the lake. Now he was no longer so excited or fearful; the long waiting had dulled him.

In the early evening, the mood of the weather changed again. First, Gwyn could see blue sky behind the gauze of cloud, and then the clouds left the mountain altogether. The lake and the ashen scree were soothed by yellow sunlight.

This was the hour when Gwyn saw that three cows were walking on the water. They were out in the middle of Llyn y Fan Fach and ambling towards him.

Gwyn stood up. He swung off the rock platform and down to the lakeside. And as he did so, the young woman appeared for the third time, as beautiful as before, passing over the mirror of water just behind the three cows.

Gwyn stepped into the lake, up to his shins, his thighs, his hips. Still the young woman came on, and she was smiling—an expression that lit up her whole face, and above all her violet eyes.

Gwyn reached out his hands and, wordless, offered her the partly baked bread.

The young woman took the bread, and Gwyn grasped her cool hand. He was nervous and breathless.

'Come with me,' he said. 'Come to the farm . . . I'll show you. Come with me . . . marry me!'

The young woman looked at Gwyn.

'I'll not let you go,' said Gwyn. He could hear his voice rising, as if someone else were speaking. 'I've waited!' He tightened his grip on the girl's hand.

'Gwyn,' said the young woman. 'I will marry you,' she said, 'on one condition.'

'Anything!' said Gwyn. 'Anything you ask.'

'I will marry you and live with you. But if you strike me . . .'

'Strike you!' cried Gwyn.

'. . . strike me three blows without reason, I'll return to this lake and you'll never see me again.'

'Never!' swore Gwyn. 'Never!' He loosened his fierce grip and at once she slid away, raised her arms, and disappeared under the surface of the water.

'Come back!' shouted Gwyn. 'Come back!'

'Gon-ba!' said the mountain. 'Gon-ba!'

Gwyn stood up to his waist in the chill water. The huge, red sun alighted on the western horizon and began to slip out of sight.

But now two young women, each as lovely as the other, rose out of the water and a tall old white-headed man immediately after them. At once they came walking towards Gwyn.

'Greetings, Gwyn!' called the old man. 'You mean to marry one of my daughters, you've asked her to marry you.' He waved towards the two girls at his side. 'And I agree to this. You can marry her if you can tell me which one you mean to marry.'

Gwyn looked from one girl to the other: their clefs of black hair, their strange violet eyes, their long necks . . .

One of the girls tossed her charcoal hair; the other eased one foot forward, one inch, two inches, and into Gwyn's memory. The sandals . . . the thongs . . .

Gwyn reached out at once across the water and took her cool hand. 'This is she,' he said.

'You have made your choice?' asked the old man.

'I have,' said Gwyn.

'You've chosen well,' the man said. 'And you can marry her. Be kind to her, and faithful.'

'I will,' said Gwyn, 'and I will.'

'This is her dowry,' said the man. 'She can have as many sheep and cattle and goats and horses as she can count without drawing breath.'

No sooner had her father spoken than his daughter began to count for the sheep. She counted in fives, 'One, two, three, four, five—one, two, three, four, five' over and over again until she'd run out of breath.

'Thirty-two times,' said the man. 'One hundred and sixty sheep.' As soon as they had been named, the sheep appeared on the surface of the darkening water, and ran across it to the bare mountain.

'Now the cattle,' said the old man. Then his daughter began to count again, her voice soft and rippling. And so they went on until there were more than six hundred head of sheep and cattle and goats and horses milling around on the lakeside.

'Go now,' said the white-headed man gently. 'And remember, Gwyn, if you strike her three blows without reason, she'll return to me, and bring all her livestock back to this lake.'

It was almost dark. The old man and his other daughter went down into the lake. Gwyn took his bride's hand and, followed by her livestock, led her down from the mountain.

So Gwyn and the girl from Llan y Fan Fach were married. Gwyn left the house in which he had been born, and his mother in it, and went to a farm a few miles away, outside the village of Myddfai.

Gwyn and his wife were happy and, because of the generosity of the old man, they were rich. They had three sons, dark-haired, dark-eyed, lovely to look at.

Some years after Gwyn and his wife had moved to Myddfai, they were invited to a christening back in Llanddeusant. Gwyn was eager to go but, when the time came for them to set off, his wife was not.

'I don't know these people,' she said.

'It's Gareth,' said Gwyn. 'I've known him all my life. And this is his first child.'

'It's too far to walk,' said his wife.

'Fetch a horse from the field then,' said Gwyn. 'You can ride down.'

'Will you go and find my gloves,' said Gwyn's wife, 'while I get the horse? I left them in the house.'

When Gwyn came out of the farmhouse with the gloves, eager to be off, his wife had made no move towards the paddock and the horse.

'What's wrong?' cried Gwyn, and he slapped his wife's shoulder with one of her gloves.

Gwyn's wife turned to face him. Her eyes darkened. 'Gwyn!' she said. 'Gwyn! Remember the condition on which I married you.'

'I remember,' said Gwyn.

'That you would never strike me without reason.'

Gwyn nodded.

'Be careful! Be more careful from now on!'

Not long after this, Gwyn and his wife went to a fine wedding. The guests at the breakfast came not only from Llanddeusant and Myddfai but many of the surrounding farms and villages. The barn in which the reception was held was filled with the hum of contentment and the sweet sound of the triple harp.

As soon as she had kissed the bride, Gwyn's wife began to weep and then to sob. The guests around her stopped talking. A few tried to comfort her but many backed away, superstitious of tears at a wedding.

Gwyn didn't know quite what to do. 'What's wrong?' he whispered. 'What's wrong?' But his wife sobbed as bitterly as a little child. Gwyn smiled apologetically and shook his head; then he pursed his lips and dropped a hand on to his wife's arm. 'What's the matter?' he insisted. 'You must stop!'

Gwyn's wife gazed at her husband with her flooded violet eyes. 'These two people,' she said, 'are on the threshold of such trouble. I see it all. And Gwyn,' she said, 'I see your troubles are about to begin. You've struck me without reason for the second time.'

Gwyn's wife loved her husband no less than he loved her and neither had the least desire that their marriage should suddenly come to an end. Knowing that her own behaviour could surprise and upset Gwyn, she sometimes reminded her husband to be very careful not to strike her for a third time. 'Otherwise,' she said, 'I must return to Llyn y Fan Fach. I have no choice in the matter.'

But the years passed. The three boys became young men, all of them intelligent. And when he thought about it at all, Gwyn believed that he had learned his lesson on the way to the christening and at the wedding, and that he and his water-wife would live together happily for as long as they lived.

One day, Gwyn and his wife went to a funeral. Everyone round about had come to pay their last respects to the dead woman: she had been the daughter of a rich farmer and wife to the priest, generous with her time and money, and still in the prime of her life.

After the funeral, a good number of the priest's friends went back to his house to eat funeral cakes with him and keep him company, and Gwyn and his wife were among them.

No sooner had they stepped inside the priest's house than Gwyn's wife began to laugh. Amongst the mourners with their black suits and sober faces, she giggled as if she were tipsy with ale or romping with young children.

Gwyn was shocked. 'Shush!' he said. 'Think where you are! Stop this laughing!' he said. And firmly he laid a restraining hand on his wife's forearm.

'I'm laughing,' said Gwyn's wife, 'because when a person dies, she passes out of this world of trouble. Ah! Gwyn,' she cried, 'you've struck me for the third time and the last time. Our marriage is at an end.'

Gwyn's wife left the funeral feast alone and went straight back to their fine farm outside Myddfai. There she began to call in all her livestock.

'Brindled cow, come! White speckled cow, spotted cow, bold freckled cow, come! Old white-faced cow, Grey Squinter, white bull from the court of the king, come and come home!'

Gwyn's wife knew each of her livestock by name. And she did not forget the calf her husband had slaughtered only the previous week. 'Little black calf,' she cried, 'come down from the hook! Come home!'

The black calf leaped into life; it danced around the courtyard.

Then Gwyn's wife saw four of her oxen ploughing a nearby field. 'Grey oxen!' she cried. 'Four oxen of the field, you too must come home!'

When they heard her, the oxen turned from their task and, for all the whistles of the ploughboy, dragged the plough right across the newly turned furrows.

Gwyn's wife looked about her. She paused. Then she turned her back on the farmhouse and the farm. Those who saw her never forgot that sight: one woman, sad and steadfast, walking up on to Myddfai mountain, and behind her, plodding and trudging and tripping and high-stepping, a great concourse of creatures.

The woman crossed over on to the swept slopes of Black Mountain just above the lonely farm where Gwyn had been born and where Megan still lived in her old age. Up she climbed, on and up to the dark eye.

The Lady of Llyn y Fan Fach walked over the surface of the water and disappeared into the water, and all her hundreds of animals followed her. They left behind them sorrow, they left a wake of silence, and the deep furrow made by the oxen as they dragged their plough up over the shoulder of the mountain and into the lake.

One Night in Paradise

O nce upon a time there were two close friends who, out of affection for each other, made this pledge: the first to get married would call on the other to be his best man, even if he should be at the ends of the earth.

Shortly thereafter one of the friends died. The survivor, who was planning to get married, had no idea what he should now do, so he sought the advice of his confessor.

'This is a ticklish situation,' said the priest, 'but you must keep your promise. Call on him even if he is dead. Go to his grave and say what you're supposed to say. It will then be up to him whether to come to your wedding or not.'

The youth went to the grave and said, 'Friend, the time has come for you to be my best man!'

The earth yawned, and out jumped the friend. 'By all means. I have to keep my word, or else I'd end up in Purgatory for no telling how long.'

They went home, and from there to church for the wedding. Then came the wedding banquet, where the dead youth told all kinds of stories, but not a word did he say about what he'd witnessed in the next world. The bridegroom longed to ask him some questions, but he didn't have the nerve. At the end of the banquet the dead man rose and said, 'Friend, since I've done you this favour, would you walk me back a part of the way?'

'Why, certainly! But I can't go far, naturally, since this is my wedding night.'

'I understand. You can turn back any time you like.'

The bridegroom kissed his bride. 'I'm going to step outside for a moment, and I'll be right back.' He walked out with the dead man. They chatted about first one thing and then another, and before you knew it, they were at the grave. There they embraced, and the living man thought, If I don't ask him now, I'll never ask him. He therefore took heart and said, 'Let me ask you something, since you are dead. What's it like in the hereafter?'

'I really can't say,' answered the dead man. 'If you want to find out, come along with me to Paradise.'

The grave opened, and the living man followed the dead one inside. Thus they found themselves in Paradise. The dead man took his friend to a handsome crystal palace with gold doors, where angels played their harps for blessed souls to dance, with Saint Peter strumming the double bass. The living man gaped at all the splendour, and goodness knows how long he would have remained in the palace if there hadn't been all the rest of Paradise to see.

'Come on to another spot now,' said the dead man, who led him into a garden whose trees, instead of foliage, displayed songbirds of every colour. 'Wake up, let's move on!' said the dead man, guiding his visitor on to a lawn where angels danced as joyously and gracefully as lovers. 'Next we'll go to see a star!' He could have gazed at the stars forever. Instead of water, their rivers ran with wine, and their land was of cheese.

All of a sudden, he started. 'Oh, my goodness, friend, it's later than I thought. I have to get back to my bride, who's surely worried about me.'

'Have you had enough of Paradise so soon?'

'Enough? If I had my choice . . .'

'And there's still so much to see.'

'I believe you, but I'd better be getting back.'

'Very well, suit yourself.' The dead man walked him back to the grave and vanished.

The living man stepped from the grave, but no longer recognized the cemetery. It was packed with monuments, statues, and tall trees. He left the cemetery and saw huge buildings in place of the simple stone cottages that used to line the streets. The streets were full of cars and buses, while aeroplanes flew through the skies.

'Where on earth am I? Did I take the wrong street? And look how these people are dressed!'

He stopped a little old man on the street. 'Sir, what is this town?'

'This city, you mean.'

'All right, this city. But I don't recognize it, for the life of me. Can you please direct me to the house of the man who got married yesterday?'

'Yesterday? I happen to be the sacristan, and I can assure you no one got married yesterday!'

'What do you mean? I got married myself!' Then he gave an account of accompanying his dead friend to Paradise.

'You're dreaming,' said the old man. 'That's an old story people tell about the bridegroom who followed his friend into the grave and never came back, while his bride died of sorrow.'

'That's not so, I'm the bridegroom myself!'

'Listen, the only thing for you to do is to go and speak with our bishop.'

'Bishop? But here in town there's only the parish priest.'

'What parish priest? For years and years we've had a bishop.' And the sacristan took him to the bishop.

The youth told his story to the bishop, who recalled an event he'd heard about as a boy. He took down the parish books and began flipping back the pages. Thirty years ago, no. Fifty years ago, no. One hundred, no. Two hundred, no. He went on thumbing the pages. Finally on a yellowed, crumbling page he put his finger on those very names. 'It was three hundred years ago. The young man disappeared from the cemetery, and the bride died of a broken heart. Read right here if you don't believe it!'

'But I'm the bridegroom myself!'

'And you went to the next world? Tell me about it!'

But the young man turned deathly pale, sank to the ground, and died before he could tell one single thing he had seen.

Oniyeye and King Olu Dotun's Daughter

A very long time ago, and soon after our forefathers had come to Yorubaland, there lived a king called Olu Dotun. This king had only one child, a very beautiful daughter, and when she reached a marriageable age, her father was unable to decide to whom she should be married. Many young men had asked for the girl as wife, but the king had refused them all. In order to rid himself of the many suitors that called at his palace, he announced one day, half in jest, that any man in the kingdom who was able to produce an animal with one hundred and fifty-two tails could have half the kingdom and the hand of his daughter in marriage.

The king's news was received with great surprise by all the hunters. One of them, called Oniyeye, who was reputed to be the finest of them all in the king's dominion, made up his mind that if such an animal existed in the world, he would hunt it down and bring it to the king.

First he went and called on an Ifa priest and asked him to find out if there really was such an animal in the world. The priest, for a small gift, promised to consult his jujus and let him know. Three days later the Ifa priest called him back. 'Yes,' said the old man, 'such an animal does exist today, but only one remains in the whole world. My juju tells me that it dwells in a far-distant hollow mountain, but where it is I do not know. Nobody can reach it except in their dreams, and if you do ever happen to dream of the animal you must make a sacrifice to the gods on waking. Beyond this I can tell you nothing more, my son.'

Oniyeye thanked the old Ifa priest and departed.

For a long time the hunter tried to find out how he could reach the hollow mountain where the animal with a hundred and fifty-two tails dwelt. At last he thought of a plan.

He told all his friends and brother hunters that he was going away on a long journey and would not be returning for two months, and so he set out with his bow and arrows, and armed with his hunter's talisman.

Setting off for the forest on foot, he travelled for several days, until he came to a district where many of the wild animals congregated.

Oniyeye searched about until he discovered an open glade. This showed signs of being frequented by many animals. He then placed his quivers under his head as a pillow and his bow under his feet and lay still, pretending to be dead.

For a long time Oniyeye lay perfectly still. Gradually, however, being on the ground and being a skilled hunter, he was able to discern movements in the undergrowth of the forest, sounds that were not made by the wind. Suddenly a tiny field-mouse appeared and watched Oniyeye for a long time from a little distance, then, growing bolder, he came up close to the hunter and looked again. All this while Oniyeye kept his eyes closed and pretended to be dead.

Now the field-mouse had often been warned about Oniyeye and of his great skill as a hunter. He was well known to the creatures of the forest, who were quick to inform each other if he was hunting in the district. They always knew Oniyeye by his talisman.

The field-mouse started to sing and call all the other animals to come and witness that the greatest of all hunters, Oniyeye, was dead and peace and safety had once more returned to the forest. He was soon heard by the monkeys, and their loud chattering attracted other animals. So one by one all the animals from the district gathered in the glade till it was full and there was great rejoicing amongst them. Not only the animals, but the birds and insects too gathered to celebrate the good news. Returning to their homes, they called on all their companions to go and look at the corpse of Oniyeye lying in the glade and spread the report that he was now dead.

The animal with one hundred and fifty-two tails learnt the news from some birds that happened to be flying home across the hollow mountain, chirping with joy. He called one of the birds and asked him if the news was correct. 'Go and see for yourself,' replied the bird. 'You will see all the other animals around the hunter's body in the glade.'

'Good, go back and announce to the animals that I, the animal of one hundred and fifty-two tails, am coming to witness Oniyeye's death, and tell them to prepare for my coming.'

The bird flew back and informed the others, and so the hunter knew that his plan had worked.

Coming down from his hollow mountain, the animal with one hundred and fifty-two tails went to the glade. When he appeared, all the other animals were impressed and prostrating themselves on the ground, hailed him as their king.

'This is a great day for all of us,' said the king of the animals. 'This man Oniyeye was the most powerful hunter in the world and because of him, my friends, I have shut myself up alone in the hollow mountain for many years. Now that I have witnessed his death I will come down, and henceforth I will live here in the forest amongst you all.' There was a roar of applause at these words, and the animals took their king to see the hunter's body.

Then the king started to boast of his great power. 'Now pick up the dead Oniyeye,' ordered the animal of one hundred and fifty-two tails, 'and carry him back to my hollow mountain while I mount him like a horse and ride home in triumph.'

At these words, Oniyeye sprang up, seizing his bow and arrows as he did so. There was a great cry of astonishment and fear from everybody, and instead of staying to help their king, the animals fled in confusion into the forest. As for the animal with one hundred and fifty-two tails, he lay there quivering before the hunter.

Oniyeye was about to kill the animal, but he begged the hunter to spare his life and said he would become his slave and work for him for the rest of his life.

So Oniyeye spared him and carried him back to King Olu Dotun.

There was great excitement and rejoicing when they reached the king's palace, and people came from far and wide to witness the strange animal with so many tails.

As for the other hunters, some had been able to find animals with as many as fifty tails and one hunter had even found one with one hundred tails. King Olu Dotun had, however, particularly announced that he would give his daughter in marriage to the man who produced one with one hundred and fifty-two. So Oniyeye married the king's daughter and was given half the kingdom to rule over. As for the animal of one hundred and fifty-two tails, he lived peacefully in captivity, and the other animals of the forest enjoyed greater security, for Oniyeye did not go hunting so often after his marriage.

Why the Hare Runs Away

This is a story of the hare and the other animals.

The dry weather was drying up the earth into hardness. There was no dew. Even the creatures of the water suffered from thirst. Famine soon followed, and the animals, having nothing to eat, assembled in council.

'What shall we do,' said they, 'to keep ourselves from dying of hunger and thirst?' And they deliberated a long time.

At last it was decided that each animal should cut off the tips of its ears, and extract the fat from them. Then all the fat would be collected and sold, and with the money they would get for it, they would buy a hoe and dig a well, so as to get some water.

And all cried, 'It is well. Let us cut off the tips of our ears.'

They did so, but when it came the hare's turn he refused.

The other animals were astonished, but they said nothing. They took up the ears, extracted the fat, went and sold all, and bought a hoe with the money.

They brought back the hoe and began to dig a well in the dry bed of a lagoon, until at last they found water. They said, 'Ha! At last we can slake our thirst a little.'

The hare was not there, but when the sun was in the middle of the sky, he took a calabash and went towards the well.

As he walked along, the calabash dragged on the ground and made a great noise. It said, '*Chan-gan-gan-gan, chan-gan-gan-gan.*'

The animals, who were watching by the lagoon, heard this terrible noise and were frightened. They asked each other, 'What is it?' Then, as the noise kept coming nearer, they ran away. Reaching home, they said something terrible at the lagoon had put them to flight.

When all the animals were gone, the hare could draw up water from the lagoon without interference. Then he went down into the well and bathed, so that the water was muddied.

When the next day came, all the animals ran to get water, and they found it muddied.

'Oh,' they cried, 'who has spoiled our well?'

Saying this, they went and took a dummy-image. They made birdlime and spread it over the image.

Then, when the sun was again in the middle of the sky, all the animals went and hid in the bush near the well.

Soon the hare came, his calabash crying, '*Chan-gan-gan-gan, chan-gan-gan-gan.*' He approached the image. He never suspected that all the animals were hidden in the bush.

The hare saluted the image. The image said nothing. He saluted again, and still the image said nothing.

'Take care,' said the hare, 'or I will give you a slap.'

He gave it a slap, and his right hand was stuck fast in the birdlime. He slapped with his left hand, and that was held fast, too.

'Oh! oh!' cried he, 'I'll kick with my feet,' and he did, but his feet became fixed, and he could not get away.

Then the animals ran out of the bush and came to see the hare and his calabash.

'Shame, shame, oh, hare!' they cried together. 'Did you not agree with us to cut off the tips of your ears, and, when it came to your turn, did you not refuse? What! You refused, and yet you come to muddy our water?'

They took whips, they fell upon the hare, and they beat him. They beat him so that they nearly killed him.

'We ought to kill you, accursed hare,' they said. 'But no—run.'

They let him go, and the hare fled. Since then, he does not leave the grass.

The Sacred Milk of Koumongoé

Far away, in a very hot country, there once lived a man and woman who had two children, a son named Koané and a daughter called Thakané.

Early in the morning and late in the evenings the parents worked hard in the fields, resting, when the sun was high, under the shade of some tree. While they were absent the little girl kept house alone, for her brother always got up before the dawn, when the air was fresh and cool, and drove out the cattle to the sweetest patches of grass he could find.

One day, when Koané had slept later than usual, his father and mother went to their work before him, and there was only Thakané to be seen busy making the bread for supper.

'Thakané,' he said, 'I am thirsty. Give me a drink from the tree Koumongoé, which has the best milk in the world.'

'Oh, Koané,' cried his sister, 'you know that we are forbidden to touch that tree. What would father say when he came home? For he would be sure to know.'

'Nonsense,' replied Koané, 'there is so much milk in Koumongoé that he will never miss a little. If you won't give it to me, I shan't take the cattle out. They will just have to stay all day in the hut, and you know that they will starve.' And he turned from her in a rage, and sat down in the corner.

After a while Thakané said to him: 'It is getting hot, had you not better drive out the cattle now?'

But Koané only answered sulkily, 'I told you I am not going to drive them out at all. If I have to do without milk, they shall do without grass.'

Thakané did not know what to do. She was afraid to disobey her parents, who would most likely beat her, yet the beasts would be sure to suffer if they were kept in, and she would perhaps be beaten for that too. So at last she took an axe and a tiny earthen bowl, she cut a very small hole in the side of Koumongoé, and out gushed enough milk to fill the bowl.

'Here is the milk you wanted,' said she, going up to Koané, who was still sulking in his corner.

'What is the use of that?' grumbled Koané. 'Why, there is not enough to drown a fly. Go and get me three times as much!'

Trembling with fright, Thakané returned to the tree, and struck it a sharp blow with the axe. In an instant there poured forth such a stream of milk that it ran like a river into the hut.

'Koané! Koané!' cried she. 'Come and help me to plug up the hole. There will be no milk left for our father and mother.' But Koané could not stop it any more than Thakané, and soon the milk was flowing through the hut downhill towards their parents in the fields below.

The man saw the white stream a long way off, and guessed what had happened.

'Wife, wife,' he called loudly to the woman, who was working at a little distance, 'do you see Koumongoé running fast down the hill? That is some mischief of the children's, I am sure. I must go home and find out what is the matter.' And they both threw down their hoes and hurried to the side of Koumongoé.

Kneeling on the grass, the man and his wife made a cup of their hands and drank the milk from it. And no sooner had they done this than Koumongoé flowed back again up the hill, and entered the hut.

'Thakané,' said the parents, severely, when they reached home panting from the heat of the sun, 'what have you been doing? Why did Koumongoé come to us in the fields instead of staying in the garden?'

'It was Koané's fault,' answered Thakané. 'He would not take the cattle to feed until he drank some of the milk from Koumongoé. So, as I did not know what else to do, I gave it to him.'

The father listened to Thakané's words, but made no answer. Instead, he went outside and brought in two sheepskins which he stained red, and sent for a blacksmith to forge some iron rings. The rings were then passed over Thakané's arms and legs and neck, and the skins fastened on her before and behind. When all was ready, the man sent for his servants and said, 'I am going to get rid of Thakané.'

'Get rid of your only daughter?' they answered, in surprise. 'But why?'

'Because she has eaten what she ought not to have eaten. She has touched the sacred tree which belongs to her mother and me alone.' And, turning his back, he called to Thakané to follow him, and they went down the road which led to the dwelling of an ogre.

They were passing along some fields where the corn was ripening, when a rabbit suddenly sprang out at their feet, and standing on its hind legs, it sang:

> *Why do you give to the ogre*
> *Your child, so fair, so fair?*

'You had better ask her,' replied the man, 'she is old enough to give you an answer.'

Then, in her turn, Thakané sang:

> *I gave Koumongoé to Koané,*
> *Koumongoé to the keeper of beasts;*
> *For without Koumongoé they could not go to the meadows:*
> *Without Koumongoé they would starve in the hut;*
> *That was why I gave him the Koumongoé of my father.*

And when the rabbit heard that, he cried, 'Wretched man! It is you whom the ogre should eat, and not your beautiful daughter.'

But the father paid no heed to what the rabbit said, and only walked on the faster, bidding Thakané to keep close behind him.

By-and-by they met with a troop of great deer, called elands, and they stopped when they saw Thakané and sang:

> *Why do you give to the ogre*
> *Your child, so fair, so fair?*

'You had better ask her,' replied the man, 'she is old enough to give you an answer.'

Then, in her turn, Thakané sang:

> *I gave Koumongoé to Koané,*
> *Koumongoé to the keeper of beasts;*
> *For without Koumongoé they could not go to the meadows:*
> *Without Koumongoé they would starve in the hut;*
> *That was why I gave him the Koumongoé of my father.*

And the elands all cried, 'Wretched man! It is you whom the ogre should eat, and not your beautiful daughter.'

By this time it was nearly dark, and the father said they could travel no further that night, and must go to sleep where they were. Thakané was thankful indeed when she heard this, for she was very tired, and found the two skins fastened round her almost too heavy to carry. So, in spite of her dread of the ogre, she slept till dawn, when her father woke her, and told her roughly that he was ready to continue their journey.

Crossing the plain, the girl and her father passed a herd of gazelles feeding. They lifted their heads, wondering who was out so early, and when they caught sight of Thakané, they sang:

> *Why do you give to the ogre*
> *Your child, so fair, so fair?*

'You had better ask her,' replied the man, 'she is old enough to answer for herself.'

Then, in her turn, Thakané sang:

> *I gave Koumongoé to Koané,*
> *Koumongoé to the keeper of beasts;*
> *For without Koumongoé they could not go to the meadows:*
> *Without Koumongoé they would starve in the hut;*
> *That was why I gave him the Koumongoé of my father.*

And the gazelles all cried, 'Wretched man! It is you whom the ogre should eat, and not your beautiful daughter.'

At last they arrived at the village where the ogre lived, and they went straight to his hut. He was nowhere to be seen, but in his place was his son Masilo, who was not an ogre at all, but a very polite young man. He ordered his servants to bring a pile of skins for Thakané to sit on, but told her father he must sit on the ground. Then, catching sight of the girl's face, which she had kept bent down, he was struck by its beauty, and put the same question that the rabbit, and the elands, and the gazelles had done.

Thakané answered him as before, and he instantly commanded that she should be taken to the hut of his mother, and placed under her care, while the man should be led to his father. Directly the ogre saw him he bade the servant throw him into the great pot which always stood ready on the fire, and in five minutes he was done to a turn. After that the servant returned to Masilo and related all that had happened.

Now Masilo had fallen in love with Thakané the moment he saw her. At first he did not know what to make of this strange feeling, for all his life he had hated women, and had refused several brides whom his parents had chosen for him. However, they were so anxious that he should marry, that they willingly accepted Thakané as their daughter-in-law, though she did not bring any marriage portion with her.

After some time a baby was born to her, and Thakané thought it was the most beautiful baby that ever was seen. But when her mother-in-law saw it was a girl, she wrung her hands and wept, saying, 'O miserable mother! Miserable child! Alas for you! Why were you not a boy!'

Thakané, in great surprise, asked the meaning of her distress; and the old woman told her that it was the custom in that country that all the girls who were born should be given to the ogre to eat.

Then Thakané clasped the baby tightly in her arms, and cried, 'But it is not the custom in *my* country! There, when children die, they are buried in the earth. No one shall take my baby from me.'

That night, when everyone in the hut was asleep, Thakané rose, and carrying her baby on her back, went down to a place where the river spread itself out into a large lake, with tall willows all round the bank. Here, hidden from everyone, she sat down on a stone and began to think what she should do to save her child.

Suddenly she heard a rustling among the willows, and an old woman appeared before her.

'What are you crying for, my dear?' said she.

And Thakané answered, 'I was crying for my baby—I cannot hide her for ever, and if the ogre sees her, he will eat her; and I would rather she was drowned than that.'

'What you say is true,' replied the old woman. 'Give me your child, and let me take care of it. And if you will fix a day to meet me here I will bring the baby.'

Then Thakané dried her eyes, and gladly accepted the old woman's offer. When she got home she told her husband she had thrown it in the river, and as he had watched her go in that direction he never thought of doubting what she said.

On the appointed day, Thakané slipped out when everybody was busy, and ran down the path that led to the lake. As soon as she got there, she crouched down among the willows, and sang softly:

> *Bring to me Dilah, Dilah the rejected one,*
> *Dilah, whom her father Masilo cast out!*

And in a moment the old woman appeared holding the baby in her arms. Dilah had become so big and strong, that Thakané's heart was filled with joy and gratitude, and she stayed as long as she dared, playing with her baby. At last she felt she must return to the village, lest she should be missed, and the child was handed back to the old woman, who vanished with her into the lake.

Children grow up very quickly when they live under water, and in less time than anyone could suppose, Dilah had changed from a baby to a woman. Her mother came to visit her whenever she was able, and one day, when they were sitting talking together, they were spied by a man who had come to cut willows to weave into baskets. He was so surprised to see how like the face of the girl was to Masilo, that he left his work and returned to the village.

'Masilo,' he said, as he entered the hut, 'I have just beheld your wife near the river with a girl who must be your daughter, she is so like you. We have been deceived, for we all thought she was dead.'

When he heard this, Masilo tried to look shocked because his wife had broken the law; but in his heart he was very glad.

'But what shall we do now?' asked he.

'Make sure for yourself that I am speaking the truth by hiding among the bushes the first time Thakané says she is going to bathe in the river, and waiting till the girl appears.'

For some days Thakané stayed quietly at home, and her husband began to think that the man had been mistaken; but at last she said to her husband: 'I am going to bathe in the river.'

'Well, you can go,' answered he. But he ran down quickly by another path, and got there first, and hid himself in the bushes.

An instant later, Thakané arrived, and standing on the bank, she sang:

> *Bring to me Dilah, Dilah the rejected one,*
> *Dilah, whom her father Masilo cast out!*

Then the old woman came out of the water, holding the girl, now tall and slender, by the hand. And as Masilo looked, he saw that she was indeed his daughter, and he wept for joy that she was not lying dead in the bottom of the lake.

The old woman, however, seemed uneasy, and said to Thakané, 'I feel as if someone was watching us. I will not leave the girl today, but will take her back with me.' And sinking beneath the surface, she drew the girl after her. After they had gone, Thakané returned to the village, which Masilo had managed to reach before her.

All the rest of the day Masilo sat in a corner weeping, and his mother who came in asked, 'Why are you weeping so bitterly, my son?'

'My head aches,' he answered, 'it aches very badly.' And his mother passed on, and left him alone.

In the evening he said to his wife, 'I have seen my daughter, in the place where you told me you had drowned her. Instead, she lives at the bottom of the lake, and has now grown into a young woman.'

'I don't know what you are talking about,' replied Thakané. 'I buried my child under the sand on the beach.'

Then Masilo implored her to give the child back to him; but she would not listen, and only answered, 'If I were to give her back you would only obey the laws of your country and take her to your father, the ogre, and she would be eaten.'

But Masilo promised that he would never let his father see her, and that now she was a woman no one would try to hurt her; so Thakané's heart melted, and she went down to the lake to consult the old woman.

'What am I to do?' she asked, when, after clapping her hands, the old woman appeared before her. 'Yesterday Masilo beheld Dilah, and ever since he has entreated me to give him back his daughter.'

'If I let her go he must pay me a thousand head of cattle in exchange,' replied the old woman. And Thakané carried her answer back to Masilo.

'Why, I would gladly give her two thousand!' cried he, 'for she has saved my daughter.' And he bade messengers hasten to all the neighbouring villages, and tell his people to send him at once all the cattle he possessed. When they were all assembled he chose a thousand of the finest bulls and cows, and drove them down to the river, followed by a great crowd wondering what would happen.

Then Thakané stepped forward in front of the cattle and sang:

> *Bring to me Dilah, Dilah the rejected one,*
> *Dilah, whom her father Masilo cast out!*

And Dilah came from the waters holding out her hands to Masilo and Thakané, and in her place the cattle sank into the lake, and were driven by the old woman to the great city filled with people, which lies at the bottom.

The Magic Mirror

Along, long while ago, before ever the White Men were seen in Senna, there lived a man called Gopáni-Kúfa.

One day, as he was out hunting, he came upon a strange sight. An enormous python had caught an antelope and coiled itself around it; the antelope, striking out in despair with its horns, had pinned the python's neck to a tree, and so deeply had its horns sunk in the soft wood that neither creature could get away.

'Help!' cried the antelope. 'For I was doing no harm, yet I have been caught, and would have been eaten, had I not defended myself.'

'Help me,' said the python, 'for I am Insáto, King of all the Reptiles, and will reward you well!'

Gopáni-Kúfa considered for a moment, then stabbing the antelope with his assegai, he set the python free.

'I thank you,' said the python. 'Come back here with the new moon, when I shall have eaten the antelope, and I will reward you as I promised.'

'Yes,' said the dying antelope, 'he will reward you and lo! your reward shall be your own undoing!'

Gopáni-Kúfa went back to his kraal, and with the new moon he returned again to the spot where he had saved the python.

Insáto was lying upon the ground, still sleepy from the effects of his huge meal, and when he saw the man he thanked him again, and said, 'Come with me now to Píta, which is my own country, and I will give you what you will of all my possessions.'

Gopáni-Kúfa at first was afraid, thinking of what the antelope had said, but finally he consented and followed Insáto into the forest.

For several days they travelled, and at last they came to a hole leading deep into the earth. It was not very wide, but large enough to admit a man. 'Hold on to my tail,' said Insáto, 'and I will go down first, drawing you after me.' The man did so, and Insáto entered.

Down, down, down they went for days, all the while getting deeper and deeper into the earth, until at last the darkness ended and they dropped into a beautiful country; around them grew short green grass, on which browsed herds of cattle and sheep and goats. In the distance Gopáni-Kúfa saw a great collection of houses all square, built of stone and very tall, and their roofs were shining with gold and burnished iron.

Gopáni-Kúfa turned to Insáto, but found, in the place of the python, a man, strong and handsome, with the great snake's skin wrapped round him for covering; and on his arms and neck were rings of pure gold.

The man smiled. 'I am Insáto,' said he, 'but in my own country I take man's shape—even as you see me—for this is Píta, the land over which I am king.' He then took Gopáni-Kúfa by the hand and led him towards the town.

On the way they passed rivers in which men and women were bathing and fishing and boating; and further on they came to gardens covered with heavy crops of rice and maize, and many other grains which Gopáni-Kúfa did not even know the name of. And as they passed, the people who were singing at their work in the fields abandoned their labours and saluted Insáto with delight, bringing also palm wine and green coconuts for refreshment, as to one returned from a long journey.

'These are my children!' said Insáto, waving his hand towards the people. Gopáni-Kúfa was much astonished at all that he saw, but he said nothing. Presently they came to the town; everything here, too, was beautiful, and everything that a man might desire he could obtain. Even the grains of dust in the streets were of gold and silver.

Insáto conducted Gopáni-Kúfa to the palace, and showing him his rooms, and the maidens who would wait upon him, told him that they would have a great feast that night, and on the morrow he might name his choice of the riches of Píta and it should be given him. Then he went away.

Now Gopáni-Kúfa had a wasp called Zéngi-mízi. Zéngi-mízi was not an ordinary wasp, for the spirit of the father of Gopáni-Kúfa had entered it, so that it was exceedingly wise. In times of doubt Gopáni-Kúfa always consulted the wasp as to what had better be done, so on this occasion he took it out of the little rush basket in which he carried it, saying, 'Zéngi-mízi, what gift shall I ask of Insáto tomorrow when he would know the reward he shall bestow on me for saving his life?'

'Biz-z-z,' hummed Zéngi-mízi, 'ask him for Sipáo the Mirror.' And it flew back into its basket.

Gopáni-Kúfa was astonished at this answer; but knowing that the words of Zéngi-mízi were true words, he determined to make the request. So that night they feasted, and on the morrow Insáto came to Gopáni-Kúfa and, giving him greeting joyfully, he said, 'Now, O my friend, name your choice amongst my possessions and you shall have it!'

'O king!' answered Gopáni-Kúfa, 'out of all your possessions I will have the Mirror, Sipáo.'

The king started. 'O friend, Gopáni-Kúfa,' he said, 'ask anything but that! I did not think that you would request that which is most precious to me.'

'Let me think over it again then, O king,' said Gopáni-Kúfa, 'and tomorrow I will let you know if I change my mind.'

But the king was still much troubled, fearing the loss of Sipáo, for the Mirror had magic powers, so that he who owned it had but to ask and his wish would be fulfilled; to it Insáto owed all that he possessed.

As soon as the king left him, Gopáni-Kúfa again took Zéngi-mízi out of his basket. 'Zéngi-mízi,' he said, 'the king seems loath to grant my request for the Mirror—is there not some other thing of equal value for which I might ask?'

And the wasp answered, 'There is nothing in the world, O Gopáni-Kúfa, which is of such value as this Mirror, for it is a Wishing Mirror, and accomplishes the desires of him who owns it. If the king hesitates, go to him the next day, and the day after, and in the end he will bestow the Mirror upon you, for you saved his life.'

And it was even so. For three days Gopáni-Kúfa returned the same answer to the king, and, at last, with tears in his eyes, Insáto gave him the Mirror, which was of polished iron, saying, 'Take Sipáo, then, O Gopáni-Kúfa, and may thy wishes come true. Go back now to thine own country; Sipáo will show you the way.'

Gopáni-Kúfa was greatly rejoiced, and, taking farewell of the king, said to the Mirror, 'Sipáo, Sipáo, I wish to be back upon the Earth again!'

Instantly he found himself standing upon the upper earth; but, not knowing the spot, he said again to the Mirror, 'Sipáo, Sipáo, I want the path to my own kraal!'

And behold! right before him lay the path!

When he arrived home he found his wife and daughter mourning for him, for they thought that he had been eaten by lions; but he comforted them, saying that while following a wounded antelope he had missed his way and had wandered for a long time before he had found the path again.

That night he asked Zéngi-mízi, in whom sat the spirit of his father, what he had better ask Sipáo for next?

'Biz-z-z,' said the wasp, 'would you not like to be as great a chief as Insáto?'

And Gopáni-Kúfa smiled, and took the Mirror and said to it, 'Sipáo, Sipáo, I want a town as great as that of Insáto, the King of Píta; and I wish to be chief over it!'

Then all along the banks of the Zambesi river, which flowed near by, sprang up streets of stone buildings, and their roofs shone with gold and burnished iron like those in Píta; and in the streets men and women were walking, and young boys were driving out the sheep and cattle to pasture; and from the river came shouts and laughter from the young men and maidens who had launched their canoes and were fishing. And when the people of the new town beheld Gopáni-Kúfa they rejoiced greatly and hailed him as chief.

Gopáni-Kúfa was now as powerful as Insáto the King of the Reptiles had been, and he and his family moved into the palace that stood high above the other buildings right in the middle of the town. His wife was too astonished at all these wonders to ask any questions, but his daughter Shasása kept begging him to tell her how he had suddenly become so great; so at last he revealed the whole secret, and even entrusted Sipáo the Mirror to her care, saying, 'It will be safer with you, my daughter, for you dwell apart; whereas men come to consult me on affairs of state, and the Mirror might be stolen.'

Then Shasása took the Magic Mirror and hid it beneath her pillow, and after that for many years Gopáni-Kúfa ruled his people both well and wisely, so that all men loved him, and never once did he need to ask Sipáo to grant him a wish.

Now it happened that, after many years, when the hair of Gopáni-Kúfa was turning grey with age, there came white men to that country. Up the Zambesi they came, and they fought long and fiercely with Gopáni-Kúfa; but, because of the power of the Magic Mirror, he beat them, and they fled to the sea-coast. Chief among them was one Rei, a man of much cunning, who sought to discover whence sprang Gopáni-Kúfa's power. So one day he called to him a trusty servant named Butou, and said, 'Go you to the town and find out for me what is the secret of its greatness.'

And Butou, dressing himself in rags, set out, and when he came to Gopáni-Kúfa's town he asked for the chief; and the people took him into the presence of Gopáni-Kúfa. When the white man saw him he humbled himself, and said, 'O Chief! take pity on me, for I have no home! When Rei marched against you I alone stood apart, for I knew that all the strength of the Zambesi lay in your hands, and because I would not fight against you he turned me forth into the forest to starve!'

And Gopáni-Kúfa believed the white man's story, and he took him in and feasted him, and gave him a house.

In this way the end came. For the heart of Shasása, the daughter of Gopáni-Kúfa, went forth to Butou the traitor, and from her he learnt the secret of the Magic Mirror. One night, when all the town slept, he felt beneath her pillow and, finding the Mirror, he stole it and fled back with it to Rei, the chief of the white men.

So it befell that, one day, as Gopáni-Kúfa was gazing at the river from a window of the palace he again saw the war-canoes of the white men; and at the sight his spirit misgave him.

'Shasása! My daughter!' he cried wildly. 'Go fetch me the Mirror, for the white men are at hand.'

'Woe is me, my father!' she sobbed. 'The Mirror is gone! For I loved Butou the traitor, and he has stolen Sipáo from me!'

Then Gopáni-Kúfa calmed himself, and drew out Zéngi-mízi from its rush basket.

'O spirit of my father!' he said. 'What now shall I do?'

'O Gopáni-Kúfa!' hummed the wasp. 'There is nothing now that can be done, for the words of the antelope which you slew are being fulfilled.'

'Alas! I am an old man—I had forgotten!' cried the chief. 'The words of the antelope were true words—my reward shall be my own undoing—they are being fulfilled!'

Then the white men fell upon the people of Gopáni-Kúfa and slew them together with the chief and his daughter Shasása; and since then all the power of the Earth has rested in the hands of the white men, for they have in their possession Sipáo, the Magic Mirror.

The Rainbow Bird
and the Crocodile and
How People First Got Fire

Long ago in the Dreamtime there was an Old Man who could do one thing no one else could do. He knew how to make fire. He was clever with fire too. He could balance it on his head, juggle it in the air, breathe it out of his mouth. But he was very mean and would not share that fire with anyone. So everyone else was cold at night, had to eat their food raw and had no way to light themselves through the dark.

One day a Boy came up to the Old Man and said, 'Hey, Old Man. I'm tired of eating my food raw and being cold at night. Please, please will you show me how to make fire?'

And the Old Man said, 'Aaarrrgh! I'm boss for fire! I'm boss! If you want to make fire you've got to use bud-bud sticks. Now go away and leave me alone!'

The Boy ran off thinking, Bud-bud sticks, what are bud-bud sticks? He looked here, there, and everywhere for bud-bud sticks but when you're looking for something and you don't know what it is how are you going to find it? He couldn't find the bud-bud sticks so he came back to the Old Man and he said, 'Hey, Old Man! I've been looking everywhere for them bud-bud sticks but I can't find them. Please, will you show me how to make fire?'

But the Old Man goes, 'Aaarrrgh! I'm boss for fire! I'm boss! Now go away and leave alone!' And the Boy ran for it. He was frightened of that old man.

But after a little while the Old Man was thinking to himself, Oh dear. Maybe I growled at that boy too much. He's only a boy after all. So he called him back and said, 'Hey, youngfella! Come here, sit down and I'll tell you a story.' So the Boy cautiously came back, sat down, and the Old Man told him a story. Maybe one story, two story, three stories. Dreamtime stories.

Then the Old Man said, 'Now I've done something for you. You've gotta do something for me.' And you'll never guess what the Old Man asked the Boy to do. He said, 'I want you to take the nits out of my hair.'

Now the funny thing is, when someone's taking nits out of your hair it makes you all sleepy, all drowsy, and as the Boy was taking nits out of the Old Man's hair he began to nod off. And the Boy thought to himself, If that Old Man falls properly asleep I can sneak out and find the bud-bud sticks and make fire for myself. But I'd better make sure he's asleep first. So he called out and said, 'Old Man! Wake up! Wake up!'

But the Old Man said, 'I'm really tired. I want to go to sleep. Go away and leave me alone.' Then he fell asleep and began to snore.

And the Boy thought, Now is my chance. He crept out of the hut and there lying on the ground were two sticks, not much longer than a foot and as thick as a finger. One of them had a little hole halfway through on one side. And somehow or other the Boy knew that these were the bud-bud sticks and he knew what to do.

He laid the stick with the hole flat on the ground with one foot at each end. Then he put the other stick down into the little hole and began to twirl it between his fingers. He twirled and twirled with all his strength until at last smoke began to rise up from where the two sticks were rubbing together. Then he reached out for some dry grass, put it on the smoke and blew gently. Suddenly, 'pouff!' There was a bright orange flame. It was his first fire. He was really excited. He peeled off some bark from a stringy bark tree, tied it into a bunch and dipped it into the flame. At last he had it. His first flaming firestick.

Then the Boy had a mischievous idea. He thought to himself, That Old Man, he's been really mean to me. I'm going to pay him back! And he took his firestick and made a big circle of fire in the dry grass all the way round the Old Man's hut. Then he took his firestick and ran off into the bush.

Now the Old Man was lying there fast asleep when suddenly his nostrils started twitching with the smoke. He sat up, he opened his eyes and looked around. He was surrounded by leaping, crackling flames and he knew that if he stayed there he'd be burned to death. Then suddenly he remembered that about fifty metres away on the other side of the fire was a billabong.

So he gathered all of his strength together and then he ran through the fire. But as he ran . . . through . . . the fire . . . he turned . . . into . . . a crocodile! And his skin got all burned and blistered on his back, went all lumpy and bumpy. But he made it through to the other side of the fire and plunged sizzling into the cool waters of the billabong . . .

And ever since then the Crocodile has lived in wet places—in the swamps and lakes and rivers and billabongs. His fire has gone out now. In fact he's frightened of fire. But sometimes if you get close to old Crocodile—but don't get too close—when he opens his jaws you can still hear him say, 'I'm boss! I'm boss! I'm boss!'

As for the Boy, now he had a good idea. Now he decided to give fire to people so whenever they wanted to make fire all they had to do was to get the wood from any tree. So he ran round the bush putting fire into the heart of every tree. But as he ran . . . round . . . the bush . . . putting fire . . . into the heart . . . of every tree . . . suddenly his legs shrank . . . his shoulders sprouted feathers . . . and he turned into a bird. When he finished he plunged the firestick into his tail and there was a ripple of colour through his feathers and he turned into a Rainbow Bee-Eater.

And still to this day there are two tassels hanging from the tail of the Rainbow Bee-Eater, and the people say that those are the remains of the firestick that was placed there all those many, many years ago in the Dreamtime of Australia.

The Boy Pu-nia
and the King of the Sharks

O n one side of the island there lived a great shark: Kai-
ale-ale he was named; he was the King of the Sharks of
that place, and he had ten sharks under him. He lived
near a cave that was filled with lobsters. But no one dared to dive
down, and go into that cave, and take lobsters out of it, on
account of Kai-ale-ale and the ten sharks he had under him; they
stayed around the cave night and day, and if a diver ventured
near they would bite him and devour him.

There was a boy named Pu-nia, whose father had been killed
by the sharks. Now after his father had been killed, there was
no one to catch fish for Pu-nia and his mother; they had sweet
potatoes to eat, but they never had any fish to eat with them.
Often Pu-nia heard his mother say that she wished she had a fish
or lobster to eat with the sweet potatoes. He made up his mind
that they should have lobsters.

He came above the cave where the lobsters were. Looking
down he saw the sharks—Kai-ale-ale and his ten sharks; they

were all asleep. While he was watching them, they wakened up. Pu-nia pretended that he did not know that the sharks had wakened. He spoke loudly so that they would hear him, and he said, 'Here am I, Pu-nia, and I am going into the cave to get lobsters for myself and my mother. That great shark, Kai-ale-ale, is asleep now, and I can dive to the point over there, and then go into the cave; I will take two lobsters in my hands, and my mother and I will have something to eat with our sweet potatoes.' So Pu-nia said, speaking loudly and pretending that he thought the sharks were still asleep.

Said Kai-ale-ale, speaking softly to the other sharks, 'Let us rush to the place where Pu-nia dives, and let us devour him as we devoured his father.' But Pu-nia was a very cunning boy and not at all the sort that could be caught by the stupid sharks. He had a stone upon his hand while he was speaking, and he flung it towards the point that he said he was going to dive to. Just as soon as the stone struck the water the sharks made a rush to the place, leaving the cave of the lobsters unguarded. Then Pu-nia dived. He went into the cave, took two lobsters in his hands, and came up on the place that he had spoken from before.

He shouted down to the sharks, 'Here is Pu-nia, and he has come back safely. He has two lobsters, and he and his mother have something to live on. It was the first shark, the second shark, the third shark, the fourth shark, the fifth shark, the sixth shark, the seventh shark, the eighth shark, the ninth shark, the tenth shark—it was the tenth shark, the one with the thin tail, that showed Pu-nia what to do.'

When the King of the Sharks, Kai-ale-ale, heard this from Pu-nia, he ordered all the sharks to come together and stay in a row. He counted them, and there were ten of them, and the tenth one had a thin tail. 'So it was you, Thin Tail,' he said, 'that told the boy Pu-nia what to do. You shall die.' Then, according to the orders of Kai-ale-ale, the thin-tailed shark was killed.

Pu-nia called out to them, 'You have killed one of your own kind.' With the two lobsters in his hands, he went back to his mother's.

Pu-nia and his mother now had something to eat with their sweet potatoes. And when the lobsters were all eaten, Pu-nia went back to the place above the cave. He called out, as he had done the first time, 'I can dive to the place over there and then slip into the cave, for the sharks are all asleep. I can get two lobsters for myself and my mother, so that we'll have something to eat with our sweet potatoes.' Then he threw down a stone and made ready to dive to another point.

When the stone struck the water the sharks rushed over, leaving the cave unguarded. Then Pu-nia dived down and went into the cave. He took two lobsters in his hands and swam back to the top of the water, and when he got to the place that he had spoken from before, he shouted down to the sharks, 'It was the first shark, the second shark, the third shark, the fourth shark, the fifth shark, the sixth shark, the seventh shark, the eighth shark, the ninth shark—it was the ninth shark, the one with the big stomach, that told Pu-nia what to do.'

Then the King of the Sharks, Kai-ale-ale, ordered the sharks to get into a line. He counted them, and he found that the ninth shark had a big stomach. 'So it was you that told Pu-nia what to do,' he said; and he ordered the big-stomached shark to be killed. After that Pu-nia went home with his two lobsters, and he and his mother had something to eat with their sweet potatoes.

Pu-nia continued to do this. He would deceive the sharks by throwing a stone to the place that he said he was going to dive to; when he got the sharks away from the cave, he would dive down, slip in, and take two lobsters in his hands. And always, when he got to the top of the water, he would name a shark.

'The first shark, the second shark, the third shark—the shark with the little eye, the shark with the grey spot on him—told Pu-nia what to do,' he would say; and each time he would get one of the sharks killed. He kept on doing this until only one of the sharks was left; this one was Kai-ale-ale, the King of the Sharks.

After that, Pu-nia went into the forest; he hewed out two hard pieces of wood, each about a yard long; then he took sticks for lighting a fire—the au-li-ma to rub with, and the au-na-ki to rub on; he got charcoal to burn as a fire, and he got food. He put all into a bag, and he carried the bag down to the beach. He came above the cave that Kai-ale-ale was watching, and he said, speaking in a loud voice, 'If I dive now, and if Kai-ale-ale bites me, my blood will come to the top of the water, and my mother will see the blood and will bring me back to life again. But if I dive down and Kai-ale-ale takes me into his mouth whole, I shall die and never come back to life again.'

Kai-ale-ale was listening, of course. He said to himself, 'No, I will not bite you, you cunning boy; I will take you into my mouth and swallow you whole, and then you will never come back to life again. I shall open my mouth wide enough to take you in. Yes, indeed, this time I will get you.'

Pu-nia dived holding his bag. Kai-ale-ale opened his mouth wide and got Pu-nia into it. But as soon as the boy got within, he opened his bag and took out the two pieces of wood which he had hewn out in the forest. He put them between the jaws of the shark so that Kai-ale-ale was not able to close his jaws. With his mouth held open, Kai-ale-ale went dashing through the water.

Pu-nia was now inside the big shark; he took the fire sticks out of his bag and rubbed them together, making a fire. He kindled the charcoal that he had brought, and he cooked his food at the fire that he had made. With the fire in his insides, the shark could not keep still; he went dashing here and there through the ocean.

At last the shark came near the Island of Hawaii again. 'If he brings me near the breakers, I am saved,' said Pu-nia, speaking aloud, 'but if he takes me to the sand near where the grass grows, I shall die; I cannot be saved.'

Kai-ale-ale, when he heard Pu-nia say this, said to himself, 'I will not take him near the breakers; I will take him where the dry sand is, near the grass.' Saying this, he dashed in from the ocean and up to where the shrubs grew on the shore. No shark had ever gone there before; and when Kai-ale-ale got there, he could not get back again.

Then Pu-nia came out of the shark. He shouted out, 'Kai-ale-ale, Kai-ale-ale, the King of the Sharks, has come to visit us.' And the people, hearing about their enemy Kai-ale-ale, came down to the shore with their spears and their knives and killed him. And that was the end of the ugly and wicked King of the Sharks.

Every day after that, Pu-nia was able to go down into the cave and get lobsters for himself and his mother. And all the people rejoiced when they knew that the eleven sharks that guarded the cave had been got rid of by the boy Pu-nia.

The Bones of Djulung

In a beautiful island that lies in the southern seas, where chains of gay orchids bind the trees together, and the days and nights are equally long and nearly equally hot, there once lived a family of seven sisters. Their father and mother were dead, and they had no brothers, so the eldest girl ruled over the rest, and they all did as she bade them. One sister had to clean the house, a second carried water from the spring in the forest, a third cooked their food, while to the youngest fell the hardest task of all, for she had to cut and bring home the wood which was to keep the fire continually burning. This was very hot and tiring work, and when she had fed the fire and heaped up in a corner the sticks that were to supply it till the next day, she often threw herself down under a tree, and went sound asleep.

One morning, however, as she was staggering along with her bundle on her back, she thought that the river which flowed past their hut looked so cool and inviting that she determined to bathe in it, instead of taking her usual nap. Hastily piling up her load by the fire, and thrusting some sticks into the flame, she ran down to the river and jumped in. How delicious it was diving and swimming and floating in the dark forest, where the trees were so thick that you could hardly see the sun! But after a while she began to look about her, and her eyes fell on a little fish that seemed made out of a rainbow, so brilliant were the colours he flashed out.

I should like him for a pet, thought the girl, and the next time the fish swam by, she put out her hand and caught him. Then she ran along the grassy path till she came to a cave in front of which a stream fell over some rocks into a basin. Here she put her little fish, whose name was Djulung-djulung, and promising to return soon and bring him some dinner, she went away.

By the time she got home, the rice for their dinner was ready cooked, and the eldest sister gave the other six their portions in wooden bowls. But the youngest did not finish hers, and when no one was looking, stole off to the fountain in the forest where the little fish was swimming about.

'See! I have not forgotten you,' she cried, and one by one she let the grains of rice fall into the water, where the fish gobbled them up greedily, for he had never tasted anything so nice.

'That is all for today,' she said at last, 'but I will come again tomorrow,' and bidding him goodbye she went down the path.

Now the girl did not tell her sisters about the fish, but every day she saved half of her rice to give him, and called him softly in a little song she had made for herself. If she sometimes felt hungry, no one knew of it, and, indeed, she did not mind that much, when she saw how the fish enjoyed it. And the fish grew fat and big, but the girl grew thin and weak, and the loads of wood felt heavier every day, and at last her sisters noticed it.

Then they took counsel together, and watched her to see what she did, and one of them followed her to the fountain where Djulung lived, and saw her give him all the rice she had saved from her breakfast. Hastening home the sister told the others what she had witnessed, and that a lovely fat fish might be had for the catching. So the eldest sister went and caught him, and he was boiled for supper, but the youngest sister was away in the woods, and did not know anything about it.

Next morning she went as usual to the cave, and sang her little song, but no Djulung came to answer it; twice and thrice she sang, then threw herself on her knees by the edge, and peered into the dark water, but the trees cast such a deep shadow that her eyes could not pierce it.

'Djulung cannot be dead, or his body would be floating on the surface,' she said to herself, and rising to her feet she set out homewards, feeling all of a sudden strangely tired.

What is the matter with me? she thought, but somehow or other she managed to reach the hut, and threw herself down in a corner, where she slept so soundly that for days no one was able to wake her.

At length, one morning early, a cock began to crow so loud that she could sleep no longer; and as he continued to crow she seemed to understand what he was saying, and that he was telling her that Djulung was dead, killed and eaten by her sisters, and that his bones lay buried under the kitchen fire. Very softly she got up, and took up the large stone under the fire, and creeping out carried the bones to the cave by the fountain, where she dug a hole and buried them anew. And as she scooped out the hole with a stick she sang a song, bidding the bones grow till they became a tree—a tree that reached up so high into the heavens that its leaves would fall across the sea into another island, whose king would pick them up.

As there was no Djulung to give her rice to, the girl soon became fat again, and as she was able to do her work as of old, her sisters did not trouble about her. They never guessed that when she went into the forest to gather her sticks, she never failed to pay a visit to the tree, which grew taller and more wonderful day by day. Never was such a tree seen before. Its trunk was of iron, its leaves were of silk, its flowers of gold, and its fruit of diamonds, and one evening, though the girl did not know it, a soft breeze took one of the leaves, and blew it across the sea to the feet of one of the king's attendants.

'What a curious leaf! I have never beheld one like it before. I must show it to the king,' he said, and when the king saw it he declared he would never rest until he had found the tree which bore it, even if he had to spend the rest of his life in visiting the islands that lay all around. Happily for him, he began with the island that was nearest, and here in the forest he suddenly saw standing before him the iron tree, its boughs covered with shining leaves like the one he carried about him.

'But what sort of tree is it, and how did it get here?' he asked of the attendants he had with him.

No one could answer him, but as they were about to pass out of the forest a little boy went by, and the king stopped and enquired if there was anyone living in the neighbourhood whom he might question.

'Seven girls live in a hut down there,' replied the boy, pointing with his finger to where the sun was setting.

'Then go and bring them here, and I will wait,' said the king, and the boy ran off and told the sisters that a great chief, with strings of jewels round his neck, had sent for them.

Pleased and excited the six elder sisters at once followed the boy, but the youngest, who was busy, and who did not care about strangers, stayed behind, to finish the work she was doing.

The king welcomed the girls eagerly, and asked them all manner of questions about the tree, but as they had never even heard of its existence, they could tell him nothing. 'And if we, who live close by the forest, do not know, you may be sure no one does,' added the eldest, who was rather cross at finding this was all that the king wanted of them.

'But the boy told me there were seven of you, and there are only six here,' said the king.

'Oh, the youngest is at home, but she is always half asleep, and is of no use except to cut wood for the fire,' replied they in a breath.

'That may be, but perhaps she dreams,' answered the king. 'Anyway, I will speak to her also.' Then he signed to one of his attendants, who followed the path that the boy had taken to the hut.

Soon the man returned, with the girl walking behind him. And as soon as she reached the tree it bowed itself to the earth before her, and she stretched out her hand and picked some of its leaves and flowers and gave them to the king.

'The maiden who can work such wonders is fitted to be the wife of the greatest chief,' he said, and so he married her, and took her with him across the sea to his own home, where they lived happy for ever after.

Tiger Story,
Anansi Story

I. ANANSI ASKS A FAVOUR

Once upon a time, and a long, long time ago, all things were named after Tiger, for he was the strongest of all the animals, and King of the forest. The strong baboon, standing and smiting his chest like a drum, setting the trees ringing with his roars, respected Tiger and kept quiet before him. Even the brown monkey, so nimble and full of mischief, twisting the tail of the elephant, scampering about on the back of the sleeping alligator, pulling faces at the hippopotamus, even he was quiet before Tiger.

So, because Tiger ruled the forest, the lily whose flower bore red stripes was called tiger-lily, and the moth with broad, striped wings was called tiger-moth; and the stories that the animals told at evening in the forest were called Tiger Stories.

Of all the animals in the forest Anansi the spider was the weakest. One evening, looking up at Tiger, Anansi said, 'Tiger,

you are very strong. Everyone is quiet in your presence. You are
King of the forest. I am not strong. No one pays any attention
to me. Will you grant me a favour, O Tiger?'

The other animals began to laugh. How silly of feeble Anansi
to be asking a favour of Tiger! The bullfrog gurgled and hurried
off to the pond to tell his wife how silly Anansi was. The green
parrot in the tree called to her brother to fly across and see what
was happening.

But Tiger said nothing. He did not seem to know that Anansi
had spoken to him. He lay quiet, head lifted, eyes half closed.
Only the tip of his tail moved.

Anansi bowed low so that his forehead almost touched the
ground. He stood in front of Tiger, but a little to one side, and
said, 'Good evening, Tiger. I have a favour to ask.'

Tiger opened his eyes and looked at Anansi. He flicked his tail
and asked, 'What favour, Anansi?'

'Well,' replied Anansi in his strange, lisping voice, 'everything
bears your name because you are strong. Nothing bears my
name. Could something be called after me, Tiger? You have so
many things named after you.'

'What would you like to bear your name?' asked Tiger, eyes
half closed, tail moving slowly from side to side, his tawny,
striped body quite still.

'The stories,' replied Anansi. 'Would you let them be called
Anansi Stories?'

Now Tiger loved the stories, prizing them even more than the
tiger-lily and the tiger-moth. Stupid Anansi, he thought to himself. Does he really think that I am going to permit these stories
to be called Anansi Stories, after the weakest of all the animals
in the forest? Anansi Stories indeed! He replied, 'Very well,
Anansi. Have your wish, have your wish, but . . .'

Tiger fell silent. All the animals listened. What did Tiger
mean, agreeing to Anansi's request and then saying 'but'? What
trick was he up to? Parrot listened. Bullfrog stopped gurgling in
order to catch the answer. Wise Owl, looking down from his
hole in the trunk of a tree, waited for Tiger to speak.

'But what, Tiger? And it is so kind of you, Tiger, to do me this
favour,' cried Anansi.

'But,' said Tiger, speaking loudly and slowly so that all might
hear, 'you must first do me two favours. Two favours from the

weak equal one favour from the strong. Isn't that right, Anansi?'

'What two favours?' asked Anansi.

'You must first catch me a gourd full of live bees, Anansi. That is the first favour I ask of you.'

At this all the animals laughed so loudly that Alligator came out of a nearby river to find out what was happening. How could weak Anansi catch a gourd full of bees? One or two sharp stings would put an end to that!

Anansi remained silent. Tiger went on, eyes half closed. 'And there is a second favour that I ask, Anansi.'

'What is that, Tiger?'

'Bring me Mr Snake alive. Mr Snake who lives down by the river, opposite the clump of bamboo-trees. Both these things you must do within seven days, Anansi. Do these two small things for me, and I will agree that the stories might be called after you. It was this you asked, wasn't it, Anansi?'

'Yes, Tiger,' replied Anansi, 'and I will do these two favours for you, as you ask.'

'Good,' replied Tiger. 'I have often wished to sit and talk with Mr Snake. I have often wished to have my own hive of bees, Anansi. I am sure you will do what I ask. Do these two little things and you can have the stories.'

Tiger leapt away suddenly through the forest, while the laughter of the animals rose in great waves of sound. How could Anansi catch live bees and a live snake? Anansi went off to his home, pursued by the laughter of Parrot and Bullfrog.

II. THE FIRST TASK: A GOURD FULL OF BEES

On Monday morning Anansi woke early. He went into the woods carrying an empty gourd, muttering to himself. 'I wonder how many it can hold? I wonder how many it can hold?'

Ant asked him why he was carrying an empty gourd and talking to himself, but Anansi did not reply. Later, he met Iguana.

'What are you doing with that empty gourd?' asked Iguana. Anansi did not answer. Still further along the track he met a centipede walking along on his hundred legs.

'Why are you talking to yourself, Anansi?' asked Centipede, but Anansi made no reply.

Then Queen Bee flew by. She heard Centipede speaking to Anansi, and, full of curiosity, she asked, 'Anansi, why are you carrying that empty gourd? Why are you talking to yourself?'

'Oh, Queen Bee,' replied Anansi, 'I have made a bet with Tiger, but I fear that I am going to lose. He bet me that I could not tell him how many bees a gourd can hold. Queen Bee, what shall I tell him?'

'Tell him it's a silly bet,' replied Queen Bee.

'But you know how angry Tiger becomes, how quick-tempered he is,' pleaded Anansi. 'Surely you will help me?'

'I am not at all sure that I can,' said Queen Bee as she flew away. 'How can I help you when I do not know myself how many bees it takes to fill an empty gourd?'

Anansi went back home with the gourd. In the afternoon he returned to the forest, making for the logwood-trees, which at this time of the year were heavy with sweet-smelling yellow flowers and full of the sound of bees. As he went along he kept saying aloud, 'How many can it hold? How many can it hold?'

Centipede, who saw Anansi passing for the second time, told his friend Cricket that he was sure Anansi was out of his mind, for he was walking about in the forest asking himself the same question over and over again. Cricket sang the news to Bullfrog, and Bullfrog passed it on to Parrot, who reported it from his perch on the cedar-tree. Tiger heard and smiled to himself.

At about four o'clock that afternoon, Queen Bee, returning with her swarm of bees from the logwood-trees, met Anansi. He was still talking to himself. Well content with the work of the day, she took pity on him, and called out, 'Wait there, Anansi. I have thought of a way of helping you.'

'I am so glad, Queen Bee,' said Anansi, 'because I have been asking myself the same question all day and I cannot find the answer.'

'Well,' said Queen Bee, 'all you have to do is measure one of my bees, then measure your empty gourd, divide one into the other and you will have the answer.'

'But that's school-work, Queen Bee. I couldn't do that. I was never quick in school. That's too hard for me, too hard, Queen Bee. And that dreadful Tiger is so quick-tempered. What am I to do, Queen Bee?'

'I will tell you how to get the answer,' said one of the bees that advised the Queen. 'Really, it is quite easy. Hold the gourd with the opening towards the sunlight so that we can see it. We will fly in one at a time. You count us as we go in. When the gourd is full we will fly out. In this way you will find out the correct answer.'

'Splendid,' said Queen Bee. 'What do you think of that, Anansi?'

'Certainly that will give the answer,' replied Anansi, 'and it will be more correct than the school answer. It is a good method, Queen Bee. See, I have the gourd ready, with the opening to the sunlight. Ready?'

Slowly the bees flew in, their Queen leading the way, with Anansi counting, 'One, two, three, four, five . . . twenty-one, twenty-two, twenty-three . . . forty-one, forty-two, forty-three, forty-four,' until the gourd was half full, three-quarters full, '. . . a hundred and fifty-two, and fifty-three, and fifty-four.' At that point the last bee flew in, filling the gourd, now heavy with humming bees crowded together. Anansi corked up the opening and hurried off to the clearing in the forest where Tiger sat with a circle of animals.

'See, King Tiger,' he said, 'here is your gourd full of bees, one hundred and fifty-four of them, all full of logwood honey. Do you still want me to bring Brother Snake, or is this enough?'

Tiger was so angry that he could hardly restrain himself from leaping at Anansi and tearing him to pieces. He had been laughing with the other animals at Parrot's account of Anansi walking alone through the forest asking himself the same ridiculous question over and over. Tiger was pleased about one thing only, that he had set Anansi two tasks and not one. Well, he had brought the gourd full of bees. But one thing was certain. He could never bring Mr Snake alive.

'What a good thing it is that I am so clever,' said Tiger to himself. 'If I had set him only one task I would have lost the stories.' Feeling more content within himself, and proud of his cleverness, he replied to Anansi, who was bowing low before him, 'Of course, Anansi. I set you one thing that I knew you could do, and one that I know you cannot do. It's Monday evening. You have until Saturday morning, so hurry off and be gone with you.'

The animals laughed while Anansi limped away. He always walked like that, resting more heavily on one leg than on the others. All laughed, except Wise Owl, looking down from his home in the cedar-tree. The strongest had set the weakest two tasks.

Perhaps, thought Owl to himself, perhaps . . . perhaps . . .

III. THE SECOND TASK: MR SNAKE

On Tuesday morning Anansi got up early. How was he to catch Mr Snake? The question had been buzzing about in his head all night, like an angry wasp. How to catch Mr Snake?

Perhaps he could trap Snake with some ripe bananas. He would make a Calaban beside the path that Snake used each day when the sky beat down on the forest and he went to the stream to quench his thirst. How good a thing it is, thought Anansi, that Snake is a man of such fixed habits; he wakes up at the same hour each morning, goes for his drink of water at the same hour, hunts for his food every afternoon, goes to bed at sunset each day.

Anansi worked hard making his Calaban to catch Snake. He took a vine, pliant yet strong, and made a noose in it. He spread grass and leaves over the vine to hide it. Inside the noose he placed two ripe bananas. When Snake touched the noose, Anansi would draw it tight. How angry Mr Snake would be, to find that he had been trapped! Anansi smiled to himself while he put the finishing touches to the trap, then he hid himself in the bush by the side of the track, holding one end of the vine.

Anansi waited quietly. Not a leaf stirred. Lizard was asleep on the trunk of a tree opposite. Looking down the path Anansi could see heat waves rising from the parched ground.

There was Snake, his body moving quietly over the grass and dust, a long gleaming ribbon marked in green and brown. Anansi waited. Snake saw the bananas and moved towards them. He lay across the vine and ate the bananas. Anansi pulled at the vine to tighten the noose, but Snake's body was too heavy. When he had eaten the bananas Snake went on his way to the stream.

That was on Tuesday. Anansi returned home, the question still buzzing about in his head: 'How to catch Snake? How to catch Snake?' When his wife asked him what he would like for supper, he answered, 'How to catch Snake?' When his son asked if he could go off for a game with his cousin, Anansi replied, 'How to catch Snake?'

A Slippery Hole! That was the answer. Early on Wednesday morning he hurried back to the path in the forest where he had waited for Snake the day before, taking with him a ripe avocado pear. Snake liked avocado pears better even than bananas. In the middle of the path Anansi dug a deep hole, and made the sides slippery with grease. At the bottom he put the pear. If Snake went down into the hole he would not be able to climb back up the slippery sides. Then Anansi hid in the bush.

At noon Snake came down the path. 'How long he is,' said Anansi to himself; 'long and strong. Will I ever be able to catch him?'

Snake glided down the path, moving effortlessly until he came to the Slippery Hole. He looked over the edge of the hole and saw the avocado pear at the bottom. Also he saw that the sides of the hole were slippery. First he wrapped his tail tightly round the trunk of a slender tree beside the track, then lowered his body and ate the avocado pear. When he had finished he pulled himself out of the hole by his tail and went on his way to the river. Anansi had lost the bananas; now he had lost the avocado pear also!

On Wednesday Anansi spent the morning working at a 'Fly-Up', a trap he had planned during the night while the question buzzed through his head: 'How to catch Snake. How? How?' He arranged it cleverly, fitting one of the slender young bamboo-trees with a noose, so that the bamboo flew up at the slightest touch, pulling the noose tight. Inside the noose he put an egg, the only one that he had left. It was precious to him, but he knew that Snake loved eggs even more than he did. Then he waited behind the clump of bamboos. Snake came down the path.

The Fly-Up did not catch Snake, who simply lowered his head, took the egg up in his mouth without touching the noose, and then enjoyed the egg in the shade of the clump of bamboos while Anansi looked on. He had lost the bananas and avocado pear, and his precious egg.

There was nothing more to do. The question 'How to catch Snake?' no longer buzzed round and round in his head, keeping him awake by night, troubling him throughout the day. The Calaban, the Slippery Hole, and the Fly-Up had failed. He would have to go back to Tiger and confess that he could not catch Snake. How Parrot would laugh, and Bullfrog and Monkey!

Friday came. Anansi did nothing. There was no more that he could do.

Early on Saturday morning, before daybreak, Anansi set off for a walk by the river, taking his cutlass with him. He passed by the hole where Snake lived. Snake was up early. He was looking towards the east, waiting for the sun to rise, his head resting on the edge of his hole, his long body hidden in the earth. Anansi had not expected that Snake would be up so early. He had forgotten Snake's habit of rising early to see the dawn. Remembering how he had tried to catch Snake, he went by very quietly, limping a little, hoping that Snake would not notice him. But Snake did.

'You there, you, Anansi, stop there!' called Snake.

'Good morning, Snake,' replied Anansi. 'How angry you sound.'

'And angry I am,' said Snake. 'I have a good mind to eat you for breakfast.' Snake pulled half his body out of the hole. 'You have been trying to catch me. You set a trap on Monday, a Calaban. Lizard told me. You thought he was asleep on the trunk of the tree but he was not; and as you know, we are of the same family. And on Tuesday you set a Slippery Hole, and on Wednesday a Fly-Up. I have a good mind to kill you, Anansi.'

'Oh, Snake, I beg your pardon. I beg your pardon,' cried the terrified Anansi. 'What you say is true. I did try to catch you, but I failed. You are too clever for me.'

'And why did you try to catch me, Anansi?'

'I had a bet with Tiger. I told him you are the longest animal in the world, longer even than that long bamboo-tree by the side of the river.'

'Of course I am,' shouted Snake. 'Of course I am. You haven't got to catch me to prove that. Of course I am longer than the bamboo-tree!' At this, Snake, who was now very angry and excited, drew his body out of the hole and stretched himself out on the grass. 'Look!' he shouted. 'Look! How dare Tiger say that the bamboo-tree is longer than I am!'

'Well,' said Anansi, 'you are very long, very long indeed. But, Snake, now that I see you and the bamboo-tree at the same time, it seems to me that the bamboo-tree is a little longer than you are; just a few inches longer, Snake, half a foot or a foot at the most. Oh, Snake, I have lost my bet. Tiger wins!'

'Tiger, fiddlesticks!' shouted the enraged Snake. 'Anyone can see that the bamboo-tree is shorter than I am. Cut it down, you stupid creature! Put it beside me. Measure the bamboo-tree against my body. You haven't lost your bet, you have won.'

Anansi hurried off to the clump of bamboos, cut down the longest and trimmed off the branches.

'Now put it beside me,' shouted the impatient Snake.

Anansi put the long bamboo pole beside Snake. Then he said, 'Snake, you are very long, very long indeed. But we must go about this in the correct way. Perhaps when I run up to your head you will crawl up, and when I run down to see where your tail is you will wriggle down. How I wish I had someone to help me measure you with the bamboo!'

'Tie my tail to the bamboo,' said Snake, 'and get on with the job. You can see that I am longer!'

Anansi tied Snake's tail to one end of the bamboo. Running up to the other end, he called, 'Now stretch, Snake, stretch!'

Snake stretched as hard as he could. Turtle, hearing the shouting, came out of the river to see what was happening. A flock of white herons flew across the river, and joined in, shouting, 'Stretch, Snake, stretch.' It was more exciting than a race. Snake was stretching his body to its utmost, but the bamboo was some inches longer.

'Good,' cried Anansi. 'I will tie you round the middle, Snake, then you can try again. One more try, and you will prove you are longer than the bamboo.'

Anansi tied Snake to the bamboo, round the middle. Then he said, 'Now rest for five minutes. When I shout, "Stretch," then stretch as much as you can.'

'Yes,' said one of the herons. 'You have only six inches to stretch, Snake. You can do it.'

Snake rested for five minutes. Anansi shouted, 'Stretch.' Snake made a mighty effort. The herons and Turtle cheered Snake on. He shut his eyes for the last tremendous effort that would prove him longer than the bamboo.

'Hooray,' shouted the animals, 'you are winning, you are winning, four inches more, two inches more . . .'

At that moment Anansi tied Snake's head to the bamboo. The animals fell silent. There was Snake tied to the bamboo, ready to be taken to Tiger.

From that day the stories have been called Anansi Stories.

The Coming
of Asin

There was once a chief among the Pilagá people by the name of Nalaraté. Nalaraté was known for his victories in war, and the men who followed him were battle-hardened warriors. Into Nalaraté's village one day there came a curious stranger. When the people saw him they laughed, for he was grotesque and ugly. Whereas other men were lean and straight, the stranger was crooked, with a large paunch. And whereas other men had long black hair, the stranger had none at all. Other men wore loincloths, but as for the stranger, he wore a fox-skin cloak over his shoulders.

'What kind of creature is this?' Nalaraté's people asked each other. 'He is not of the Toba tribe, nor of the Matacao, nor the Tereno. He must be a tribe all by himself, for where could there be other people like him?' They mocked him this way, but the stranger simply listened and made no answer. Finally one of the Pilagá asked him, 'Who are you?'

'My name is Asin,' the stranger answered quietly.

He remained in the village and built himself a small shelter of boughs and grass. The people tolerated him as a curiosity, and they treated him as a beggar. If a man caught a fish that was too small to cook, he might toss it to Asin, and Asin would take it humbly and express his thanks. But though the people didn't send Asin out of the village they abused him in many ways. Sometimes, for sport, the men would wipe their hands on Asin's fox-skin cloak and make a great joke of it when he complained.

One day Asin went to the house of the chief. Nalaraté said, 'Do not enter here. What is in my house that you want to steal?'

Asin answered, 'I only want to borrow a comb from your daughter.'

Nalaraté laughed. 'Since you have no hair on your head, what could you do with a comb?'

But Nalaraté's daughter overheard them talking, and she said to Asin, 'Here, I will lend you the comb.'

Asin took it and thanked her and went down to the river. The girl picked up her water jars and followed him, curious as to what he would do with a comb. When she came near the river, she hid among the trees and watched Asin. She saw him remove his fox-skin cloak. As Asin stood there in the water he changed instantly into a handsome young warrior with long black hair, which he combed with the comb the girl had lent him.

'He is handsome and he has great powers!' the girl said to herself. 'I will have him for my husband.'

Asin finished combing his hair. Then he transformed himself again into the ugly stranger, and put the fox-skin cloak back on his shoulders. After he had left, the girl filled her water jars and carried them home.

When Asin came to Nalaraté's house to return the comb, the girl said, 'Sit down with me here.'

Asin replied, 'Why do you want me to sit with you? I am ugly.'

The girl said, 'Even though my father will object, I will have you for my husband.'

Asin answered, 'Very well, then. Let us sit where people can see.'

The girl put a skin on the ground in front of the house and they sat on it together, signifying that they were married. When people saw them sitting there, they said, 'The chief's daughter has lost her mind. She is married to Asin.'

When Nalaraté came he was angry. He ordered his daughter to leave Asin and choose another man of the village, but she refused, saying, 'He is my husband now.'

That night, Asin demonstrated his magic powers. From under the fox-skin cloak he brought out a mosquito netting to protect them from insects. He brought out food, and they ate. He brought out a beautiful red skirt-cloth and gave it to his wife.

When the girl's mother saw what Asin could do, she said, 'I didn't protest when you married Asin. What can he bring out from under the fox skin for me?'

The girl said, 'Ask for whatever you want, he will give it to you.'

The mother said, 'It is the beautiful red skirt-cloth that I want.'

'Take it,' Asin said, and she took it. Then Asin reached under the fox-skin cloak and brought out a yellow skirt-cloth for his wife. He brought out ears of corn and a honeycomb full of honey and gave them to the girl's mother, and she was grateful. She said again, 'I wasn't one of those who objected to Asin's living here.'

Nalaraté was at a drinking party with the warriors of the village. When he returned early in the morning he said, 'Get my things ready, we are going on an expedition against the Matacao tribe.'

Asin said, 'I will come with you.'

The chief replied scornfully, 'No, how could I take you? You would be a hindrance. You are no warrior. You don't even have a horse. If you had a horse, could you even make it go in the right direction? And if you arrived at the place of battle, what could you do but cause us shame and misery? No, stay here with the women. As for my daughter, she chose a beggar instead of a warrior. She will starve. I will give her nothing.'

Nalaraté and his warriors mounted their horses and rode away. When they were out of sight, Asin said, 'Now I will go.'

He mounted his donkey and followed the war party. When he had left the village behind, he clapped his hands together, *tao*, and his donkey changed into a fiery iron horse. He clapped his hands again, *tao*, and changed himself into a handsome young man as his wife had seen him at the river. When night came, Nalaraté's warriors made camp. Before Asin entered the camp, he changed his iron horse back into a donkey, and himself into an ugly man without hair.

The war party saw him then, and they made jokes and asked, 'Why did you come?' They threw him some scraps of food, which he took. After a while he mounted his donkey and rode on ahead of the war party. He spent the night alone at a watering place. He brought out food from under his fox skin and he ate until he was satisfied.

In the morning he again joined the warriors, and he rode at a distance behind them. The men joked about Asin. Then they sighted the camp of the enemy. Nalaraté ordered Asin to return to the village. He said, 'Go back at once before you cause us trouble and shame.'

Asin stopped and waited, as the Pilagá men went cautiously forward. Then he changed himself into the warrior with the flowing black hair, and he changed his donkey into the fiery iron horse. He rode fiercely past the Pilagá men into the camp of the enemy and fought with them. Nalaraté's warriors stopped and watched the battle, asking each other, 'Who is this man? Who is this man?'

One of them cried out, 'It is Asin! He changed his donkey into a fiery iron horse!'

Then the Pilagá went forward to join the battle, but by the time they arrived Asin had scattered the enemy and rounded up all the horses. They met him coming back, driving the horses before him. He did not speak to the Pilagá, but went on and left them behind.

Asin returned to the village. He said to his wife, 'Let us leave this village where I have been mistreated.' His wife agreed. Her mother said, 'I will come too.' So Asin took them and his horses to a new place on the edge of a river and made a new house.

When Nalaraté arrived home he found his house empty. The women of the village told him how Asin had gone away with his household.

The men blamed Nalaraté, saying, 'It is your fault, you abused him. And he is the greatest of warriors.'

Nalaraté was angry. He said, 'If you want him for your chief, follow him.'

Many of the men did. They took their families and went to the place where Asin had built his house. There they built a new village. And Asin was the chief.

Nalaraté decided he would destroy Asin for the grief he had caused him. But Asin learned of the plot, and he called all the men of the village together and spoke to them. He said, 'There is a wind coming. It will be cold. Go and brace your houses, and put heavy thatch on the roof.' They went and prepared their houses. Then Asin clapped his hands, *tao*, and the cold wind came. It swept across the country. People became cold and sought refuge inside their houses. But the wind blew away the thatch from the roofs. Only in Asin's village did the roofs remain. Everywhere else people were punished by the cold and the wind. In his own house Asin clapped his hands, *tao*, and made a fire. People came to him begging for an ember so that they could have a fire in their houses too. To those people who were his friends, Asin gave firebrands. When his enemies came and begged for fire, he turned them away. Nalaraté himself came, but Asin said, 'First you merely abused me; then you planned to kill me. Why should I give you fire?' Nalaraté went away and was cold.

All those who hadn't abused Asin had fire and were warm, but the others suffered and died. The rivers froze, and snow covered the land.

At last the wind stopped, and the ice and snow melted, and Asin came out of his house. He went to Nalaraté's village and found the people dead. He changed the old men into yulo birds and mazamorras birds, and they flew away. He changed the old women into chaja birds, and they flew away. He changed the middle-aged people into hawks and vultures, and they flew away. And the children he changed into ducks and herons, and they flew away. Asin found Nalaraté where he had taken refuge from the cold in a well, and he changed him into an alligator.

This is the legend of Asin, who was abused because of his appearance.

The Legend of the Yara

It is said that many years ago a young brave named Jaraguari lived on the banks of the Amazon River. This young man was as cheerful as the sun-dappled water of the great river, yet as strong and agile as the yellow-black jaguar, lord of the forest. He was the son of the chieftain of a small village. Each year, this village had a ceremony that celebrated a young man's rite of passage into the rank of warrior where manhood was honoured and a boy's skills as a hunter were tested. No more exquisite a hunter than Jaraguari had ever emerged. The villagers wondered at his boldness which surpassed that of all the other young braves who envied his courage and dexterity. None of them could approximate the uncanny precision with which he pierced the thick, hairy hide of a white-lipped peccary.

Jaraguari had in his keen eyes the strength of the great river. His disposition was as contented as the rhythmic waters that lapped along the shores of his village. The elders of the village loved Jaraguari because he treated them with kindness and respect. And the girls of the village dreamed at night of his handsome good looks, his grace, and his courage.

Paddling his canoe or *ubá* downriver with the prow barely disturbing the still waters, Jaraguari would set forth each day to fish, delighting in the skittish egrets that followed his trajectory. The river animals feared some of the braves because they fished by poisoning the waters with the sap from the deadly *timbó* plants. The poison killed the *piava*, the *pintado*, and the piranha fish. But the fish appreciated that Jaraguari would not poison them. Jaraguari would use one of his sharp arrows to spear the giant *pirarucu* fish. He was nimble and elegant, and he respected the nobility of the many freshwater fish. When he returned each night at twilight, his mother would see him from the shore, standing proudly in the bow of his *ubá* surveying the day's catch.

Once a young man reached the rank of warrior, he was finally able to wear a necklace made from the teeth of the jaguars he had killed in the hunt. It was several moons after Jaraguari became a warrior that his mother glimpsed him returning very late one night. The stars were already dimming in the sky.

The next day Jaraguari seemed changed. He was pensive and reserved. Although his mother was concerned by his mood, he insisted on leaving that day at his usual hour, cutting the same route to Tarumã Point, where he remained until well past dusk. Each night thereafter, silent and solitary, he would return to shore, lost in his thoughts.

Astounded by the changes in her son, Jaraguari's mother finally asked him, 'What sort of fishing are you doing, my son, that goes on until so late an hour? Are you not afraid of the treacherous tricks of the jungle spirits? Have you never heard voices in the angry winds? Is that why you are so sad, my son?'

His mother's words were a warning to him. When she saw Jaraguari huddled in his hammock, staring into the dead of night, hour after mournful hour, contemplating the realm of darkness, she feared what might be happening to him. Jaraguari's response to her warning was silence.

'Son, where is the happiness that animated your life? Not long ago joy danced from your eyes. Now it has travelled to a place far from you and me.'

'Mother,' was all Jaraguari managed to say, in a voice so pathetic he could barely be heard.

Jaraguari's mother and the chieftain watched as their son, once so fresh and full of sap, withered away. He still accompanied his father on the hunting forays, and even in his present state he did not tremble at the scream of a puma. But as a day lengthened into dusk, he would abandon the young braves still setting snares and casting their nets, and return to his canoe. With great haste he would speed through the murky waters toward Tarumã Point.

Jaraguari's mother knew that in the great river there was believed to be the Yara, or the Spirit of the Water. A woman of unusual beauty, she had light pink skin, vivid eyes, and green-gold hair falling the length of her body. The Yara tormented the souls of the men who crossed her path by slowly drawing them to her irresistible songs. Her alluring power could fill the rivers with pink and red and deep purple light. It was well known that no warrior could withstand the Yara's enchantment. Whoever saw her was instantly attracted by her grace and charm. In fear of her power, when the sun began to set, the braves stayed away from lakes and rivers where she could be found singing her eerie melodies. The unfortunate beings who were captured by her haunting incantations and beauty were dragged down to the depths of the waters.

For this reason, Jaraguari's mother stood her ground, and, though her heart was heavy with forebodings, she berated her son. 'The evil water spirits have poisoned your soul. Your father and I want you to leave this village with us, and we will find a life where the bird of happiness will once again dance in your eyes.'

As if witnessing a marvellous spectacle, Jaraguari suddenly came to life, his eyes wide open. 'Mother, I saw her. I saw her swimming amidst the flowers, floating like the lilies in the lagoon. She is as beautiful as the moon in the clearest of skies. Mother, her hair is the colour of other worlds we know nothing of, and her face is pink like the rosy spoonbill feathers dusting the sullied plain. Her eyes are like two gem-stones, more fiery than the precious emerald, and her song hushes the roar of the waterfall so the river can hear her. When she looks into my eyes, I want to follow her to where the water divides and she descends to her home. There is nothing in the river a man will ever see more beautiful than the Yara. And I want to hear her song once more.'

Upon hearing her son's words, the alarmed mother threw herself on the ground, sobbing, and cried out to her son, 'Flee from this place, my son! Never again let your canoe reach Tarumã Point. You have seen the Yara. She is fatal. Run away, my son. Death will leap from her green eyes and kill you.'

The young man did not reply. He silently walked away from the village, already enchanted.

The next day, just as the *murucututú* birds flew from their day nest on the river's edge, Jaraguari's canoe glided quietly towards Tarumã Point, cleaving the darkening water. The lads fishing on the banks of the river saw him pass and cried out, 'Come, everyone, come and see Jaraguari!'

The women with water jars balanced atop their heads and all the little boys chasing crabs rushed to the promontory where in the distance Jaraguari's canoe could be seen cutting through the water towards the horizon. The horizon seemed to be fed by flames from the setting sun. The nearer the canoe came to the horizon's edge, the more it appeared ready to hurl itself into the emblazoned sky.

Standing beside the young warrior was a woman of such great beauty, it was as if she were aglow herself from something luminary within. Her pale pink limbs stood out as filigree cast in relief against the blood gleam of the disappearing sun. More stunning than her beauty was the colour of her long hair. As bright a green as parrot's plumage was the Yara's iridescent hair which shone like a halo of light around them both.

In the distance could be heard the screams of the braves and maidens. 'It's the Yara. The Yara!' they shouted as if in one voice. They ran to the village and some could not resist looking back to see their chieftain's son traversing the night waters of the river into the realm of darkness.

The Hungry Peasant,
God, and Death

Not far from the city of Zacatecas there lived a poor peasant, whose harvest was never sufficient to keep hunger away from himself, his wife and children. Every year his harvests grew worse, his family more numerous. Thus as time passed, the man had less and less to eat for himself, since he sacrificed a part of his own rations on behalf of his wife and children.

One day, tired of so much privation, the peasant stole a chicken with the determination to go far away, very far, to eat it, where no one could see him and expect him to share it. He took a pot and climbed up the most broken side of a nearby mountain. Upon finding a suitable spot, he made a fire, cleaned his chicken, and put it to cook with herbs.

When it was ready, he took the pot off the fire and waited impatiently for it to cool off. As he was about to eat it, he saw a man coming along one of the paths in his direction. The peasant hurriedly hid the pot in the bushes and said to himself, 'Curse the luck! Not even here in the mountains is one permitted to eat in peace.'

At this moment the stranger approached and greeted, 'Good morning, friend!'

'May God grant you a good morning,' he answered.

'What are you doing here, friend?'

'Well, nothing, señor, just resting. And, Your Grace, where are you going?'

'Oh, I was just passing by and stopped to see if you could give me something to eat.'

'No, señor, I haven't anything.'

'How's that, when you have a fire burning?'

'Oh, this little fire; that's just for warming myself.'

'Don't tell me that. Haven't you a pot hidden in the bushes? Even from here I can smell the cooked hen.'

'Well yes, señor, I have some chicken but I shall not give you any; I would not even give any to my own children. I came way up here because for once in my life I wanted to eat my fill. I shall certainly not share my food with you.'

'Come, friend, don't be unkind. Give me just a little of it!'

'No, señor, I shall not give you any. In my whole life I have not been able to satisfy my hunger, not even for one day.'

'Yes, you will give me some. You refuse because you don't know who I am.'

'I shall not give you anything, no matter who you are, I shall not give you anything!'

'Yes, you will as soon as I tell you who I am.'

'Well then, who are you?'

'I am God, your Lord.'

'Uh, hm, now less than ever shall I share my food with you. You are very bad to the poor. You only give to those whom you like. To some you give haciendas, palaces, trains, carriages, horses; to others, like me, nothing. You have never even given me enough to eat. So I shall not give you any chicken.'

God continued arguing with him, but the man would not even give Him a mouthful of broth, so He went His way.

When the peasant was about to eat his chicken, another stranger came along; this one was very thin and pale.

'Good morning, friend!' he said. 'Haven't you anything there you can give me to eat?'

'No, señor, nothing.'

'Come, don't be a bad fellow! Give me a little piece of that chicken you're hiding.'

'No, señor, I shall not give you any.'

'Oh yes, you will. You refuse me now because you don't know who I am.'

'Who can you be? God, Our Lord Himself, just left and not even to Him would I give anything, less to you.'

'But you will, when you know who I am.'

'All right; tell me then who you are.'

'I am Death!'

'You were right. To you I shall give some chicken, because you are just. You, yes, you take away the fat and thin ones, old and young, poor and rich. You make no distinctions nor show any favouritism. To you, yes, I shall give some of my chicken!'

The Spirit-Wife

A young man was grieving because the beautiful young wife whom he loved was dead. As he sat at the graveside weeping, he decided to follow her to the Land of the Dead. He made many prayer sticks and sprinkled sacred corn pollen. He took a downy eagle plume and coloured it with red earth colour. He waited until nightfall, when the spirit of his departed wife came out of the grave and sat beside him. She was not sad, but smiling. The spirit-maiden told her husband, 'I am just leaving one life for another. Therefore do not weep for me.'

'I cannot let you go,' said the young man, 'I love you so much that I will go with you to the land of the dead.'

The spirit-wife tried to dissuade him, but could not overcome his determination. So at last she gave in to his wishes, saying, 'If you must follow me, know that I shall be invisible to you as long as the sun shines. You must tie this red eagle plume to my hair.

It will be visible in daylight, and if you want to come with me, you must follow the plume.'

The young husband tied the red plume to his spirit-wife's hair, and at daybreak, as the sun slowly began to light up the world, bathing the mountaintops in a pale pink light, the spirit-wife started to fade from his view. The lighter it became, the more the form of his wife dissolved and grew transparent, until at last it vanished altogether. But the red plume did not disappear. It waved before the young man, a mere arm's-length away, and then, as if rising and falling on a dancer's head, began leading the way out of the village, moving through the streets out into the cornfields, moving through a shallow stream, moving into the foot-hills of the mountains, leading the young husband ever westward towards the land of the evening.

The red plume moved swiftly, evenly, floating without effort over the roughest trails, and soon the young man had trouble following it. He grew tireder and tireder and finally was totally exhausted as the plume left him further behind. Then he called out, panting, 'Beloved wife, wait for me. I can't run any longer.'

The red plume stopped, waiting for him to catch up, and when he did so, hastened on. For many days the young man travelled, following the plume by day, resting during the nights, when his spirit-bride would sometimes appear to him, speaking encouraging words. Most of the time, however, he was merely aware of her presence in some mysterious way. Day by day the trail became rougher and rougher. The days were long, the nights short, and the young man grew wearier and wearier, until at last he had hardly enough strength to set one foot before the other.

One day the trail led to a deep, almost bottomless chasm, and as the husband came to its edge, the red plume began to float away from him into nothingness. He reached out to seize it, but the plume was already beyond his reach, floating straight across the canyon, because spirits can fly through the air.

The young man called across the chasm, 'Dear wife of mine, I love you. Wait!'

He tried to descend one side of the canyon, hoping to climb up the opposite side, but the rock walls were sheer, with nothing to hold on to. Soon he found himself on a ledge barely wider than a thumb, from which he could go neither forward nor back. It seemed that he must fall into the abyss and be dashed into pieces. His foot had already begun to slip, when a tiny striped squirrel scooted up the cliff, chattering, 'You young fool, do you think you have the wings of a bird or the feet of a spirit? Hold on for just a little while and I'll help you.'

The little creature reached into its cheek pouch and brought out a little seed, which it moistened with saliva and stuck into a crack in the wall. With his tiny feet the squirrel danced above the crack, singing, '*Tsithl, tsithl, tsithl*, tall stalk, tall stalk, tall stalk, sprout, sprout quickly.' Out of the crack sprouted a long, slender stalk, growing quickly in length and breadth, sprouting leaves and tendrils, spanning the chasm so that the young man could cross over without any trouble.

On the other side of the canyon, the young man found the red plume waiting, dancing before him as ever. Again he followed it at a pace so fast that it often seemed that his heart would burst. At last the plume led him to a large, dark, deep lake, and the plume plunged into the water to disappear below the surface. Then the husband knew that the spirit land lay at the bottom of the lake. He was in despair because he could not follow the plume into the deep.

In vain did he call for his spirit-wife to come back. The surface of the lake remained undisturbed and unruffled like a sheet of mica. Not even at night did his spirit-wife reappear. The lake, the land of the dead, had swallowed her up. As the sun rose above the mountains, the young man buried his face in his hands and wept.

Then he heard someone gently calling: 'Hu-hu-hu,' and felt the soft beating of wings on his back and shoulders. He looked up and saw an owl hovering above him. The owl said, 'Young man, why are you weeping?'

He pointed to the lake, saying, 'My beloved wife is down there in the land of the dead, where I cannot follow her.'

'I know, poor man,' said the owl. 'Follow me to my house in the mountains, where I will tell you what to do. If you follow my advice, all will be well and you will be reunited with the one you love.'

The owl led the husband to a cave in the mountains and, as they entered, the young man found himself in a large room full of owl-men and owl-women. The owls greeted him warmly, inviting him to sit down and rest, to eat and drink. Gratefully he took his seat.

The old owl who had brought him took his owl clothing off, hanging it on an antler jutting out from the wall, and revealed himself as a manlike spirit. From a bundle in the wall this mysterious being took a small bag, showing it to the young man, telling him, 'I will give this to you, but first I must instruct you in what you must do and must not do.'

The young man eagerly stretched out his hand to grasp the medicine bag, but the owl drew back. 'Foolish fellow, suffering from the impatience of youth! If you cannot curb your eagerness and your youthful desires, then even this medicine will be of no help to you.'

'I promise to be patient,' said the husband.

'Well then,' said the owl-man, 'this is sleep medicine. It will make you fall into a deep sleep and transport you to some other place. When you awake, you will walk towards the Morning Star. Following the trail to the middle anthill, you will find your spirit-wife there. As the sun rises, so she will rise and smile at you, rise in the flesh, a spirit no more, and so you will live happily.

'But remember to be patient; remember to curb your eagerness. Let not your desire to touch and embrace her get the better of you, for if you touch her before bringing her safely home to the village of your birth, she will be lost to you forever.'

Having finished this speech, the old owl-man blew some of the medicine on the young husband's face, who instantly fell into a deep sleep. Then all the strange owl-men put on their owl coats and, lifting the sleeper, flew with him to a place at the beginning of the trail to the middle anthill. There they laid him down underneath some trees.

Then the strange owl-beings flew on to the big lake at the bottom of which the land of the dead was located. The old owl-man's magic sleep-medicine, and the feathered prayer sticks which the young man had carved, enabled them to dive down to the bottom of the lake and enter the land of the dead. Once inside, they used the sleep medicine to put to sleep the spirits who are in charge of that strange land beneath the waters. The owl-beings reverently laid their feathered prayer sticks before the altar of that netherworld, took up the beautiful young spirit-wife, and lifted her gently to the surface of the lake. Then, taking her upon their wings, they flew with her to the place where the young husband was sleeping.

When the husband awoke, he saw first the Morning Star, then the middle anthill, and then his wife at his side, still in deep slumber. Then she too awoke and opened her eyes wide, at first not knowing where she was or what had happened to her. When she discovered her lover right by her side, she smiled at him, saying: 'Truly, your love for me is strong, stronger than love has ever been, otherwise we would not be here.'

They got up and began to walk towards the pueblo of their birth. The young man did not forget the advice the old owl-man had given him, especially the warning to be patient and shun all desire until they had safely arrived at their home. In that way they travelled for four days, and all was well.

On the fourth day they arrived at Thunder Mountain and came to the river that flows by Salt Town. Then the young wife said, 'My husband, I am very tired. The journey has been long and the days hot. Let me rest here awhile, let me sleep a while, and then, refreshed, we can walk the last short distance home together.'

And her husband said, 'We will do as you say.'

The wife lay down and fell asleep. As her lover was watching over her, gazing at her loveliness, desire so strong that he could not resist it overcame him, and he stretched out his hand and touched her.

She awoke instantly with a start, and, looking at him and at his hand upon her body, began to weep, the tears streaming down her face. At last she said, 'You loved me, but you did not love me enough; otherwise you would have waited. Now I shall die again.' And before his eyes her form faded and became transparent, and at the place where she had rested a few moments before, there was nothing.

On a branch of a tree above him the old owl-man hooted mournfully, 'Shame, shame, shame.' Then the young man sank down in despair, burying his face in his hands, and ever after his mind wandered as his eyes stared vacantly.

If the young lover had controlled his desire, if he had not longed to embrace his beautiful wife, if he had not touched her, if he had practised patience and self-denial for only a short time, then death would have been overcome. There would be no journeying to the land below the lake, and no mourning for others lost.

But then, if there were no death, men would crowd each other with more people on this earth than the earth can hold. Then there would be hunger and war, with people fighting over a tiny patch of earth, over an ear of corn, over a scrap of meat. So maybe what happened was for the best.

Hankering for a Long Tail

O ne time, when the summertime had come and the hot sun liked to burn up everything, mosquito and sandfly and gnat, always buzzing, used their mouths too much and bothered Brer Rabbit too much. He didn't have anything to brush off the pests, so he began jumping around uselessly and soon ran out of breath.

So he went to scheming to see what he could do to get rid of them. He noticed Brother Bull Cow standing under a tree, chewing his cud in a satisfied way, and every time those bugs lit on him, Brother Cow switched his tail and knocked them, and they flew away and left him alone. Just then Brother Horse came along the road, and a fly buzzed around his haunches, and he just switched his tail and killed it dead.

Brother Rabbit was eating himself up with envy, vexed because he didn't have a long tail. He thought that when things like that were handed out he should have gotten a tail like they had. It made him mad to remember how he had been obliged to cry and beg with Sister Nanny Goat just to fool her into giving him even that stumpy little bit of cottontail he had now. There isn't any way in this world to take away the shame of having something that is nothing at all, like his stub of a tail. Fly and flea just buzz around, laughing at that poor excuse for a switch. A long tail would also have made a fine figure of a fellow! But there wasn't any way to go back to those times; the question he faced was how he was to get a sizeable tail right now.

He went home and he thought about it and thought about it until suddenly he hatched out a plan. It was a right bodacious plan too, but then Brer Rabbit is a right bodacious creature. There isn't anything so outrageous that he won't try to do it at least one time. And Brer Rabbit put on his store clothes, with his blue breeches and his yellow shoes, all fine. And he cocked his hat and took the path that went to Heaven to ask God if he wouldn't be so kind as to give him a long tail like those other creatures have.

It wasn't easy for Brer Rabbit to find the way because everybody he asked seemed to have a different notion about how to get there. Brer Rabbit listened to everyone and paid no attention to most of them, but kept a steady head about him and kept pushing on. And, by and by, it seemed as if the narrow path kind of rambled and rambled in front of him. And he went on and on until at last he was right at the front gate of Heaven and at the head of the long avenue of the Beautiful City. And he pushed in and walked along the grand boulevard and at last there he was, right in front of the Big House.

That house sure is big! Brer Rabbit had to walk a mile or more around the veranda to the back porch plaza. When he got there he took off his hat and he put it on the step. He took his bandana and dusted his yellow shoes and wiped his forehead and threw the rag into his hat. Then he reached over and knocked on the floor of the porch at the back door. Tap! Tap! Tap!—sort of easy-like.

His heart almost failed him, but nothing happened. He waited a little while. Then he rapped again. Maybe God isn't in—but no fresh tracks led away from the house. He decided to rap again, a little louder this time. And this time, God hollered out in the house in a great big voice, 'Who is there?' Brer Rabbit was really scared.

He said in a timid kind of whisper, 'It is me, sir.'

God eyeballed him and said, 'Who is me?'

'Well just me, Brer Rabbit, sir.'

And God asked mighty severely, 'What do you want, Brer Rabbit?'

'Just a little something, sir. Won't take you barely a minute to do it.'

'Humph! What sort of business are you up to now?' God said. 'Sit down and I'll be out right away.'

Brer Rabbit sat down on the steps. And after a long time while he mostly wished he had never come, God finally came out. The first look Brer Rabbit had of God, he was so scared that he almost took off and ran away. But when he thought about how badly he wanted that long tail he held his ground.

He jumped off the step and displayed his best manners, pulling his forelock and scraping the gravel with his feet. 'Now, Brer Rabbit,' God said, sort of gruffly, 'what is the thing that you want so badly that you have gotten bold enough to come way up here like this?'

Brer Rabbit pulled his forelock again and answered, 'Master, this weather is so hard on us poor creatures, I don't see how we survive. Looks like Brer Mocking Bird is the only one that can enjoy himself, and he has to go away out to the top of a tree in the woods before he can jump around and sing the way he does. We who have to stay on the ground have Satan's own time. Every sort of devilish biting and stinging and troubling thing just trying to stay alive, we have to contend with. The gnats, and green head flies, and sandflies, and the redbugs, and the ticks, and the chiggers, and all kinds of varmints like that bother us from first day clean to dark. They work from can to can't, and they work faithfully! And when darkness comes and they leave off, the mosquitoes and the gallinippers join hands to take their place and suck out blood and annoy us until the first day brings its light.

'Even then, Master, some creatures make out better than the rest because they have a real tail, not just a leftover stump like Sister Nanny Goat gave me. I noticed what nice tails Brother Bull Cow and Brother Horse were given. When a fly bothers them, all they have to do is wave their tails in the air and the flies and the mosquitoes are scared if they don't fly off. *Ping!* That long tail cracks down and they are dead. Now, sir'—Brer Rabbit got mighty bold and brash, but his voice came out as sweet as molasses—'I just came here to ask you to do something for me, Master! Please, sir, if you could be so kind as to give me a long tail so that I can brush away those pesky critters too.'

God cast his eyes down at Brer Rabbit and squinched up his forehead and looked him over. Then he puckered up his mouth like he had been biting a green persimmon. And he said, 'You are made like you are made. You have been contrary about that tail from the first day. Sister Nanny Goat did just as I told her, and she was kind to give you any tail at all. Even with all the blessings you already have you come here to me to get a tail like the very best of creatures have. Hmm! You are mighty little to have a long tail. Brother Horse and Brother Bull Cow are big and stand high off the ground, but your belly mostly drags in the dust. You can jump around in the grass to keep those flies off.'

'That's what I have been doing, sir, but it just wears me out.'

God looked at him closely. 'You just want to be in high fashion, don't you?'

'Who, sir? Why do I have to think about fashion, sir! I am thankful for what I have got. The flies are the only thing that brought me here!' But Brer Rabbit was so scared he couldn't keep from trembling just a little bit.

God kind of smiled at him and then sort of squinched up his face. 'Well, you are smart enough to get here, and that is more than most, so I reckon I'll set you a task to see just how smart you are. That will keep you from bothering me for a while. And if you do it, I might give you a long tail.'

With that he turned around and went into the house. He came right back out again with something in his hand.

Brer Rabbit jumped up from where he had been sitting and became polite again. God gave him a crocus bag and said, 'Take this bag and bring it back to me full of blackbirds.'

Poor Brer Rabbit cried out at that. But God looked sour at him, cocking his eye, and Brer Rabbit shut up.

Then God gave him a hammer and said, 'Knock out Brother Alligator's eye teeth with this hammer and fetch them to me.'

This time Brer Rabbit was so upset that he could only grunt.

Last, God took a little calabash and said, 'This you must fill with Brother Deer's eye water. You understand? Now, you get away from here. And don't come back bothering me until you have done the whole lot.' Then he turned on his heel and went back in the house and slammed the door.

Brer Rabbit felt so cut down to size that he could scarcely pick up his hat to put on his head and go home. His heart was heavy and he dragged his feet along the ground. He walked along and he thought. He shook his head and he thought. How could he catch blackbirds by the sackful? He wasn't a hawk! Why would anyone with good sense go anywhere near Brother Alligator's mouth—so how could he knock out his teeth with a hammer?

And getting Brother Deer's tears! Brother Deer is so foolish and skittery, if you just ask him about anything he gets scared and runs off. God fixed it so that it's mighty hard to get a long tail. It didn't look like he was ever going to get his.

Now, you know, Brer Rabbit is little, but he is as quick as a whip. And he worked his mind day and night on how to get a sack full of blackbirds. At last he figured out a scheme. During the fall, the white folks burn off the rice-field bank where the grass grows all summer and stands heavy. The fire just goes along, and the smoke rolls along ahead of it, and then all the birds living in the grass get foolish about the smoke and fly about like crazy.

So when they started that year, Brer Rabbit went down on the bank and got a big clump of grass, just a little way in front of where they were beginning to burn. And when the fire came that way and the heavy smoke reached them, the birds flew around madly, lighting on one bush and then another, just running away. At last they came down right in front of Brer Rabbit's clump of grass. He jumped out and caught a bird and put it in the sack, and he jumped around again and caught some more. The birds were so slippery he got his sack full at last, and he was very proud.

Next, he began to think about the problem of Brer Alligator's teeth. One fine day, he got his fiddle and he went down to the rice field by the river. Now Brer Rabbit worked the fiddle in his own devilish way at all the dances and picnics in the country, and made people lose their religion. And a whole lot of them had been turned out of their churches because they had crossed their feet to his dancing tunes, because when Brer Rabbit played, there aren't any feet around that can take any notice whether they are crossing or not!

Now, this day, Brer Rabbit sat down on a stump and started to play and sing and pat his foot. And when he did that something began to move, because he knew no animal could resist that music, expecially Brer Alligator. Brer Alligator, who was way down at the bottom of the river, yelled at him and came to the top of the water, poked his big eyes out, and looked about to see who it was playing like that. But Brer Rabbit didn't pay any attention to him. He sang and he played and he patted his foot.

Right away that music started to pull Brer Alligator out of the water, and he swam over to the bank. Still Brer Rabbit didn't pay any attention to him. He went on singing and playing and patting his foot just like no one was around.

Brer Alligator crawled out on the edge of the marsh and then climbed right up on the bank and sat down by Brer Rabbit; he popped his eyes up at him and listened.

Brer Rabbit stopped at last. Brer Alligator praised him to the sky for his singing and fiddling. Then he asked Brer Rabbit, 'Can you teach me how to play like that? I sure would like to play and sing like that, yes sir!'

Brer Rabbit made like he was thinking a little while and then said to him, 'Can't say about the singing because it depends on how a man's mouth is made if he can learn to sing or not.'

'Look in my mouth, Brer Rabbit, and tell me if it is right.' Brer Rabbit pretended like he didn't care. He told him it was hard to teach anyone to sing anyway. 'Do, Brer Rabbit!' he begged him. But Brer Rabbit pretended like he hadn't heard him. He just kind of scratched his head and started to hum a tune.

'Brer Rabbit! Man! You've got to stop that just for a minute. Look and see if I have the kind of mouth that you can teach how to sing,' Brer Alligator kept on begging.

Brer Rabbit just yawned and stretched himself and looked down at Brother Alligator, shaking his head and making clucking sounds.

'All right, then, maybe I can, but you have to listen to me close and do just as I say.'

'Sure! Sure! Brer Rabbit. Anything you say!'

'Then shut your eyes tight till I tell you to open them again.'

Brer Alligator shut them. 'Open your mouth wide—*real* wide —and hold it that way.' And Brer Alligator did just as he was told.

Brer Rabbit grabbed a little lightwood knot, and he jammed it into Brer Alligator's jaws to keep them wide open, clear back by the corners of Alligator's mouth, so he couldn't shut it down. And he said, 'Bite on that a minute and hold still.'

Then he whipped out his little hammer that God had given him and—*Crack! Crack!* He knocked out both of Brer Alligator's eye teeth. And then just as quickly he ran off with them.

Brer Alligator hollered and yelled and thrashed around looking for Brer Rabbit. But Brer Rabbit didn't pay any attention to him. He just scampered on home. And every time he thought how Brother Alligator's jaws might have scrunched down on him, he had to wiggle himself to feel if he was all there. Brer Rabbit was mighty satisfied with himself then, yes sir.

The last thing Brer Rabbit had to do was to get that calabash full of Brother Deer's eye water, and then he would have all the tasks done. But he knew that getting the eye water would be the hardest task of all. He could hardly sleep again because he was so bothered by the problem. He couldn't think of anything except to ask Brer Deer directly to help him. But that wasn't any use because Brer Deer knew Brer Rabbit too well and would figure out that he was going to play some kind of trick on him. Deer would take off so fast when he saw Brer Rabbit that no one would even be able to catch up with him to argue the point.

The problem got so hard Brer Rabbit almost gave up the whole thing, but then he saw Brer Horse and Brother Bull Cow with their nice long tails switching and swinging and it reminded him of how fine he would look, walking on the Big Road, if he just had one of those long tails. He could sure sashay along the road and shake that tail about and just look so handsome. So he began to scratch his head again and think about it some more. Man, he is a schemer, that Brer Rabbit! And finally he got a notion.

Brer Deer lived way down deep in the woods. A long time ago, he used to live in the settlement. He and Brer Dog even planted land together. But Brother Deer, or one of the family, had a fight with Brer Dog; and what with one thing or another it got to be such a goings-on that Brer Dog and his family made Brer Deer and his family run away every time they got a chance. That's what made Brer Deer begin a little place way off by himself. Poor Brer Deer was scared of nearly all the animals because of that experience; in fact, he was the most frightened creature in the woods.

Brer Rabbit counted on that, and he went deep in the woods till he came to a little clearing where Brer Deer had his house. And he found Brer Deer lying down in the hot sun in his yard. Brer Rabbit passed the time of day with him. They talked a little bit about crops and weather and who had been turned out of church, and who had gotten killed at the picnic, and such things.

At last Brer Rabbit said, 'Brer Deer, you know I am your friend, right?'

'Sure, Brer Rabbit, I know that well.'

'You know I always do stick up for you, right?'

'Yes, man!'

'Very well, then, I have to inform you that they have been throwing your name about so much up in the settlement that I had to come and tell you about it.'

'What! What did they say?'

'They said that you are no good at jumping any longer—that Sister Nanny Goat takes the prize for jumping nowadays.'

'Now! Brer Rabbit—who could say that? Why, I can jump three times higher than that no-count little thing!'

'Brer Dog said you couldn't, and I told him that just wasn't so. And I came here to give you the chance to show me how you can still jump higher than anyone. Now I saw Sister Nanny Goat jump a bush almost as high as that one over there, and she could jump it good, too. Can you jump that high?'

Brer Deer sucked his teeth and shook his head and just kind of smiled. He said, 'Man! When I was a little fellow, before I could ever walk, I could jump bushes like that one.'

'Well then, why don't you go on? That bush goes awful high up in the air for anyone to jump! But if you can make it, I would sure like to see it, so I could pass the word along in the street to Brer Dog.'

Brer Deer got up and he ran down his yard and then he came back over the bush just high and fine and graceful. Brer Rabbit looked astonished. He whistled. He slapped his leg praising Brer Deer for how high and far he could jump. 'That isn't anything,' said Brer Deer, and he jumped over another bush a little higher, just to show what he could do.

Brer Rabbit loudly sang out his praises. 'Brer Dog is sure going to have to shut his lying mouth now when I carry the tale to everyone about how fine you jump. Man! you look nice doing that! I reckon you could even jump that big bush yonder?'

And Brer Deer took that one as well. So Brer Rabbit pointed to higher and higher bushes, till at last he fixed on one that wasn't a bush—it was more like a young tree, and it had a heavy fork and was all tangled up with jasmine and cat briar and snailox and supplejack and other kinds of vines.

When he looked at the tree with jasmine, Brother Deer sort of hesitated. But Brother Rabbit encouraged him with so much praise that he reared back and jumped it. He leaped very high in the air—but he didn't quite make it. He landed slam bang right in the middle in the big fork!

The jump knocked his breath out of him. When he twisted around to get out, he got so tangled up in that jacktwine and briar that it got harder to move. He hollered for Brer Rabbit to come help him.

Brer Rabbit made sure that he was caught fast and he said, 'Man, I can't help you. You're too heavy and you might fall on me and bust my back. But I will go right away to the settlement and find some help to get you out.'

With that, he ran down the path until he was out of sight and then he threw himself on the ground and he rolled and cackled and laughed at the way he had fooled Brer Deer and the way he was going to get his way now. Brer Rabbit laughed till he was crying.

And then he got up off the ground and pulled his handkerchief out of his pocket and ran back to Brer Deer wailing and sobbing. 'Brer Deer, you better get out of that bush now. Don't waste a minute because Brother Dog—' And he made out like he couldn't speak, he was crying so.

'What's the matter, Brer Rabbit?' Brer Deer was so scared that his voice trembled.

'You better come out right now because Brother Dog and his whole family are right behind me, and they're going to kill you and eat you if you stay in that bush. When I got close to the settlement, I saw them running down the path coming this way.'

Brer Deer shook and kicked himself. He pulled and he pushed but all he did was tangle himself more tightly in the jacktwine. 'Get out of that bush, Brer Deer! Get out of that bush before they get here and kill you right in front of my eyes.' And Brer Rabbit bowed his head and mopped his eyes with his handkerchief.

Then Brother Deer burst out crying. He struggled and cried, and then he struggled and then he cried some more. And all that time Brother Rabbit made out as if he was helping him out, but all he was doing was tangling the vines around Brother Deer's foot. Then he held out that little calabash that God had given him and caught every drop of that eye water which ran out of Brer Deer's eyes.

Every time Brer Deer looked like he might let up, Brer Rabbit screeched out, 'Oh, poor Brother Deer! You are going to be caught today!' And Brer Deer would bawl out some more.

But even so, the calabash wasn't quite full yet, so Rabbit called out, 'I see them getting closer, Brer Deer, howling for your meat! Hurry, Brer Deer, and get loose, or no one can save you!'

Brer Deer struggled the best he could, but he couldn't move himself and he went on crying. And so with all of that Brer Rabbit filled the calabash with eye water. Then he picked up the little calabash and he wiped his own eyes and he didn't say anything else. He just walked away and left Brer Deer high up in the tree fork.

Now that Brer Rabbit was all done with the tasks God had given him, he didn't waste any time. He went home, put on his store clothes, and picked up the three things that God had asked for. He took the path to God's house and all the way he swaggered.

When he got there this time he didn't go to any back door, no sir! He walked right up to the front door, and knocked bold and loud. *BAM! BAM! BAM!*

God was in the house and hollered out, 'Who is there?'

And Brer Rabbit answered, 'It's me, sir, Brer Rabbit!'

'What?' God's voice sounded kind of curious. 'You're back already, are you? You haven't done all the tasks I set you to do?'

'Yes, sir.'

'You mean to tell me you got all those things I told you to get?'

'Yes, sir. They are all right here, sir.'

'Take care with your foolishness, Brother Rabbit! You don't lie to me?'

'No, sir. I have them all, sir.'

God didn't make any sound for a while, but after such a length of time he came out to the door. Brer Rabbit kind of puffed himself up. He felt so pleased with himself that he was just grinning all over his face. Then he noticed that God looked vexed. And Brer Rabbit straightened up his face, put down the sack of blackbirds, then reached down in his side pocket and pulled out a little handkerchief and unwrapped Brer Alligator's two eye teeth, and handed them to God. There they were for sure, and the blood was still on them. And he hunted in his coat-tail pocket and pulled out the calabash full of Brother Deer's eye water.

God tasted it, and smelt it, and then he said, 'You are smart, aren't you, Brother Rabbit! Very well, then!' He pointed to a loblolly pine tree out in the yard. 'You go and seat yourself underneath that pine tree till I can fix you up.' And he turned around and went into the house and slammed the door after him. *BAM!*

Now Brer Rabbit went and did as he was told and sat down under that tree. But he didn't like the way God had slammed the door at all. And he didn't like the way God had talked to him. And he noticed that God's eyes showed red like fire when he looked at the pine tree. And Brer Rabbit couldn't rest easy because he was getting more and more scared. He scuffled around on his haunches—little bit by little bit—till he got to the other side of the tree trunk from the Big House, and sneaked away real quietly, keeping the tree between him and the house, till he got away over in the corner of the yard where he could hide himself under a heavy sucklebush.

Well, sir! He was hardly in the sucklebush before, *BRAM! BRAM! BRAM!* Out of the clear sky that didn't have so much as a cloud in it came the biggest thunder and lightning bolt that ever was seen. Wow! It just crashed down on the loblolly where Brer Rabbit had been! And the next minute, where that pine tree stood, there wasn't anything at all except a pile of kindling, and that was afire. Brer Rabbit didn't stop for anything! He took his feet in his hands and hit the avenue to the Big Gate and he screamed.

About that time, God in the Big House looked out of the window and saw a little something just running lickety-split down the avenue. And he looked close and sure enough it was Brother Rabbit. He leaned out of the window and put his two hands to his mouth and he hollered: 'Ah-hah! Ah-hah! Ah-hah! You think you are so smart, eh! You are so drat smart! Well, get a long tail yourself.'

The Two Old
Women's Bet

One time there were two old women got to talkin' about the menfolks: how foolish they could act and what was the craziest fool thing their husbands had ever done. And they got to arguin', so finally they made a bet which one could make the biggest fool of her husband.

So one of 'em said to her man when he come in from work that evenin', says, 'Old man, do you feel all right?'

'Yes,' he says, 'I feel fine.'

'Well,' she told him, 'you sure do look awful puny.'

Next mornin' she woke him up, says, 'Stick out your tongue, old man.' He stuck his tongue out, and she looked at it hard, says, 'Law me! You better stay in the bed today. You must be real sick from the look of your tongue.'

Went and reached up on the mantelpiece, got down all the bottles of medicine and tonic was there and dosed the old man out of every bottle. Made him stay in the bed several days, and she kept on talkin' to him about how sick he must be. Dosed him every few minutes and wouldn't feed him nothin' but mush.

Came in one mornin', sat down by the bed, and looked at him real pitiful, started in snifflin' and wipin' her eyes on her apron, says, 'Well, honey, I'll sure miss ye when you're gone.' Sniffed some more, says, 'I done had your coffin made.'

And in a few days she had 'em bring the coffin right on in beside the old man's bed. Talked at the old man till she had him thinkin' he was sure 'nough dead. And finally they laid him out, and got everything fixed for the buryin'.

Well, the day that old woman had started a-talkin' her old man into his coffin, the other'n she had gone on to her house and about the time her old man came in from work she had got out her spinnin' wheel and went to whirlin' it. There wasn't a scrap of wool on the spindle, and the old man he finally looked over there and took notice of her, says, 'What in the world are ye doin', old woman?'

'Spinnin',' she told him, and 'fore he could say anything she says, 'Yes, the finest thread I ever spun. It's wool from virgin sheep, and they tell me anybody that's been tellin' his wife any lies can't see the thread.'

So the old man he come on over there and looked at the spindle, says, 'Yes, indeed, hit surely is mighty fine thread.'

Well, the old woman she'd be there at her wheel every time her old man come in from the field—spin and wind, spin and wind, and every now and then take the shuck off the spindle like it was full of thread and lay it in a box. Then one day the old man come in and she was foolin' with her loom, says, 'Got it all warped off today. Just got done threadin' it on the loom.' And directly she sat down and started in weavin'—step on the treadles, throwin' the shuttle and it empty. The old man he'd come and look and tell her what fine cloth it was, and the old woman she'd weave right on. Made him think she was workin' day and night. Then one evenin' she took hold on the beam and made the old man help her unwind the cloth.

'Lay it on the table, old man—Look out! You're a-lettin' it drag the floor.'

Then she took her scissors and went to cuttin'.

'What you makin', old woman?'

'Makin' you the finest suit of clothes you ever had.'

Got out a needle directly and sat down like she was sewin'. And there she was, every time the old man got back to the house, workin' that needle back and forth. So he come in one evenin' and she says to him, 'Try on the britches, old man. Here.' The old man he shucked off his overalls and made like he was puttin' on the new britches.

'Here's your new shirt,' she told him, and he pulled off his old one and did his arms this-a-way and that-a-way gettin' into his fine new shirt. 'Button it up, old man.' And he put his fingers up to his throat and fiddled 'em right on down.

'Now,' she says, 'let's see does the coat fit ye.' And she come at him with her hands up like she was holdin' out his coat for him, so he backed up to her and stuck his arms in his fine new coat.

'Stand off there now, and let me see is it all right—Yes, it's just fine. You sure do look good.'

And the old man stood there with nothin' on but his shoes and his hat and his long underwear.

Well, about that time the other old man's funeral was appointed and everybody in the settlement started for the buryin' ground. The grave was all dug and the preacher was there, and here came the coffin in a wagon, and finally the crowd started gatherin'. And pretty soon that old man with the fine new suit of clothes came in sight. Well, everybody's eyes popped open, and they didn't know whether they ought to laugh or not, but the kids went to gigglin' and about the time that old man got fairly close, one feller laughed right out, and then they all throwed their heads back and laughed good. And the old man he'd try to tell somebody about his fine new suit of clothes, and then the preacher busted out laughin' and slappin' his knee—and everybody got to laughin' and hollerin' so hard the dead man sat up to see what was goin' on. Some of 'em broke and ran when the corpse rose up like that, but they saw him start in laughin'— laughed so hard he nearly fell out the coffin—so they all came back to find out what-'n-all was goin' on.

The two old women had started in quarrelin' about which one had won the bet, and the man in the coffin heard 'em, and when he could stop laughin' long enough, he told 'em, says, 'Don't lay it on me, ladies! He's got me beat a mile!'

Jean Labadie's Dog

Jean Labadie stood in the chicken yard and counted chickens. 'If the weasels aren't getting my chickens,' Jean Labadie said, 'you can bet your life my good neighbour André Drouillard is getting them.'

Jean Labadie decided he would catch André Drouillard in the act of absconding with his poultry. So for three nights he slept in the chicken yard with his shotgun by his side. But nothing happened. André's sixth sense must have warned him.

Jean Labadie got tired of sleeping with the chickens, and he went back to sleeping in the house. But he was determined to do something about the chicken stealing. The only thing was, he didn't know what. You can't just ask a man if he's stealing your chickens, even if he is. Therefore, Jean Labadie didn't do anything for a while.

Then one day he was helping André Drouillard clear the brushwood along the fences. While he was working, he found a pile of chicken feathers. Jean Labadie looked at them closely, thinking that they looked mighty like the feathers his own chickens had worn before they'd disappeared. Still and all, you couldn't tell a man, 'These look like my chickens' feathers.' So Jean Labadie didn't say anything about them. He just kept cutting brush and thinking.

'If André thought I had a dog,' Jean Labadie said to himself, 'maybe he'd keep away from my chicken yard.' So right then and there, Jean Labadie made up a big lie. He invented a dog. He said to André, 'Have you seen my big black dog yet?'

'Dog?' André said. 'You don't have any dog.'

'I didn't use to have a dog,' Jean Labadie said, 'but now I do. I just bought him from the Indians. Somebody's been stealing my chickens, so I went out and got myself a dog. He's big and black and mighty mean, and I don't think anyone will do any more prowling around my chicken yard.'

'Well, well, so you've got a dog now,' André remarked.

Jean Labadie looked up.

'See, there he goes now, black as coal, with his big red tongue hanging out.'

André looked. 'I don't see any dog,' he said.

'What do you mean, you don't see any dog?' Jean Labadie said. 'There he goes, right across that ridge.'

'Where?' André asked.

'Look, man, look. Don't you see him lifting those big black paws one after another?'

'Yes, yes, I see him now!' André said, straining his eyes for a sight of the big dog with the hanging red tongue and the paws going one after another. 'Yes, he looks mighty mean, slinking along the fence like that.'

Jean Labadie said nothing more about the dog he had just invented. André Drouillard was a little quiet about it all, but once in a while he looked up towards the ridge to catch a glimpse of the animal.

Jean was right about one thing. There were no more chickens stolen from his chicken yard. He was pretty pleased with himself.

Then one day he met André on the road.

'I saw your big black dog today,' André said. 'He was running along the fence, his red tongue hanging out, and his big feet going one after another. I got out of his way pretty fast, you can bet your life.'

Jean Labadie was amused, but he was also a little disgusted with André's imagination. If the big black dog was running around the countryside, who was guarding the chicken yard?

André met Jean Labadie again on the road one day and said, 'Jean, I saw your big black dog this morning. He was on the other side of town chasing rabbits.'

Jean said, 'Must be some other dog, André. My big black dog is at home guarding the chicken yard.'

'If it wasn't your big black dog whose was it?' André said. 'Doesn't your dog have a big red tongue that hangs out? When he runs, doesn't he fan the air with his feet?'

'Well, it sounds like my dog,' Jean said, 'but just the same he's at home now watching the chicken yard.'

'You'd better chain him up,' André said. 'People in town are complaining about your letting a wild Indian dog like that run loose.'

Jean wanted to ask how people found out about his dog, but he decided to keep quiet. If he had a dog, people obviously had to know about it.

A few days later André stopped Jean Labadie again. This time he spoke sharply. 'You're going to have to do something about that vicious dog of yours. Today on the road he came at me and snapped at my legs. I had to beat him off with a stick.'

Jean Labadie didn't know whether to laugh or call André Drouillard a liar. The big black dog had gotten pretty real by now. Finally he said, 'All right, I guess I'll have to chain him up.' He put his fingers in his mouth and gave a loud whistle. 'Here boy! Here boy!' he called to the dog. André Drouillard looked around nervously and left in a hurry.

For a while Jean Labadie heard no more about it. Then one day when he was in the store buying roofing nails, Madame Villeneuve came up to him and said, 'Jean Labadie, you ought to be ashamed the way you let that fierce dog run loose in town.'

'He's a fierce dog, that's true,' Jean Labadie replied, 'but he's chained up at home.'

'Maybe he *was* chained up,' Madame Villeneuve said, 'but he's not chained up any more. He's running around with his red tongue hanging out, making his big black paws go this way and that way. He even bared his teeth at me this afternoon.'

Jean Labadie began to worry. It looked like things were getting out of control with the dog. He thought maybe he ought to get rid of him. So he said to Madame Villeneuve, 'I'll tell you what I'll do, Madame Villeneuve. Tomorrow morning I'll take that dog back to the Indians.'

'It's about time,' Madame Villeneuve said.

The next morning Jean hitched his horse and got in the cart. He waited until he saw André Drouillard, then he whistled loudly and made a great show of getting the dog in with him. As he drove past André's house, André shouted, 'Taking him back, Jean?'

'Back where I got him,' Jean Labadie replied, and he drove down the road and headed for the Indian village.

He spent the day talking with his Indian friends, and in the late afternoon he headed for home. As he came around the bend near André Drouillard's house, a feeling of foreboding came over him. He saw André waiting at the gate.

'What's the matter?' Jean Labadie asked.

'Plenty's the matter,' André said. 'Your big black dog's come home. Beat you here by an hour. I was just coming out to milk, and what should I see but the dog coming up the road, his big red tongue hanging out of his mouth.'

Jean Labadie exploded. 'André Drouillard,' he shouted, 'you're a liar! I just left that big black dog with the Indians!'

'Oh?' André said coldly. 'Now you're calling your neighbours liars?' And he turned and went into the house.

Jean Labadie groaned. After all the pains he'd gone to, he had messed everything up. Now he had called André Drouillard a liar. He might as well have called him a chicken thief in the first place.

The way it turned out, Madame Villeneuve saw the big black dog running behind her house. Henri Dupuis saw him skulking behind the store. Delphine Langlois saw him running through the graveyard. And everyone was angry at Jean Labadie. But Jean figured there was no use taking the dog to the Indian village again, he'd just come back.

A few days later, when Jean Labadie was sitting in front of the blacksmith's shop, André Drouillard came riding up at a great pace on his horse. 'Where is Dr Brisson?' André shouted. 'Somebody get Dr Brisson!'

'What's the matter?' everyone called out at once.

André raised a bleeding hand and pointed it at Jean Labadie. '*His* big black dog bit me!' he said.

Jean sat there with his mouth open. Seeing a dog that isn't there is one thing. Being bitten by such a dog is something else again. He closed his mouth and went over where everyone was looking at André's bleeding hand.

'It doesn't look like a dog bite to me, it looks more like an axe cut,' Jean Labadie said.

This made everyone angry. 'First he lets his wild Indian dog run loose,' they said, 'and then when someone gets bitten he says it's an axe cut!'

Jean felt very helpless about the dog. At last he said, 'My friends, I think we'll have to put an end to this matter once and for all. I'll give André two chickens for the damage to his hand. And what's more important, I think I'll have to shoot that big black dog.'

The crowd was silent. Jean Labadie said, 'Follow me.' He walked down the road to his house, with the crowd behind. He went in the door and came out a minute later with his gun. 'Stand here,' Jean Labadie said, 'and watch me kill the big black dog.'

He went out by the barn and whistled. He whistled again. Then he called out, 'Here he comes!'

The crowd moved back toward the fence to get out of the way. Madame Villeneuve said tensely, 'I see him behind the barn, with his big red tongue hanging out!' And André Drouillard said, 'Also with his big old feet going up and down!'

Jean Labadie raised his gun to his shoulder, aimed carefully, and fired. 'Got him,' he said. Delphine Langlois fainted.

'There,' Jean Labadie said softly, brushing a tear from his eye, 'I've done it. My big black dog is gone for good.'

Everyone agreed that Jean Labadie's dog was done for, and they turned and went away. André Drouillard headed for home with two fat chickens under his arm.

As for Jean Labadie, when the people looked over their shoulders they saw him sadly digging a grave for the only dog he ever had.

Glossary

butt: cask (holding from 108 to 140 gallons)
chapati: unleavened bread
choom: tent of skins
chunked: chucked, threw
dervish: man of Muslim faith who has taken vows of poverty
dreidel: a Jewish four-sided spinning-top; the game played with it
fakir: man of Hindu or Muslim faith sworn to poverty
ghoul: evil spirit who robs graves and eats corpses
gourd: large fruit used as vessel when dried and hollowed out
hacienda: large estate
hamal: porter
Hanukkah: 8-day midwinter Jewish festival commemorating the rededication of the Temple. Also known as the Festival of Lights
jinn (or *djinn*): supernatural beings in Muslim legend that can take human or animal form, and influence human affairs
ju-ju: a magic charm or fetish used by some West African tribes; or the magic the charm works
kimono: long Japanese robe with sleeves
kismet: fate
kvass: a Russian fermented drink made from barley or rye
loblolly: tree (*Pinus Taeda*) that grows in swamps of the southern United States
mica: small glittering scales of mineral usually found within granite
muezzin: public crier who proclaims the hours of prayer from the slender tower of a mosque, known as a minaret
peccary: one of the swine family
pueblo: village; terraced building(s) housing a number of families
samisen: a Japanese musical instrument akin to a banjo, but with three strings
sesame: kind of seed, yielding oil
scree: steep slope of stones on a mountainside
tabor: small drum
wazir: minister

Acknowledgements

Roger D. Abrahams: 'Why the Hare Runs Away' from *African Folktales*, Copyright © 1983 by Roger D. Abrahams; and 'Hankering for a Long Tail' from *Afro-American Folktales*, Copyright © 1985 by Roger D. Abrahams, both reprinted by permission of Pantheon Books, a division of Random House, Inc. **Inea Bushnaq**: 'The Nightingale that Shrieked' from *Arab Folktales* edited and translated by Inea Bushnaq, Copyright © 1986 by Inea Bushnaq, reprinted by permission of Pantheon Books, a division of Random House, Inc. **Italo Calvino**: 'One Night in Paradise' from *Italian Folktales: Selected and retold by Italo Calvino* (1980), Copyright © 1956 by Giulio Einaudi Editore, s.p.a., English translation by George Martin, Copyright © 1980 by Harcourt Brace & Company, reprinted by permission of Harcourt Brace & Company and The Wylie Agency. **Richard Chase**: 'The Two Old Women's Bet' from *The Grandfather Tales*, Copyright © 1948, renewed 1976 by Richard Chase, reprinted by permission of the publisher, Houghton Mifflin Co. All rights reserved. **Padraic Colum**: 'The Boy Pu-Nia and the King of the Sharks' from *Legends of Hawaii* (1937), reprinted by permission of the publisher, Yale University Press. **Kevin Crossley-Holland**: 'To Tell the Truth', Copyright © Kevin Crossley-Holland 1998, first published in this collection, and 'The Pied Piper of Hamelin' first published in *Tales from Europe* (BBC Books, 1991), both reproduced by permission of the author c/o Rogers, Coleridge & White Ltd, 20 Powis Mews, London W11 1JN; 'The Three Blows', from *British Folk Tales* (1986), reprinted by permission of the publishers, Orchard Books, a division of the Watts Publishing Group, 96 Leonard Street, London EC2A 4RH. **Harold Courlander**: 'The Coming of Asin' and 'Jean Labadie's Dog' both from Harold Courlander (ed.): *Ride with the Sun* (McGraw Hill, for the United Nations Women's Guild, 1955), reprinted by permission of the United Nations Women's Guild; 'The Tiger's Whisker' from *The Tiger's Whisker and Other Tales and Legends from Asia and the Pacific* (Methuen, 1960), copyright holder not traced. **Mercedes Dorson** and **Jeanne Wilmot**: 'The Legend of the Yara' from *Tales from the Rain Forest*, Copyright © 1997 by Mercedes Dorson and Jeanne Wilmot, reprinted by permission of The Ecco Press. **Charles Downing**: 'The Power of Love' from *Armenian Folk-tales and Fables* (OUP, 1972). **Richard Erdoes** and **Alfonzo Ortiz**: 'The Spirit Wife' from *American Indian Myths and Legends*, Copyright © 1984 by Richard Erdoes and Alfonzo Ortiz, reprinted by permission of Pantheon Books, a division of Random House, Inc. **Abayomi Fuja**: 'Oniyeye and King Olu Dotun's Daughter' from *Fourteen Hundred Cowries* (OUP, Ibadan, 1962). **Helen** and **William McAlpine**: 'The Tongue-Cut Sparrow' from *Japanese Tales and Legends* (OUP, 1958), reprinted by permission of Mrs Lily L. Gillespie and Mrs Mary Johnson, executors of the Estate of the authors, c/o Millar, Shearer and Black, Cookstown, Northern Ireland. **Eric Maddern**: 'The Rainbow Bird and the Crocodile and How the People First Got Fire,' retelling of an aboriginal tale, used by permission of the author. **Eric** and **Nancy Protter**: 'The Magic

Acknowledgements

Brocade' from *Folk and Fairy Tales of Far-Off Lands* (Duell, Sloan & Pearce, 1965), Copyright 1965 by Eric and Nancy Protter, reprinted by permission of JCA Literary Agency. **A. K. Ramanujan**: 'Why the Fish Laughed' and 'And then, Burrah!' from *Folktales from India* Copyright © 1991 by A. K. Ramanujan, reprinted by permission of Pantheon Books, a division of Random House, Inc. **Philip Sherlock**: 'Tiger Story, Anansi Story' from *West Indian Folk-tales* (OUP, 1966), reprinted by permission of Oxford University Press. **Jacqueline Simpson**: 'The Dead Man's Nightcap' from *Icelandic Folktales and Legends* (1972), reprinted by permission of the author and the publisher, B. T. Batsford Ltd. **Isaac Bashevis Singer**: 'Zlateh the Goat' from *Zlateh the Goat* (Harper & Row, 1966), reprinted by permission of HarperCollins Publishers, Inc. **Frances Toor**: 'The Hungry Peasant, God, and Death' from *A Treasury of Mexican Folkways* Copyright © 1947, 1975 by Crown Publishers, Inc., reprinted by permission of Crown Publishers, Inc. **Barbara K. Walker**: 'Trousers Mehmet and the Sultan's Daughter' from *A Treasury of Turkish Folktales for Children*, Copyright © 1988 by Barbara K. Walker, reprinted by permission of Linnet Books/The Shoe String Press, Inc., North Haven, Connecticut, USA. **Irina Zheleznova**: 'Kotura, Lord of the Winds' from *Folk Tales from Russian Lands* (Dover, 1969), by permission of Dover Publications, Inc.

Although we have tried to trace and contact all copyright holders before publication this has not been possible in every case. If notified we will rectify any errors or omissions at the earliest opportunity.

We also acknowledge with thanks the following out-of-copyright material: **C. Fillingham-Coxwell**: 'Vasilissa the Fair' from *Siberian and other Folktales* (London, 1925). **Joseph Jacobs**: 'The Son of Seven Queens' from *Indian Fairy Tales*. **Andrew Lang**: 'The Forty Thieves' from *The Blue Fairy Book*; 'Stan Bolovan' from *The Violet Fairy Book*; 'The Sacred Milk of Koumongoé' from *The Brown Fairy Book*; 'The Magic Mirror' from *The Orange Fairy Book*; 'The Bones of Djulung' from *The Lilac Fairy Book*.

The editor is grateful to Margaret Lockerbie Cameron, Keith Harrison, Ron Heapy, David Lumsdaine, Eric Maddern, Linda Waslien, and Gillian Crossley-Holland for their valuable advice and pursuit of elusive tales.

The illustrations are by:
Sarah Young pp 1, 4–5, 7, 13, 15, 18, 19, 27, 28, 33, 34, 44, 45, 49, 213
Ron Tiner pp 54, 57, 61, 66, 72, 75
John Millington pp v, 85, 88, 92, 98–99, 102, 103, 105, 108, 114, 123, 126
Karen Perrins pp i, viii, 127, 130, 131, 133, 134, 141, 142, 147
John Gosler pp iii, 152, 155, 156, 157, 161, 214
Hannah Firmin pp 162, 166, 172, 177, 181, 183
Rosamund Fowler pp 184, 189, 190, 201, 202, 205
Clare Hemstock pp 148, 151

And Then, *Bhurrah!*

Astoryteller was tired of telling stories, but the children and the grown people who were around him were not yet tired of listening to them. They asked for more.

So he began to describe how a vast number of birds were sitting on a tree. People asked as usual at a pause, 'And then?'

He said, 'One bird flew from the tree with a sound like *bhurrah!*'

'And then?'

'*Bhurrah!* went another bird, flying from the tree.'

'And then?'

'Another bird went *bhurrah!*'

'And then?'

'*Bhurrah!*'

This went on until nothing was heard but 'And then?' and '*Bhurrah!*' Finally someone asked, 'How long is this going to go on?' The storyteller answered, 'Till all the birds are gone.'

Syllable-leaves, and branches of happening,
Trunk of time:
May the storytree blossom with our bright
Understanding.